STRANGER THAN FULHAM

Matthew Baylis was born in Nottingham, educated in Liverpool and Cambridge and currently lives in London. A former storyliner for BBC1's 'EastEnders', he now works as a freelance journalist.

Matthew Baylis

STRANGER THAN FULHAM

V

VINTAGE

Published by Vintage 2000

2 4 6 8 10 9 7 5 3 1

Copyright © Matthew Baylis 1999

The right of Matthew Baylis to be identified as the author
of this work has been asserted by him in accordance with
the Copyright, Designs and Patents Act, 1988

First published in Great Britain in 1999 by
Chatto & Windus

Vintage
Random House, 20 Vauxhall Bridge Road,
London SW1V 2SA

Random House Australia (Pty) Limited
20 Alfred Street, Milsons Point, Sydney
New South Wales 2061, Australia

Random House New Zealand Limited
18 Poland Road, Glenfield,
Auckland 10, New Zealand

Random House (Pty) Limited
Endulini, 5A Jubilee Road, Parktown 2193,
South Africa

The Random House Group Limited Reg. No. 954009
www.randomhouse.co.uk

A CIP catalogue record for this book
is available from the British Library

ISBN 0 09 927354 3

Papers used by Random House are natural, recyclable
products made from wood grown in sustainable forests.
The manufacturing processes conform to the environ-
mental regulations of the country of origin

Printed and bound in Denmark by
Nørhaven A/S, Viborg

FOR MAGGIE

Southport

August 1995

1

All six foot nine inches of Gus are splayed out, naked on the sofa, and I am on the floor. I can sense the brooding presence of his genitals just behind my neck and it unsettles me, but there's nowhere else to sit and still see the TV. It's the summer – before my last year at college – and we're in our parents' house, in the big sitting room that opens out on to the garden.

'It's shite this slate,' Gus observes. 'See if you can't get summat else.' And he flips the burnt-out end of the reefer into the ashtray. I twist round to look at him. A fly buzzes over Gus' head, thinks better of it and moves off to the sticky patch on the coffee-table.

'Don't you know anyone you can score off?' I ask, tentatively, because it's nearing that golden hour of *Take The High Road* and *Young Doctors*.

But Gus – who has that valuable manner of always looking like he might know everything and anyone, even if he doesn't – just screws up his sand-burnt face. He spits on the carpet, as if concluding a transaction with some armed Kikuyu. 'Basically mate, I'm not into any of that business any more,' he says. 'Can't be doing with it. Know what I mean?'

I do know what he means. It is another mark of Gus' glibness that he assumes I feel any different. Tapping nervously on doors, putting on a rough accent, loafing, self-consciously, around toilets for some demi-villain to deal you a gramme of dog-muck. When you're fifteen or so, round here, it's the closest you get to glamour, but it's been a long while since 'any of that business' gave me a thrill.

3

I sigh, unsure what to say. I don't want an argument. I've only had one proper argument with Gus in my life, and that was five days ago.

He has been issuing orders ever since he arrived – though they were not the cause of the argument. Just a week ago, I was revelling in the prospect of a whole summer to myself, pretending the house was mine while my father subjected my mother to an apparently joyless tour of Eastern Germany. In a blaze of extravagance that is as rare as it is rash, they've just bought themselves a satellite dish and a new, halfway decent TV. And lurking amongst the three hundred or so German, Czech and Polish channels which some techno-klutz has managed to programme irrevocably into the memory, there's still a number of retro gems, like *UK Gold* and *Bravo*. So within a few hours of dumping my stuff in the hallway, I'd dragged the sofa into position and devised a rewarding schedule of round-the-clock vintage *Falcon Crest*, *The Sullivans* and other broadcast delights.

The honeymoon was sweet, but brief. In less than twenty-four hours, Gus appeared, fresh from his recent circuit of the Karakoram, with time to kill before his company sent him on elsewhere. He'd been over to see Sue, our big sister in Widnes, and she'd somehow let slip that the house was free of parents.

Sue and Gus have always got on in a way I can never quite fathom. She laughs about him, has no time for his breezy liberty-taking, feeds him, whatever enigmatic hour he turns up, always the same dish: beans, bacon and poached egg on toast. But never lets him stay the night.

They keep in touch. Sue gets postcards from him, and he sends her parcels from time to time. Gifts for the kids – usually entirely inappropriate: fertility masks that give them nightmares, wooden beads that invariably get stuck in tiny nostrils and earholes. But she forgives him. The glue of their friendship

4

can only be the age-thing. Gus is fourteen years older than I. Sue fifteen. So they have shared a past which I have not. Memories of a time when they were both prone to wet patches down the front of their trousers, and the fear of puppets. It levels all the differences.

But still she can't put up with him for long and hence, I guess, Gus ended up at my parents' house a few nights ago, just as *Coronation Street* was starting.

'Now then,' he said, elbowing past me as I opened the front door. Which seemed a novel way to resume a conversation after nine years.

Gus' last evening in this house was in 1980, and was characterised by three events: Gus attempting to dismantle a motorbike engine – on the kitchen floor – with the aid of our mother's tea-trolley; Gus punching my father in the mouth; Gus declaring, to a delighted audience of neighbours, gathered in the street either side of our driveway, that our father was a killer.

Gus stayed in Southport a full seven years after that, living in bedsits and flats in the grottier streets near the station. He carried on working at the Arts Centre, mending the projectors and doing the lighting. Occasionally, we would run into each other when I went to see a film and the conversations would be, however hard I tried, gruff and awkward. I heard from Sue (to whose washing machine he made regular visits) that Gus said he couldn't stand to be left in the same room as me, and he thought I would grow up into a nasty piece of work. And after I heard that, I never made much of an effort with Gus.

In that whole time, our father had just one conversation with Gus. They were showing something on the big screen at the Arts and Gus was in charge of fixing the letters on to the sign outside. My father and I rode past on bicycles. It was just before my thirteenth birthday, and – it having been finally conceded that I could have my own TV – we were on our way to look at the second-hand sets in the market. My father stopped with a rubbery squeal of brakes. 'Daaaaad,' I said, imploringly. But he ignored me. He did that long throaty cough of his. Like a seal who has something awkward to confess. And Gus, twenty feet above us, recognised it and looked down. His face screwed up as if he'd inhaled a wasp.

'I E,' our father called up. 'It's I then E. Not Sp*e*ilberg. It's Sp*ie*lberg.'

Which was typical of my father – forever advising shopkeepers on punctuation and policemen on protocol. One time he warned a meaty crew of roadworkers drilling at the end of our street to wear their earmuffs, or face an early onset of deafness. Fortunately, they were already too deaf to hear him. But Gus was not. He paused, and looked at the letters, a fair foot each in height, which he was sliding into a metal grille. 'Up yours,' he said. 'Killer.'

And a few weeks after that, Sue told me that Gus had got his HGV and had taken a job driving big safari-buses round Asia.

Now my parents are, in their way, a relatively free-thinking pair: my father likes to announce when he's 'going for a shit', or 'a piss', and my mother once even called our milkman a twat (though admittedly she never knew it was any ruder than a twit). But after that final filial smack in the mouth, we had a taboo. No one, either in drink or in anger, ever dared mention Gus again. And now, at a point in my life when I mostly pretend I am an orphan, I've suddenly reacquired a brother. He just eased his way into the house a week ago, wearing only a tiny pair of khaki shorts and his desert boots, sat down at the kitchen table, lit a Duty-Free, and told me to switch the telly off.

Normally I wouldn't switch Corrie off if the Israeli airforce landed in KwikSave car park, but I did turn the volume down the night he arrived, because there's something about Gus that makes him hard to resist. As I suspect a fair few women would tell you. My long, lean brother with his vast hands that can strip an engine in seconds or punch an obstreperous Pathan to the floor. Who drives enormous trucks round the steppes of Asia. Trucks full of well-heeled, horny girls on their years off, or taking a break from nursing and teaching and keen, if not really to experience some danger, then at least to sleep with someone who looks as if he has.

A lifestyle that breeds insurmountable arrogance. I keep telling myself that, every time Gus changes the channel on the TV without asking, or takes gargantuan swigs from the last milk bottle. After all, he announced in his mock-Manchester dialect, shortly after we heard the lost, mournful trumpet wail of Corrie's end-credits, that he didn't blame me for 'any of what happened in the past', said I was 'basically a good kid – probably' and suggested we could be mates. Relieved, and shyly flattered, I slipped a delicate hand into one of his callused paws in order to shake on the deal. 'Sound one,' Gus observed, happily, as we shook. Eight years spent in exotic locations have had the curious effect of making him sound more Northern than ever.

Gus' dialect is a mystery to many, if not to me. In the North, if people suspect that you might, privately, be spreading 'batter' on your bread instead of 'booter', then you are labelled, irrevocably, as a wrong'un – at worst, a London-type, at best, a snob. Even if, like the Strange family, you live in Calvinist simplicity and didn't even get satellite till 1995. To prevent perpetual exile, both Gus and I abandoned the Home Counties vowels of our parents. For me, it was barely conscious – I started school here, so the transition to fluent North was easy. But Gus was fifteen when we moved, so his efforts had to be stronger. His accent became something of a local phenomenon, sounding closer to a Salford tower block than a seaside town. Even the aforementioned, insulted milkman (who comes from Salford himself) used to confess to finding Gus quite hard to understand.

People never know we're brothers. Our accents are different. He's eight inches taller than me, eats three times as much and hates soap operas. Gus the panther. Me some bumbling woodland thing – badger or boar. I alone picked up the blue, myopic eyes of our father. And the slim hands of some anorexic piano teacher. We grew up in different decades. But even if I'm slightly miffed that Gus got the seventies and I was left with the eighties (naff clothes, naff music and largely, naff telly), I'm intrigued by those little shreds of past we share.

We've talked a lot, for hours, smoking away in the sitting room and in the kitchen and the garden, and it's come out that we can each remember things that the other thought were dreams. I remember, at Harlech Castle, Gus setting himself alight on the Primus stove, and our father rolling him in the nettles to put the flames out. Gus has his own, less romantic counterparts from my past (*. . . Dick Whittington ad ye right up on the stage an ye just picked yer nose and all this blood started coming out. In the fuckin' footlights it was . . .*) but I don't hold it against him. It's exciting, in a way, finding out what things you have in common and what you don't. Even if the list of Don'ts is bigger.

And he has a stack of stories better than any of the year-off kids at college. Dragged at gunpoint, after crashing into a local bus, down to the jail in a Pakistani hill-village, until his co-driver paid the ransom in tobacco and eggs. A Canadian woman who smoked something very strong, went 'loop-the-loop' and was later spotted wandering, sarongless, in a very wicked quarter of Kathmandhu. You only have to watch his easy movements, look at Gus' green eyes, old in a still-boyish face, to know he's come a long way.

At college, one of the chief occupations of my peers consists of condemning the nebulous beast they call 'society' for its failings, whilst confident that, one day, 'society' will reward them with groovy jobs and smart flats in the capital. Gus, meanwhile, has never been anywhere near a university, except perhaps to screw some year-off girl who has given him her new address. But he's got a groovy job, and his contempt knows no bounds. So it thrilled me when, on his first day, he went down to KwikSave wearing only his underpants. And at the end of that day, when he went to sleep on the floor – boots wrapped in his faded denim shirt for a pillow. A deeply spiritual soul, Gus hates a great deal of things: material possessions (except cigarettes), techno music, advertising, newspapers, and all forms of hypocrisy.

Gus' unnaturally strong feelings concerning newspapers were the cause of our only argument. This summer, the whole town, including myself, has been shaken by something dark that happened down on the sand dunes. And nowhere was our collective shock more visible than in the pages of our local paper, *The Clarion*.

Normally, the local press perpetuates the impression that we live in a dignified resort where commerce and culture flourish, and God bestows his blessings on all right-thinking citizens. That the town boasts more intravenous drug users per square foot than Leeds is never mentioned. (I know it for a fact – half of them were in my class.) Nor does anyone talk about the brown foam on the beach that sends dog-walkers home with a fever and their dogs home with worse. The darker side of Southport life tends to be, like a grandma's farts, tactfully ignored. People prefer it that way. But when, shortly before Gus' homecoming, a teenage girl was abducted by four men at a bus stop in the early hours of the morning, and raped in the sand-dunes, *The Clarion* had no option but to devote itself to the story. And when it had run out of things to say, it handed the microphone, so to speak, over to the people – opening up a hotline, so that readers could call in with their comments on the crime. We cannot blame *The Clarion* for doing that – it would have seemed far more callous to have gone back to the Flower

9

Show and the rusty tramlines and the other civic trivia that traditionally fill its pages.

The kid wants – *had* wanted, anyway – to be a veterinary nurse and was spending her summer holidays shovelling dung at a stable off the Formby by-pass. She was on her way there when it happened. She was out of hospital by the time the paper picked the story up, but she still couldn't tell the police much. One of the men did worse things to her than all the other men. He was fat, and had a tattoo – and there simply isn't the room to arrest every townsman who meets that description.

I came downstairs, on the morning of Gus' second day here, to find him sitting by the telephone in the hall, the newspaper spread out in front of him. He was already stoned and had decided to call the hotline.

'Why does your article say she was pretty?' he demanded, crossly. 'Or that she was wearing ski-pants? Or she begged 'em to stop?' Then he took a deep breath. Clearly no one on the other end was answering him. 'I'll tell you why. So the same cunts what are going on about chopping the rapists' knobs off can read it and then go off and have a wank about it. Thank you.' He paused. Someone was speaking to him. 'Eh? My name. Oh. P.P. Strange. Yeah. P like in er Uttar Pradesh.'

And after having assigned our father's name to his tirade, Gus spent the rest of that day surrounded with an almost boozy glow of triumph. It was as if he had effected the perfect act of civil disobedience: mischief mingled with righteousness. I couldn't get through to him – this was some private, peculiar campaign of his own.

'What good is it going to do?' I tried asking him.

'What good are *you* gonna do?' he replied crossly. 'Sitting there like a ponce. Like you know fuck. You're still wet,' he said, forcefully. I was taken aback. Because suddenly, it seemed,

I had replaced the media as the target of his fury. I shook my head. And Gus threw the newspaper at me, hard.

'How many times do I have to tell you? Don't fucking do that!'

'What? I was just shaking my head.'

He pointed at me, suddenly furious. 'Not that. *That!* You're still doing it now. That – that shuffling. I hate it.'

I looked down at my feet, half-covered by the crumpled newspaper. They were motionless.

'I'm not shuffling.'

'Well you were. Just stop it. It spooks me. It's gay.'

'Why have we gone from talking about the newspaper to me being gay?'

Gus mumbled something as threatening as it was incoherent, and I left the room, hurt and angry – numbed by the ferocity of his attack. Gus sat on the sofa all the rest of the day, glowering, and smoking a chain of heavy spliffs. That was the row.

Then later, much later, as the sky was turning pink, I was in the kitchen alone, chasing some macaroni around a bowl and torturing myself with the *TV Times* and the seductive booming of the TV from the living room next door when Gus came in to empty the ashtray. He looked at my food.

'Macaroni,' he said, in a sort of comedy Italian voice.

'Yep,' I said – staring down at the bowl.

'Ey,' he said. I looked up.

'Soz, like,' he offered, sheepishly. 'I mean – about all that. Daft really. I just sort of got a bit carried away like.'

I waited a minute. A little ache of anger began in the centre of my back, flared into a sting and ebbed away.

'S'alright,' I said.

And, because it seemed to be the sort of thing brothers might do when they have buried a quarrel, we went down to the Saracen's Head. Gus taught me how to squirt lager through the gaps in my teeth.

We've done that again since – I've even passed up the first six episodes of *Atherfold Road* to go down and watch my brother shoot pool. The quarrel is forgotten. But for all these bonding exercises, I'm wondering if – whatever Gus says about us being mates – he really understands what that means. Perhaps because, in his lifestyle, there aren't that many opportunities for mates. Very swiftly, he's taken up a rough, hectoring tone with me – like we are on one of his trips and he is Group Leader. I mightn't have minded if he'd ever performed any of the other functions of Big Brother: seeing off bullies, giving you rides on his motorbike, repairing your Scalextric and so on. But Gus never did anything like that for me. When I was growing up, Gus was always one of three things: Out, In His Room, or Gone. His brotherly attentions now (*'If I find out you've ever gone and got into smack and that I'll kick your arse down the street, kiddah . . .'*) are a little on the late side.

And every now and then, just engaged in the most innocent practices, sitting watching TV, or washing up, I catch him looking at me. And there's something very wrong about the look. Sometimes I reach for a cloth, or lunge to grab the remote before him and he pulls back. This six-foot-nine, big-booted tree trunk of a man actually *flinches*. I make him flinch. And I don't like it. I want him to know it's not like he said. I haven't turned into a nasty piece of work.

There's a film they showed us in first year anthropology. *Onka's Big Moka*. Onka lives in Papua New Guinea. Like every other man in his village, Onka is obsessed with being a Good Man. Every time they get Onka to talk about his wives, or his pigs, or the chest-pummelling ritual, Onka slyly manages to bring the topic back to Good Men and What They Do. For Onka, a Good Man is someone who has many, many *Mokas*. Unfortunately, when they showed us the film, I was staring at the girl next to me who kept sucking her pen-top like it was a

Cadbury's Flake and I missed finding out what a *Moka* was. But like Onka, I want to be a Good Man, and I remind myself of that, secretly, in the mirror nearly every morning.

By noon, of course, I've usually managed to swear at some undercover vicar or tread on a pregnant mother's bunions and generally shown myself, in a very public manner, to be quite a shit. But that only means, to make up for it, I have to engage in sporadic acts of selflessness and saintly endurance, to prove to myself, really, that whatever bleak things I did before, I'm better now. A Good Man. So today, on the seventh day of his visit, as Gus, stretched out on the sofa, finishes smoking the last of my pot and makes it clear he wants more, I just agree.

It's hardly the sacrifice of the month. I'm only going to visit Gibbo, who, despite being a bit frightening, is in his mid-forties, and so well-established he's practically on the Mersey Board of Trade and Commerce. So I set off for the market, at a brisk walk.

I'm going with my money, I should add. There've been problems with the transfer of Gus' salary.

Gibbo is a burly, hirsute man who deals in speed and pot, with the aid of mobile phone and mountain bike. He wears camouflaged trousers and has a collection of knives which is stored in a cupboard at his mum's house. He is what people call 'quite a character', meaning he is utterly mad. If you ever thought it was wise to be wary of those people who seem to hide secrets behind their eyes, Gibbo would disprove you in an instant. There's absolutely nothing either in or behind Gibbo's eyes, and believe me, that's a deal scarier.

Scary he may be, but Gibbo's never ripped anyone off. And scoring is a doddle. You just ring him on his mobile and say something like:

'Gibbo – *any joy mate?*'

And provided Gibbo says yes, you say:

13

'*Caff in the market like yeah?*'

And you sit in the darkest seats at the back of the market café, and wait for Gibbo to come to you, all oily and smelling – so I always fancy – of foxes.

The only difficulty lies in remembering the right sort of private, vague vocabulary in which to do the deal. Decades spent stewing in drugs have skewed Gibbo's world-view somewhat and he believes his operations to be subject to close monitoring by Interpol. You have to call pot 'joy' and speed 'luck' or he gets all mardy and hangs up.

Today, I walk to the café in the market, and order a coffee at the counter. There's some odd creature serving, buttoned into a huge parka with the hood done up. Like some ghastly chrysalis, gestating in the steamy fug of the café. I hand it some money and the creature paces back to the vast, chrome coffee-frother, belching gouts of steam.

'I'm just going to use the phone.' And I reach in my pocket.

The chrysalis jerks its head to the corner of the café. 'Someonth uthing it. Do you want thugar?'

Thugar?

Everything slows. Someone's turned the volume down on my life. I *know* this voice, this snot-clogged lisp – it's a part of my mythology, bigger, more significant than a Sid James laugh or an Elsie Tanner snog.

The chrysalis turns to me. Staring into the depths of the parka hood, I can make out a pale smear, like a grub in folds of moss. It sniffs – ululates with the accumulation of phlegm, and swallows, satisfied. I know him now.

School dinners. A thousand youths, bellowing for primacy over the scrape of steel on china. And at my elbow, that same eerie voice. *Can thum-buddy path the thalt?*

'Lamb? Is that you in there?'

John Thomas Longfellow-Lamb shakes the furry fronds of his parka hood, denying it, as he always did, and tries to pace

14

away. 'I'm bithy,' he hisses, nervously, but there's no one else around.

'Look – I know it's you. There's no need to be nervous. I won't hurt you.'

Lamb pauses a moment, and then unzips his hood. His face is unchanged, still geisha-white, streaked with a fatty sweat. Still the twin smudges of cocoa caught in the down at the corners of his mouth. *Lamb eats shit* we used to cry *for breakfast!* He wipes his brow with a long, delicate hand, his eyes flicker, almost seductively, over my face and then away. He makes to pull the hood back over.

'Aren't you a bit hot in there?' I ask, trying to be jovial in his unrelenting silence.

Lamb ignores me. 'Do you want thugar?' he asks again, more insistently.

'Yes. I mean no.' He plainly doesn't want this conversation, and who can blame him. But I have to have it. 'Look—'

And he does. For the first time, I think, since our first day at school, Lamb looks up from the earth and straight at me. It makes me flinch. 'I'm sorry about what they did. We did.'

Lamb carries on looking at me, an unending, chilling dog-eye stare from beetle-black eyes. Over in the corner, a fat child replaces the telephone and heads for the counter where we are standing, but Lamb ignores him.

'You're only thorry becoth you think one day I might be under your bed or your dethk with a knife or gun,' whispers Lamb. Then he turns from me and pulls his hood back up before facing the child.

This isn't how it was supposed to happen.

'Look. Can you—' I think desperately of a way to re-establish contact. 'Have you got change for the phone?'

'I'm therving thumb-one,' Lamb says, coldly, inclining his head to the child.

'What doughnuts have you got?' the child asks.

15

And that's that, I know. *Negotiations terminated at 2.38 p.m.* In *Neighbours*, a soul can move from intention, through crime, to full atonement in a week. But not in the market café. This obviously *is* how things were meant to happen. A fat boy buys doughnuts, and an older, sadder one drifts away from his redemption.

Lamb ignores me as I quit the café and walk through the market to the street outside. There's a man selling the new *Clarion* from a booth by the exit – and even he gives me change, guardedly, as if he might know exactly the number and depth of the skid-marks on my conscience. Thank God for Gibbo, whose provender helps us all forget. I call him from the box by the bandstand. Sometimes he meets you there if the café's too crowded. It's such a relief to be away from Lamb, I barely mind when Gibbo tells me he's not coming into town at all today.

'Can't,' he says, blankly. 'Someone's nicked me bike.'

But keen not to lose custom, he makes an alternative suggestion. 'Come Round Ours,' he says.

And it sinks in. This is my only choice. A five-quid cab ride. Two buses. Or a three-mile walk in the blazing heat. And my finances will only stretch to one of these options.

Gibbo is proud of his house, so proud that, like many home-owners, he's given it a name. Round Ours he calls it. No one else shares his affection, least of all me.

Round Ours is miles from anywhere, further even than where Jill, my ex-girlfriend used to live, an old, free-standing hulk, out on the Marsh Lane, which leads off towards Halsall, Preston and a string of further drizzly woollyback settlements. This region, the flat, sandy intersection of Merseyside and Lanca-shire, is riven by sectarian strife. Two distinct tribes live shoulder-by-shoulder in Southport, filling its pubs, clubs and casualty units with nightly discord and skip-loads of shattered glass. The *woollybacks*, or *woollies* – descendants of Lancashire folk, divested of their farms and mills. And the *scallies* – people of Liverpudlian stock, whose pioneering parents sought a better existence, or just a garden, eighteen miles up the road. Each group holds the other in contempt. To the scallies, the woollies are a collection of inbred sheep-shaggers, surviving on state benefit and raw potatoes. To the woollies, meanwhile, the scallies are car-radio-thieving, shellsuited scum. Those who belong to neither must ally themselves visibly with one of them, and be consistent.

Because Sue married Billy, my allegiance went south, towards Liverpool. I claim to like The Beatles (even 'I Wanna Hold Your Hand') and to be completely at ease in Toxteth. Accordingly, I always skit the woollies, and the places where they live. (One of the reasons Jill gave yrs. truly the push two summers ago.) The only time I don't skit the woollies is when I am within a hundred yards of Gibbo, whose dad, people say, made a fortune from turnips – before someone shot him.

Gibbo's produce has its merits, but the business of fetching it from Round Ours has none. These are what I'd call the chief drawbacks. Firstly, that Gibbo might decide he doesn't know you, and banish you from his property with a monkey wrench. Secondly, that Gibbo is usually to be found in his garage, underneath some rusting jalopy which he will try to sell you for a very low price. Like some lazy bear who has grown overfond of Twiglets, Gibbo can get pretty insistent. The roads leading from Marsh Lane back into town are dotted with these rotting hulks, which have been foisted on some reluctant pothead and then abandoned as the engine catches fire. Thirdly, Gibbo is prone to thirty-minute breaks in the conversation while he stares blankly at the TV. I stare blankly at the TV a lot as well, but at least I make sure there's some decent low-rent soap on while I'm doing it. Gibbo's set is stuck on BBC 2, so the silences can get pretty tiresome.

Not quite as tiresome as the fourth hazard, which is that Gibbo might have injected some speed, and might want to discuss politics. These discussions are in fact two- or three-hour monologues on the subject of the Middle East. Conducted in a low drone, they are notoriously difficult to follow. (Particularly as Gibbo is both a keen fan of Mossad *and* a card-carrying anti-Semite.) Pauly, the keg-lad from the Saracen's Head, once famously gave the wrong response during one of these monologues and was struck with a demi-john.

Gibbo is standing in his doorway as I come up the drive, and makes a strange click by way of greeting. 'We're in't back,' he murmurs. He's wearing his grey Parachute Regiment sweat-shirt, beneath which his belly fights for fresh air like a bag of doomed puppies. A cackle of laughter floats up from the rear of the house.

'I'm just after a quarter,' I say, shifting from foot to foot and wanting to get things over quickly. Gibbo shrugs, as if to say that it matters neither more nor less whether I should be after a quarter-ounce of pot or a fragment of the True Cross.

'In't back,' he says again, stonily.

Gibbo's front door is, technically, an easy boundary to cross. It is true that every bus stop in town boasts a row of griping pensioners, whose chief gripe is that it's no longer safe to leave your door open. But they know nothing of Gibbo, who doesn't even have a front door and doesn't mind, because no person would ever be dim enough to walk in uninvited. Even the police usually telephone to say they're popping by.

We pass through a scanty curtain made from hanging strips of coloured plastic, and I follow him down a bacon-scented hallway to the lounge at the back. The lounge is too hot, too bright, and it has men in it. All of them, sweating like bulls, look up when I go into the room, stare at me, then resume their activities – which are, variously, watching TV, staring at the floor, and smoking the sort of spliff which looks, and smells, as if it may have a child's arm rolled up inside it.

Gibbo belly-brushes me as he lumbers by on his way back to the armchair. He sits down heavily, begins picking his bare feet, placing shards of skin on the chair-arm. A heavy, tense silence descends. All of the men stare fiercely at the TV – a burbling Celt is joyously announcing that the current heatwave is set to last for ever.

I look around for a place to sit, but there's nothing, not even the usual stack of dusty *Fiesta* mags. I lean up against the radiator and then jolt away from it, alarmed, my palms burning from the contact. Gibbo's got his heating on full.

When at last, some Bangladeshi programme surfaces, heralded by a burst of amplified sitar music, Gibbo seems to remember I'm still standing at the edge of his lounge and lobs a soulless glare in my direction. 'It's slate,' he says, gruffly.

Slate is the poorest variety of pot – dry and powdery, its chief effect is a slight headache. Gibbo's slate is years old and has mould on the edges. This is probably the reason someone shot his dad.

'Slate, yeah fine,' I say. *Too chirpy. Not cool.* 'No sweat. Anything.'

For some reason, this makes everyone in the room snigger.

'He's gagging for it,' notes one sturdy, ginger-haired bloke in a check shirt. Another woollie – he could be a farmer, though more likely he does sod all.

'Like yer lickle girlfriend,' says Gibbo, softly. They all laugh again. Gibbo reaches down under the seat, for the huge gherkin jar where the measured deals of pot are stored.

'She were gaggin' for you alright Ev,' says a further man – a little dark hawk in paint-spattered denims.

'Aye well,' the Farmer responds. 'She'll have sand in places she never fuckin' dreamt about.'

'Ey!' shouts the Hawk, pointing at the TV. 'What's he doing on the box? It's that Paki from the Taj Mahal!'

And everyone laughs. Even the fat man at my elbow who takes up most of the sofa, and hasn't said anything up till now. Everyone except me.

I can feel a burning substance gather in my throat, like the leavings of grapefruit juice. Even though they didn't mean me to, I know what they are talking about. Gagging for it. Sand in places . . . I know I'm right. *The girl in the sand-dunes.*

'What youse after?' Gibbo says briskly, putting an end to the laughter. I tear my stare away from the fat man's arm – on one doughy wrist he sports a crude gaol-tattoo of a marijuana leaf. Underneath it the legend (or maybe the command) SMOKE.

'Quarter,' I say, hoarsely.

Outside again, I rush crab-like over the road to the smelly brook that runs towards the ship canal, and spit a nameless gruel from my stomach. A warm breeze from the west carries

20

the kippery scent of the dunes inland. 'Co...
Hawk called out as I left. I think I never, never ...

When I get home, Gus has eaten the last of the eggs, and ...
disgustedly watching *Countdown* on the kitchen portable....
run all the way and, being neither lean or healthy, I am close ...
death. Wheezing, I put the greasy, film-wrapped little package...
on the table next to Gus' feet and listen to the hammerings in
my chest.

'More slate,' he says, accusingly. 'May as well go and sniff a
biro.'

'That's the last I'm ever getting,' I say, still trembling.

Gus doesn't seem to hear. 'Yer brains'll drop out,' he says,
pointing at my head. I suddenly notice a tickling sensation on
my top lip and wipe it. My hand comes away covered in blood.

'I thought they'd stopped,' this just a distracted mutter as I
stare at the rusty stain on my hand. Gus is fingering the pot,
flipping it over and over in his palm. 'Might work if I get really
pissed first,' he opines. Unfurling himself to his full, belittling
height, he takes two fags off me and, miraculously having no
more cash flow problems, stalks off down to the Saracen's.

After a moment with my head tipped back, letting the blood
trickle down my throat, I grab my keys and run, slower this
time, after my brother. He's at the bar, just taking his first sip of
a half of Guinness as I run in. 'I've got to talk to you!'

Gus inclines his head invitingly. But so does Pauly, bored, on
the other side of the bar. So I lead Gus over to the dark corner
by the dart-board, and by a wall pitted with the wounds of
errant darts, I tell Gus, still trembling, what I heard in Gibbo's
lounge. Gus listens, impassively. I finish. He flips a beermat
over and over between mighty, horned fingers. 'Gorra fag?' he
asks. I shake my head. He shrugs. 'Don't say nothing to no
one,' he suggests, casually, as if telling me how to change a tyre.
'Keep yer head down. Don't go there again.' Then he yawns

. His eyes alight upon a pair of outsized
ing Hooch by the pool table. 'Fancy a

head down? That was them, Gus. I
. I've got to tell someone. The police.'
. I was just there buying some blow,
blokes going on about how they did
. Clever.'

the hotline. In confidence. I could give a false
name . . .'

'Fuck false names, kiddah.' He leans in, squinting. 'If them
lads find out you grassed – you're dead. You know what
happens to grasses, don't you? It's not worth it, man. Just leave
it.'

'But—'

'Stuff happens, right? I seen whole villages burned down to
the ground. Nuns drowned. Kids with their brains blown out.'

'Where?' This seems a little fantastical. *Drowned nuns?* He's
a tour leader, not a UN War Crimes Investigator.

'Never mind. Point is, kid. She'll get better. It's not worth it
for you.' Then something strikes him. ' 'Less there's a reward,
mind you. Is there one?'

'I can't believe I'm hearing this. You disgust me sometimes.'

Gus shrugs, unconcerned. 'Aye well,' he says. 'Happen I'll
just go then.' Haughtily, he drains his drink to the lees, gathers
up his tobacco and leaves.

For all my disgust, I know he has a point. I could be wrong.
People say trust your instincts – but how do you trust your
instincts when your instincts tell you to doubt everything,
including, if necessary, your own instincts? Then again, if I *am*
right, and the men are being that careless, someone else, a
braver someone, will definitely hear them, and grass on them.
And it *is* grassing. Things happen to grasses.

There were only three men, not counting Gibbo. What if Gibbo had nothing to do with it and when the three others go down, he remembers me, and tells the fourth one where I live? Or comes himself, because *he's* the fourth man, with a selection of instruments from the cupboard in his mum's house?

But I can't ignore it. Can't just shrug and say 'stuff happens'. Ten years ago, maybe, things were different. In those days, I was a wiseguy and a wag. Ever at the margins with a sharp remark and a comedy mime. It was the way boys like me – silent at home, poor at sports and fighting, and in all respects otherwise unmarked with the stamp of victory – could still triumph. That's why I was too late for Lamb. If that shrivelling moment in the market café was meant to teach me anything, it was this: Good Men do not fear the things under their desks.

There's no one on the phone here. I've got twenty pence in my pocket. But Gus was right. Don't draw attention to yourself. That's just asking for trouble. I'll do it from home.

It's like a little chapter in my life has closed. I feel lighter, less burdened, as I cross Roe Lane and head down the avenue to home. Strange the Great Sinner has perished. Strange the Good is here, amongst you, down from his mountain.

In through the drive. Past my father's ancient silver Volkswagen and through the gate to the back. The door's open. Bags are on the doorstep.

Volkswagen?

'Aah,' says my father, as if pointing out some curious architectural anomaly, as he ventures out into the driveway to meet me. 'You're here. I rather thought it was the police.'

'The police?'

'Yes – we appear to have been ah burgled.'

23

3

'Thank you for calling *The Clarion*. The hotline is closed until 9 a.m. tomorrow. If you wish to place an advertisement, please ring . . .'

I replace the phone and head back into the kitchen. My mother, a blur of tropical colour and ethnic jewellery, is darting backwards and forwards, ladling some thick, greasy stew into bowls. She casts me a worried glance and flicks past me to the larder.

'It's really most tiresome of you,' says my father, continuing the sentence I walked out on a few minutes back. 'I presume you don't leave your doors open at your ah—'

'No I don't. I just forgot. As I said.'

'The Devil finds work for I-just-forgot,' observes my mother, in mid-ladle. 'Oh *bugger*.' She drops the ladle and runs out into the garden to shout at a marauding cat.

I sit down. My father peers at me, an almost rabbinic spectacle, with his long white hair and tiny watchmaker's glasses. 'And while I appreciate that irresponsibility is something of an ah hallmark of Youth, I do feel that you might have acquired some semblance of maturity up at the ah—'

'University?'

'Quite. I mean – is it *customary* for undergraduates to ignite the furniture? They don't do it at the Polytechnic. Not since I've been there, at least.'

I curse Gus in my head. Apparently surprised by our parents' viciously early homecoming, he has managed to snake out of

24

the French windows with his kit bag, leaving them to believe they have been burgled. Where he is now is anyone's guess. I am every bit as alarmed as he must have been. They're a whole ten days too early – I was going to tackle the hole in the sofa next week. And the melted microwave. Now I'm trapped, alone, in the middle of a full-scale inquest.

'That cat is *evil*!' exclaims my mother, returning inside. 'It's got a dybbuk in it. I'm going to leave an onion out there tonight.'

'An onion?' enquires my father, distantly.

'Yes. They're very powerful,' says my mother, with certainty. She looks at me closely, as I spoon a little of the stew from the bowl. My father shrugs, indifferent to his wife's mystical rantings.

I shift my chair closer to the table, anxious that my mother doesn't see the blood on the lino from my earlier crisis. She has a pathological horror of blood. Not blood in general, I should add. Just mine. Which made it difficult to bond with a child who suffered perpetual nosebleeds.

My mother eats standing up, by the window, taking birdlike spoonfuls while she flits, in ceaseless fervour, around the room. She is a nervous, uneasy sort of woman, worse, it seems, when I am in her presence. A faint musky breeze wafts on my face as she flaps her arms, making tiny, precise alterations to the layout of her kitchen. Every now and then, she hovers, with a certain trepidation, behind my left shoulder, as if she would like to make adjustments to me also, but then thinks better of it.

'Have you had a productive vacation?' asks my father. He is awkward with me, too – always was, but today for some reason he seems to be striving for contact, by treating me as if I was a largely absent member of his Middle High German seminars. I am tempted to tell him about Gus, but decide against it. It's better to take the blame for the open doors, the sofa and, in time, the broken microwave, than speak of him in their presence. They'd only pretend they didn't know who I mean.

'We purchased you a small gift of sorts,' says my father, formally. He waves his hand over his shoulder. The tip of the mighty white scar, that snakes the length of his left forearm, is visible for a second, before he brings his hand back to the table. 'Lilly – where's the ah?'

In a nanosecond's worth of rustling, my mother has placed a parcel at my elbow, done up with string. I undo the knot carefully. I can feel four anxious eyes upon me. '*Look at him undoing the string!*' hisses my mother, as if this was some weird skill I'd picked up from a spell on Mars. My father clears his throat. They have always done this – whispered and nudged each other in secret dread as I reach to tie my shoelaces or pour a drink, as if there is something unpronounceably odd about my manner. As perhaps there is.

Two all-too familiar items. A Swiss Army Knife. And a blue, hooded top. I hold it aloft. There is a logo across the chest: *Sports International Club*. I look at my parents carefully, wondering, as I always do, if this could be a hint of irony.

'We thought you could row in it,' says my mother, hopefully.

'Thanks,' I say, deeply puzzled.

'How *is* the rowing?' asks my father.

'Erm. Well. I've never exactly rowed.'

'Oh,' says my father. They both look hurt. 'We rather thought you must do.'

'No – but I could. Now I've got this,' I say, brightly. 'Thanks.'

There is an awkward silence. My father rubs his head disconsolately, the gesture of some god whose creation has let him down rather badly. My mother sniffs.

'And I love the pen-knife,' I say, with strained enthusiasm. 'It's even got a magnifying glass.'

26

My father cheers up at this. 'We *knew* you would like one,' he says.

I keep quiet, honourably declining to mention the dozen Swiss Army knives discarded in my bedroom cupboard.

'Don't run about with the blade open,' says my mother, snatching the half-eaten bowl of stew from in front of me. 'I saw a terrible thing once where—'

'Lilly. *Darling*,' pleads my father. And she falls silent. This is my father's escape net. He puts up with the endless superstitious chatter, the folklore, the curses and the amulets. The mawkish accounts of suffering witnessed on the TV. Because he knows that, if it all gets too much, it can be silenced with a raised palm and a gentle plea of *Darling*.

Later, I set my alarm to wake me for nine, and stick a Post-It to the end of my bed, so I won't forget to ring *The Clarion*. Not that I could. Even in the midst of this untimely interruption, that conversation at Round Ours is still with me, sharpened and amplified by the stumbling, pause-ridden encounters after it.

After foraging in the kitchen, I make my way back upstairs, but pause a moment in the open doorway of the sitting room. They are lying together, like lovers, on the damaged sofa, in front of some German film. They don't notice me. A sudden moment of action on the screen, a gunshot, and my mother flinches. My father bends his head to kiss the top of her hair.

There is a wet plop as a fragment of the sandwich I have made falls to hit my shoe. I stoop to retrieve it. My parents shoot apart, like baby-sitting teenagers caught mid-snog.

'Sorry,' I say, awkwardly. I have intruded.

'Not at all,' says my father, with effort. He waves a hand at the screen, embarrassed. 'Sägebrecht. I'm doing a short course on her next term.'

I smile weakly. It has always perplexed me why, of all the languages my father knows – Russian, Czech, even Persian, for

Christ's sake – he had to end up teaching *German* at John Moore's.

'I'm off to bed. See you in the morning.'

'Shut the window or your spirit might fly out with the seagulls,' counsels my mother, helpfully. I turn to leave them in that familiar, pregnant silence. And as I turn, the stillness is shattered, by a terrible, ear-splitting crash from the kitchen.

We run in there. The kitchen window lies in shards across the lino. And at the centre of them is a pale pink brick. I glance fearfully towards the jagged hole that was our window, into the darkness of the garden. There's no one there.

My mother is distraught. She sits at the table, pale and trembling, like a child. My father makes her drink brandy. 'It's that cat,' she says, firmly. 'I knew it was up to no good.'

'Lilly. Darling. Cats can't throw bricks.'

My mother shakes her dark curls petulantly. 'It's a *symbol*,' she says. 'Of evil.'

She is persuaded to go upstairs and rest. Stands, on thick, cork-soled sandals, wobbling, her glass in one hand, like some tragic, exotic actress.

'They rob us,' she says. 'They smash our windows. Where has all this evil come from?' My father flashes her a tiny, fearful glance.

'*Darling.*'

And she is silent. She puts the glass down on the table and goes upstairs. I help my father clear up with dustpan and brush. He is sombre with fear – does everything with uncertainty, is afraid to go out to the dustbins alone. His is akin to the reaction of *The Clarion* when the news of the sand-dunes broke, a sorry disbelief, a sense that, as my mother said, something wicked is out there, stalking in our garden. And I know what it is.

He wants to call the police, but I persuade him to wait until the morning. I will be gone by then, I have to be gone. Because, scratched on to the surface of the brick, unseen by my father, as

I take it out to dump it in the wasteground beyond the garden, is a message. One word, illuminated in the security lights of the garage. *Skum*.

It can only mean one thing. This is a warning, to me. From Gibbo and the Hawk and the Farmer and the Fat Man. What sort of a man would write *Skum* on a brick? Only the man who would write *Smoke* on his arms. They know what I know, and they're covering their backs. A modest indication of the terrors that await me if I speak.

So when the alarm rings in the morning, I stuff all my clothes in a couple of holdalls. Leaving a scribbled excuse to my parents, I go and stay with a friend in Macclesfield until the new term starts, and I never ring the hotline at all.

London

September 1996

1

The Pendennis Press sits on the top floor of a white, wedding-cake building at the bottom, or the top of the Shepherd's Bush Road. You go through a whole parade of space-age security measures to get in there, but once inside, the hallway and the staircases are closer to those Soho alcoves whose doors advertise 'Models' in felt pen.

The upper floor, the office itself, is another surprise. It has clearly been designed by someone with a passion for naff sci-fi movies. The light switches are little touch-sensitive pads, raised just nanometres from the ice-white walls, the lights themselves semi-spheres, buried like meteors in the ceiling. The desks are dark, speckled iron, kidney-shaped, arranged in a weird symbol – the flag of South Korea or something Masonic. All about you, hi-tech banks of machinery bleep and snicker. The smell in there is a strong cocktail: ozone, warm women and new plastic.

When I come into the office, Tara's lying full-length under one of the cosmic desks. The bosses, Noakes and Fielding, must be befogging some dowager in a nearby winebar – there's no sign of them, and the atmosphere is relaxed. Minty is scanning some lengthy document in on the scanning machines, while with the other hand she flips vaguely through the pages of *Ms London*. In between her berry-coloured velveteen bosom and her ivory neck, she cradles the phone and talks to a man called Hugo, who, it seems, is being difficult about a forthcoming trip to Dorset.

Over on the other side of the photocopier, Jo, who does the illustrations, is also on the phone, also speaking to a Hugo. She croons and whispers and blows soft kisses, as if perhaps Hugo isn't some arrogant-haired stockbroker, but a toothless lamb sucking at her nipple.

Jo has adopted the perplexing habit of phrasing every sentence as a question. 'I'm like, Jo?' she queried, distantly, when we were first introduced. Provided Jo is speaking, or has a set of line-drawings or reproduction postcards in her hand, I can be confident of getting her name right. In all other situations, things get tricky. Seated alongside one another, Jo and Minty descend into a single disturbing blur of blondeness. At university, we used to call their kind 'rahs', in recognition of the sound that is made when a hundred of them are gathered together. It must be hell for the waiters in Harvey Nichols, serving not two, but an entire attic full of these strident, stripey-bloused grandees.

Tara is the only one I like. I squat down under her desk to talk to her. She looks like the sort of girl who might have got herself abducted by the wicked Fu Manchu: sickly white like the ash on a skinny roll-up. To her black cocktail dress there still cling the stale whiffs of the night before.

'I'm not too well, darling,' she says. Tara always calls me darling. She is one of those dark-haired, elongated girls who seem to be some cross between a cat and a horse – all tiny ears and big nostrils. I look at her lying there on the fawn carpet, stretched out like Black Beauty with a bout of colic. 'I'm *v.* hungover.'

Q., V. and F. – these are Tara's favourite adverbs. I can tell she's not well, and make the mistake of saying so.

'Thanks,' she spits back. 'You're a true gent.' A true gent being one who, when faced with a haggard woman dying under a desk, still makes allusions to her beauty. 'Get me some arsing pills will you?'

From my painful squatting position, I glance around the room.

'In my bag,' Tara murmurs. Pointing with theatrical effort to a slim leather lozenge at her feet, black, like her hair, her shoes and her spiderous legs. À la Scooby-Doo, I gulp – gripped with a surge of reluctance.

My mother, into whose purse I had dipped, not infrequently, as a lad, always told me it was bad form for a gentleman to look in a lady's bag. I never listened, and one Friday night, thieving for cash in the dark of their bedroom, I encountered some fiendish intra-uterine device. It was damp. After that, I always stole – at far greater risk – from my father and still have a sturdy dread of handbags.

Tara watches me dithering. 'Oh Jesus,' she groans. 'Give it here.' I pass it over. 'Honestly. *Boys*.' She unzips it, still staring up at the desk. I dare a teensy glimpse inside as her slim white hand rummages about. Nothing. It contains nothing except a packet of humbugs and a hundred pairs of black tights. And a few, loose Paracetamol.

I go to the kitchenette out on the landing and fetch her a cup of lukewarm water.

'Oh well done.' She swallows the pills, jerking her head back violently to help them down. Gives me that funny long, sideways look of hers. I am never certain what it means, but sometimes, smashed in the evenings on wine, I conjure it up and imagine that Tara might, just might fancy me. If she was twice as smashed as me, anyway.

'Forgot to ask,' she gargles, throatily, as the pills slip down. 'How you settling in?'

Tara has platoons of friends, including the son of the Finnish ambassador, and Helen Mirren. Whole districts of the capital are given over to housing them. It was Tara who put me on to the flat I'm in right now – she could charge fees for lodging people in the homes of London's more noxious classes.

'Fine. Haven't met Thingy yet.'

'Rory.'

The memory of Rory makes me smile.

When Tara first gave me his number, just over six weeks ago, I phoned Rory Rolfe in Cambridge, where he is managing some medieval madrigal troupe. A painfully posh man whose breeding has taught him to gush at everyone in sight, be they a docker or a duke. He practically ejaculated when I told him I wanted to move in.

'That's TOTALLY tremendous!' he shrieked. 'COMPLETE-LY.'

'Are you sure it's okay? I mean – you haven't met me or anything.'

'I don't need to! If you're a friend of Tara's, then I'm sure you'll be COMPLETELY WONDERFUL!'

I did begin to have reservations at that point.

'Well if you're sure . . .'

'I SO am!' he cried.

'So f. what?' Tara bristles now from her floor-side refuge. 'His first name's Rory and his last name's Rolfe. I suppose you'd rather he was called Vinny Macmanaman or Akko or something.'

Tara is inclined to get shirtily defensive of her friends. And she abhors that Northern name-snobbery which we ingest with our Vimto: *Oh, Rory is it? Well in't that awfully fuckin' nice?*

'And what do we call him for short?' I ask her, mock-belligerent. 'Roars? Or Rolfie?'

'No. Worse,' she says crossly. And rolls over, turning a slender back to my face. I stand up.

Minty jerks her honey-coloured head at the side office, the narrow room occupied by Noakes and Fielding, to indicate that the manuscripts are in there. I go in. Just one manuscript, sitting on the table in its yellow folder. But it's a fat one, which at fifty pence a page might keep me in kebabs for a while yet.

My job is to edit. I have had no formal training as an editor, cannot even spell particularly well. But that doesn't matter. My

36

job, really, is to cover the manuscripts with cryptic markings in red pen – not too much, not too little, the quantity of correction depending entirely on the temperament of the author. A comma here, a semi-colon there, and at my most daring, the odd ♫ in the margins. After this, the manuscripts, or 'em ess ess' as Noakes calls them, are returned to the authors who, being mostly illiterate, psychotic, and often both, are thus assured that their works are in the hands of experts. Once they believe this, we charge them money to publish their books. This is what we do at the Pendennis Press – by a combination of careful wording and bare-faced deceit, we make dreams come true.

I arrived here, fresh from Euston, a torn scrap of the Monday *Guardian* in my hand. They hired me. For three reasons: I have a degree from a British university. Noakes, being from some colony or other, feels this tantamount to being royalty. I have a penis – not a very useful one – but this, according to Noakes, means I am tenacious and capable. An agent of order. 'We started giving them to the girls,' he told me on the day of my interview, meaning manuscripts, I assumed, rather than penises. 'But they get distracted. Start playing with their hair or looking at the builders out of the window.'

Lastly, I have a pocketful of very fine-tipped red pens, which Noakes covets. Every time I present him with a finished manuscript, he gazes at my markings with boundless awe. Sometimes even strokes them with a stubby fingertip. 'Sheesh,' he says, shaking his wheaty head. 'You boffins.'

Today, the manuscript for editing is a children's story. 'Simon Snake is Attacked by a Bat' – accompanied by a series of wax crayon drawings which might do credit to a three-year-old, but make me worry about the authoress, a retired Economics lecturer from Goole. I know Simon Snake well. In my time, I have also edited the escapades of his woodland chums Larry Lion, Herbert Hamster and Karla Kangaroo.

Soon, this inspired scribe will run out of creatures, and I await with reservation the publishing debut of Terry Tapeworm.

There's a yellow Post-It on top of the folder. Noakes has written it. Fat, uncertain writing, like a P.E. teacher's. 'Strange: Wait', it says. So I sit in the swivel chair and wait.

Every manuscript has some note from Noakes on it. *Strange: Easy on the commas*, it will say, after some particularly unsettling stream-of-consciousness rant has passed through my fingers and I have foolishly attempted to render it sane. *Note: Author is Latvian* another time or *N.B. Experimental – just tick*. I am given to making mental notes to myself all the time and, gradually, they have started to resemble Noakes' own: *Strange: Have a shower*.

Jo, who in some bid for individuality has turned up the collar of her blouse, comes in and briefly fixes me with the kind of stare we reserve for the Stilton-ish mulch between a lover's toes. She makes a bit of cross banging and clattering in a drawer in the corner before emerging with a solitary pink paperclip, which she sticks in her teeth. As she is walking away she turns round and removes the paperclip.

'We had, like, an author on the phone about you this morning?'

'Who?'

'Anspaugh. "Hi Fiddly Dee – An Auditor's Life For Me"?'

I nod with trepidation. I can guess what's coming. 'Was it about the missing pages at the end? I couldn't find them anywhere, Jo, honestly. I'm not sure they were even there.'

Jo does the famous public-school flick with her fringe.

'He doesn't er … mind? He says you gave him an idea. Wants to rewrite it all. In, like, rhyming couplets?' She teeters back to her desk.

In the outer office, I can hear the crystal tones of Minty, clear and confident, Captain of Hockey, still berating her own, hapless Hugo. 'What's the Five Nations got to do with bloody anything?' she wants to know. 'It's not for another five months.'

Then from behind her I hear and feel a definite shiver, a perceptible twang on the strings of atmosphere. If that is too mystical, let me also say that I can hear my boss, Dennis Noakes, unzipping his kagoule and demanding in a loud voice: 'Why's that girl not at her work-station?'

'I'm under it,' snaps a crotchety voice.

Suddenly Noakes is in here with me, beaded with perspiration. Fussing with elastic bands as he tells me darkly that Certain Girls are skating on thin ice. He always speaks to me in a low voice, occasionally glancing over his shoulder at imaginary spies. This, combined with his bulky frame and dark-circled eyes, suggests a deeply paranoid panda.

'Girls,' he tells me, as he sits down and begins to unwrap a large slice of sticky cake, 'just can't be left unsupervised. They start chattering.' Then he begins a lengthy discourse on the subject of girls chattering, even sketching me a little graph on the back of an envelope to demonstrate how the chattering of different girls tends to peak at different times. Minty's when hungry, just before lunch. Jo's when full, just after. Except the chattering of Tara, which is a constant, unless she is sleeping. I am unsure how Noakes can know what Tara does when she's asleep, but I give him the benefit of the doubt.

' 'Course, if you get a dominant male in the work arena, it all changes. They get their heads down and get stuck into it.' There have been studies, he adds, which prove it.

He continues for some time in this vein, his speech rich with allusions to Thru-Put and Performance Quotients. He eats the whole slice of cake and starts on a flat plinth of gaily coloured nougat. 'Fielding's a hundred per cent behind me. Well, thirty-five per cent, since he only shows up thirty-five per cent of the time. Freelance just isn't tax-healthy, but we've got the nod from the *number-crunchoes* . . .'

I am not listening. I wish I was back in Fulham, sitting at the kitchen table with my flatmate. But Noakes' last words shake this little vision into nought. He's stopped. Exploring the further reaches of his teeth with a probing finger. Looking at me keenly, and plainly expecting an answer.

I ask if he'll repeat what he just said. And he does. And when he's finished, I rather wish he hadn't started.

'You might look a bit rough round the edges. But you've got the makings,' he tells me, 'of the best editor in London. You really *care* about the authors. And that's rare in a young bloke these days. Precious rare.'

He is suggesting something foul, something at odds to me – like offering a starter home to a *!Kung* Bushman. The offer is this: an end to freelance editing. And in its stead wage-labour, nine to five, in an air-conditioned office in Shepherd's Bush. I, Alastair K. Strange, who quit his job as bottom-checker in the choc-ice factory after only four hours, am being head-hunted.

And what a head to hunt. I'm not a dominant male at all. Any traces of dominant-maleness were rooted out and abolished by my first girlfriend and the Gender Studies module I did in the second year.

'I'm not sure—'

But Noakes does not hear me. A greying jungle of hair protrudes, like headphones, from each ear, obscuring the bulk of sounds that pass his way.

'Wanted to get my bid in first,' he chunters on.

Lucky for me, Noakes is enough of a jerk to believe I might have other prospects to consider. He says to call him. When I've had a think about it. His dental excavations hit the jackpot and his worried eyes light up. He extracts a sliver of almond from between his front teeth and examines it, glistening on his finger-tip. Then he seals the em ess (the 'pre-edit', as he is calling it today) in a transparent wallet, and accompanies me to the door as he informs me of his plans for a disposable, foil-wrapped book which will perish within forty-eight hours of opening.

It's all a long way from what I want, I think, as I go down the stairs. Past the other offices. The ever-perplexing perspex doors of Iranian Fruit Concentrates. Down another floor. Past Nawaz Immigration Consultants and Modelling Agency. Roger Cook, I often think, could make a whole series in this building, waddling from floor to floor with his camera crew.

A long way from what I want. Or ever wanted. And then, as I step out into the babel of Shepherd's Bush on a Monday, a scary little thought hits me right between the eyes. I am exiled here. Like the morose Kurds in the kebab shop. I have nowhere else to go.

It's lunchtime when I leave the office, and Shepherd's Bush appears to be hosting some conference for the internationally mal-coordinated. Its streets are jammed with gaily clad visitors from all corners of the earth, all of whom have one thing in common: a singular inability to walk down a street in a straight line. As I am practically rugby-tackled at the zebra-crossing by a robust Slavic lady in a gold windcheater, I wonder how Onka would cope with this every morning and night, without turning into a thoroughly Bad Man.

Noakes' offer has knocked me off-beam. After three years as a student, and a period as one of that legion now glossily termed JobSeekers, I am chemically unable to get dressed before *Neighbours*. And what would happen to such cult TV delights as *Tour of Duty* or *Riviera* if Alastair K. Strange had to get up early in the mornings? They'd fold in a week. I want it all to stay like it is now – manuscripts for cash once a week and telly, all night, every night.

I am like Kenton, the barman on *Jacaranda Cove*, who spent his lottery win on singing lessons and still ended up off-key. Just no good at work. I escaped scrutiny at school and again at the university by bullshit alone. It was said that I was clever, but I was unmasked, at last, three months ago, when I left with my degree and had to find work. Billy put in a good word for me at the choc-ice factory. I lived with Sue and checked the bottoms of choc-ices in a freezing hall in Widnes for £2.50 an hour. Earned ten pounds, less stoppages. Came home. Argued with

42

Billy and caught the train to London from Runcorn. That was my working life.

What's more, I have this idea that some day, flipping through a crumpled *Guardian* on the floor of a tube-train, I'm going to find an advert, which will say: *Alastair Strange (or similar) required. To sit on own arse, drink tea and make incisive comments about trash TV drama. Attractive package (inc. wife).* And because that dangerous idea is rooted in my mind like a tumour, nothing else will do. Billy said similar when I quit the factory and he came home for his lunch and found me there, still in my hair-net and white overalls, watching Quincy unearth another poisoner. 'I dunno what they taught you at that posh school of yours Allie but they filled you fulla shit.'

Noakes is a pushover, and I can cope with Minty and Jo, the Aryan bitch-queens. But Fielding – the ageing little hooray who constitutes the largely absent other half of the Pendennis Press management – despises me more than he despises his authors and his Filipino servants. On that fiercely hot July day when Noakes recruited me for the freelance editing, he introduced me to Fielding – who was trying to sneak away early with some heavy suitcases. And Fielding gave me a look that suggested he would sooner have hired an oyster.

I am totting up these observations on the fingers of my left hand as I make my way back towards Fulham. On my right hand, I note some contraries. I cannot go home, as I do not have one. I cannot go to Sue's. The Housing Benefit, meanwhile, won't meet the rent Rory demands – it barely covers the cost of a gym locker in Neasden – but I don't want to move. I love my new lodgings off the North End Road – the flat, with its high ceilings and huge kitchen, and the nautical railings on the steps outside. I like Martha, who rents the other spare room. I even have a certain affection for the weird Sikh who lives down-stairs, and shouts abuse all night at his TV. Maybe it wouldn't be so bad . . .

I catch sight of my reflection in a shop window. I am dressed in my smartest clobber, and still manage to look like the least groovy kid at the sixth form disco. What did Martha say, just yesterday as she rifled, without excuse, through my cupboard to borrow some socks? *Cute face, Stranger. Shit wardrobe.* When girls say things like this to you, you have to take action. Which would be easy, if I knew how to shoplift.

My legs appreciate the long walk back to the flat. They seem to know whenever their owner might be on the brink of getting trapped in the real world and start to twitch and cramp of their own accord. The only option to quiet them is to run. Or at least embark on some brisk walking.

In the Aussie soaps, the long walk is used as a device to show that the characters are working their problems out. If Tug wants a place on the welding course at Tec, Tug needs to tell Flathead that it wasn't him who stole the exam papers. But to do that, he has to say who it was. Which means dobbing on a mate. (Something akin to buggery, or teetotalism in the Australian Decalogue.) And the mate was Shoni – whom Tug quite fancies. So we see Tug, in the distance, tramping down the beach, his pugnacious little face screwed up in an effort of concentration, the knot of his problems simplifying with every step on the sand.

The long walk option has never worked like that for me. When I start trying to solve problems, I start talking out loud. And then people start to pop up from behind bushes or underneath cars, and other improbable locations, and I start to feel like I might be a little crazy. So the problem, whatever it was, gets left far behind.

I'm going to ask Martha. That's the only option. With her talent for the hitherto unthought-of, I can't possibly go wrong. Whatever she says, I'll do it.

*

Back home, she is still in her stripey pyjamas, sloppily eating mashed banana from a bowl. Her brow is plastered with a wine-coloured substance; her head is turbaned with a carrier bag from the newsagent's. She can't hear me come in, of course, because she's got the radio and the telly on full blast and is humming some tune somewhere in between the two. She hates it quiet.

But at least she smiles when she sees me coming down the hall, which is a good start – because when I left this morning, I put my foot in it by asking one of the questions I'd decided I would not ask and left her looking glum.

I prefer it when Martha smiles. When she is in a mood ('having a monk on' she calls it, for Yorkshire-based reasons inexplicable to outsiders), she resembles those Chinese finger traps that imprison the digits more fiercely with every tug. I become like some street-hardened TV cop trying to prevent a toddler from bawling: place improper items of laundry on my head, do feeble impressions of de Niro, joke about the shape of fruit. And with every attempt, Martha will enter a new plane of bleakness. I am relieved she is smiling now.

'It's definitely a lot . . . *plummier*, isn't it?' she asks, pulling a damp strand of hair out for my perusal.

'Well . . . in a red plum sort of way,' I say, putting my bag down on an empty chair.

She winces, as if I have just failed a little test. 'Fuck off,' she says, gently, examining the dark strand in annoyance.

'Well you asked.'

'Yeah. And that was the wrong bloody answer.'

Martha has a great dollop of mahogany hair – all earth and apples and Shire County haylofts – whose sheen and hue she spends a great deal of time and money trying to obliterate with various radioactive compounds, which, thankfully, make not a blind bit of difference.

'I don't know why you bother. It's great hair.'

'I could marry you sometimes.' This is some further peculiarity of Rotherham speech – she says it to me as often as Londoners say *j'naat ameen* and *innit*.

I turn the TV and the radio down, just enough to stop my eyes rattling in my skull, and sit at the table. Martha bristles slightly.

'Took your time,' she says, licking a fragment of banana from her sleeve. A lass of healthy proportions, she regards eating as a sacred activity. 'Want some tea?'

'Wouldn't mind.'

'You know where the kettle is.' She reaches for her spoon again, smiling.

'Don't laugh at your own jokes.'

'I wasn't. I broke the kettle.'

Martha is queen of the unexpected answer and a veritable princess of the pointless point. When she first met me, I told her I came from Southport. 'No wonder you're here then,' she replied. Nobody ever said that to me before. They usually say, 'Ooh, that's where the sea never comes in isn't it?' Unless they are Southern. In which case they tend to cock their heads to one side like a little dog and say 'Wassat? Stockport. 'Snear Leeds, innit?' Which it isn't.

Then, a few mornings later, she came and stood by me at the sink while I was brushing my teeth, and said that Zebedee must have, at some time, been quite a respectable man's name, because it was in the Bible. And even if it was a weird observation with which to kick off the day, you could hardly help but agree.

There are, I know, those irritating, consciously kooky girls who make a lot of effort to sound interesting even just buying a can of Fanta. But Martha is not like that. You might have thought there'd come a time when, by virtue of them being so invariably unpredictable, her comments got to be a pain in the arse. But somehow I am immune.

'What you got today? More mucky books?' She pulls my folder over and fumbles inside. The first manuscript I brought home happened to be some dentist's frantic celebration of fellatio, and since then I've had a tough job convincing Martha that I don't specialise in editing hard-core smut.

'It's more *Woodland Tales*.'

'Good,' she says, licking her broad lips as if in anticipation of a literary feast. 'I always like them.'

'They offered me a job,' I say. She ignores me, sticking her tongue out of the corner of her mouth. I repeat myself.

'A what?'

'A job. Full-time. Nine to five. Editing, writing reports. What do you think?'

'Why you bloody asking me?' she says, almost crossly. 'What d'you think *I* know about jobs?'

It is difficult understanding precisely how Martha manages in the world. Originally, she was working in some charity shop in Brook Green whose chief objective was saving the badger from extinction. And then, suddenly, she became a relief barmaid in the Pickled Newt, a run-down, rather scary establishment just up the road in Baron's Court. I don't press her any more. I'm not really interested, or I make a point of not being. How many times was it – in those first, tense weeks at university – that I stood in some roomful of chattering fucks and the first haughty question I faced was 'What do you *do*?'

Doing has, for me, a lot in common with grid references, in that I'll never understand either. There was a time, at university, when I had friends. People who saw no value in drinking Pimms until they puked. But even those people would still turn up at my room in the middle of *Emmerdale*, and say 'What are you *doing* tonight?' As if you were supposed to be.

Before long, they all started drifting off, being all proactive and self-improving. You would spot them in the street sometimes and say, 'Fancy a smoke?' and they would shake

47

their heads and say, 'No mate – I'm too *busy*. I've just been made Treasurer of the Flat Earth Society.' And then, you were left with the dregs. No girls. Just a bunch of underwashed, malnourished boys who spent every waking hour making bucketbongs and discussing the molecular structure of Skunk Weed. I lost touch with them, too, once I gave up smoking pot. Condemned to hermitude – all because I never understood this *doing* thing.

Martha and I spend a lot of time, practically every day, in our kitchen, doing absolutely nothing, except talking and smoking and watching the soaps on the portable, sitting around the big round table on which some miscreant has scratched the legend *Roo is a poo*. The kitchen has huge wide windows, and someone – Rory, I assume – has carefully laced a string of fairy lights around them.

We sit here for hours, smoking with that grim determination usually only encountered in Russians, drinking Whisky Queers, talking and feeling safe as the traffic roars down below us like the sea. Whisky Queers are a drink invented by Martha. It is just whisky and ginger beer, but we sink enough to make them a tradition. They seem to have cured my nosebleeds.

Martha predictably abandons the *Woodland Tales* and starts scribbling stuff in her big, black notebook. She draws pictures sometimes, but she won't draw me. Says I'm too ugly for her pencil. Which might be a joke. You never know.

'What will you do if you don't take the job?' Martha asks, suddenly, putting her pencil down. I shrug.

'I don't know. Maybe go up North again.'

'Really?' she asks sharply.

'No. Not really. I don't know why I said that.'

'No,' she says, reddening slightly, looking back down at her sketch book. 'Neither do I.'

There is an awkwardness in the air again. To dissolve it, I check the rat-trap behind the cooker, but once again, it has claimed no victims. I bought it a few weeks back after Martha came squealing into my bedroom, swearing that a small grey rodent had run out of the cutlery drawer and up her arm. She wouldn't set foot in there again until I went out and purchased a very expensive rat-murdering device, which is loaded with enough venom to polish off a village. Martha was still reluctant to enter the kitchen, and so, after a few, lonely evenings, I pretended I had found, and disposed of, a rat corpse. I am just praying that my fib won't come true.

It grows late – the clock on the oven says 1:30 p.m., which means it's at least three or four. We've smoked all of my cigarettes, and an old one Martha found in her cavernous handbag: Park Drive, which they only sell to very old Irishmen, so God knows how she got it.

I still don't want to deal with Noakes' offer. And Martha, conveniently, still won't tell me what to do. The back of my mouth tastes metallic – I'm hungry – and the cupboard and the fridge are practically bare – a tube of harissa, some wine, and a slim can of 'Mirage' – *the drink for mysterious people.* No wonder the rat's moved on.

So Martha, her damp and utterly undifferent hair combed back and imprisoned under a knitted hat, comes with me all the way to the Tesco Metro in Hammersmith and watches with mounting horror while I fill the trolley with seven cans of beans, a jar of garlic puree and a kilo of the bleakest Cheddar.

'It saves time. And energy,' I protest, marooned in a chilly aisle. 'You don't use up your brain thinking what to eat.'

'And what do you do with it instead?' she asks, archly. ' 'Sif I needed to ask.'

I'm thinking of a reply to this, but she's already moved on and started eyeing up the orange squash.

'Like this?' she asks, holding up a bottle.

'Prefer lemon.'

She makes a face and puts the bottle back. 'There was a lad in our street like you. Back in Rotherham,' she says. 'He'd only eat Campbell's Cream of Mushroom Soup.'

'Oh yeah?'

'He was autistic,' she adds, pointedly, and moves off.

I am a touch put out by this. All the way there, Martha walked close to me. Just a few inches shorter than me, she kept pace, knocking against my shoulders companionably as we went along. Inside the Metro, I doubled up, involuntarily, at the huge sign which says, like some accusatory *Evening Standard* headline, *John West Dressed Crab*. Martha pretended this was not funny. But later, further up the aisles, I caught her engaged in her own act of levity – slyly slipping crazy things into the trolley when she thought I was not watching: six bottles of vermouth, a bumper pack of Huggies.

'The gob on you,' she observes, coming back to the trolley with her own contribution to the shopping – a mighty, twenty-four-roll pack of bog paper, enough for a troop ship full of dysentery victims.

'Do you think that'll be enough?' I ask, drily.

'I'm not running out again,' she says. 'Had to use one of your manuscripts the other day.'

I don't really mind her stealing Mr Anspaugh's ending. Nor the autistic-slur. I even like it when Martha is rude to me – particularly about my clothes (which she nevertheless borrows with pointed frequency). It has been a familiar sort of rudeness from the start. And she has never once said the word 'Zeitgeist', or tried to convince me that Joni Mitchell is actually a great poet. She's a nice lass.

Some people, especially girlfriends and English teachers, have a misplaced horror of 'nice'. They like to say it's a cop-out, a term for vicars and old ladies. But I learned early in life that men cannot cope with 'beautiful' and 'pretty', 'stunning' and 'cute', 'striking' and 'sexy' and the esoteric distinctions between them. I remember Jill's derision when I tentatively ventured that a certain new starlet on Brookside was 'quite beautiful'. She looked at me like I was something stuck to the bottom of her mules and barked, 'No she's NOT. She's just *pretty*.'

Martha, mind you, is about as nice as they get before you really have to think of another word.

I leave her at the cash desk while I run back to find shampoo. When I come back, she has paid, and is waiting outside. I gesture to her through the window – suggesting I ditch the shampoo – but she shakes her head. So I wait in the queue, impotent, while the man in front of me attempts to pay in a mixture of credit cards, vouchers and zloty. I watch Martha, tramp-like, in my long overcoat and her knitted hat.

Whatever she looks like, I reckon I fancy Martha. In fact, there's no 'reckon' about it. What would you call the little knot of air which lodged in my chest when she first put my coat on, first borrowed a pair of my socks? It was pride. I felt like I'd won something. And even with my track-record, I know that the autumn, and not the spring, is the time when lasses can be found. New classes, courses, jobs and lodgings. The sight of the first pair of woolly stockings gives even Strange a glimmer of hope.

Outside the supermarket, the air smells a little cooler, smoky, the first real whiff of autumn. I am so caught up in private happiness I do not notice that someone is bothering Martha.

A thin, gingery sort, in a green padded vest, is talking to her, leaning snakishly across, his lips a tongue's-breadth from her ear. He has no visible eyelashes and blinks patiently, like a lizard on a warm rock. I hold back, listening, wanting to know, in spite of myself, what dark and nasty magic he is trying out. Martha, gazing ahead at me as she sips a can of Coke, makes a brief plea for assistance with her eyes.

'Are you ready?' I say, two octaves deeper and four shades more Northern than is necessary.

The man glances my way, assesses my threat-rating as precisely zero and continues. 'How comes you don't want to come for a drink, then?' All in this sugary, perky purr, as if he is taming a kestrel. 'You was smiling at me before.'

Martha turns and gazes blankly at the man.

'I wasn't smiling at you,' she says. 'I was just chewing the dead skin off my lower lip.'

The fuck-you-soon grin disappears. Ginger Vest straightens up, flexes himself. You can nearly hear the sinews crack. 'Now come on,' he says, testily. 'Don't get arsey. That's getting arsey. I'm here being pleasant, and you start giving it. That's giving it, saying that. That's out of order, gell. Well out of order.'

Aa'a vordag-el. W'laa'a vordah.

Martha takes a casual, at-your-ease sip from her can. Then she turns and spits it, in a fine arching plume, at the man's breast. It spatters there, a perfect map of Brazil on the green front of his flak-jacket, then meandering down to his narrow waist.

'Come on,' she shouts, haring down the walkway like a child after a bus, the shopping slung over her shoulder. Ginger Vest turns to me and licks his lips, tasting revenge.

'Here,' I say, thrusting the shampoo into his puzzled hand. 'It might get the stains out.' By the time he knows what I have given him, Martha and I are on the Fulham Palace Road, coughing, helpless with laughter and exertion.

Soon it's night, and she has made us some Indian potato thing to eat with a couple of bottles of wine we found at the back of Rory Rolfe's larder. In a ground-breaking move, I have turned the TV off.

Sitting at the table, across from the blue formica breakfast bar, I just happen to remark that the Indian Potato Thing (this is the only name Martha will bestow on the dish) could maybe do with a little salt. And quite without warning, she tosses the glass salt cellar at me. It hits me on the forehead, and makes a small cut.

'I thought you were going to *catch* it!' she protests, as I dab at my forehead with a tea-towel. 'I forgot you were such a joey.'

Joey as in Deacon: Blue Peter's very own palsied saint. Misappropriated by a million under-elevens as the rudest word they knew. I haven't heard the word since junior school.

'I bet you heard it a lot then,' Martha observes, giving the bristly top of my head a defiant rub. 'I bet when they picked the teams there was always just you left, and some really fat kid with allergies.'

'He wasn't fat,' I say, 'just allergic. And weird. Deeply weird. Like a boy from Mars or something.'

'Were they mean to him?'

I give a shrug. 'Boys are just like that,' I say, all knowledgeable. 'Shitty. Just the way it is.'

Martha pushes her plate away in annoyance. Her eyes narrow up. 'Hate it when you say stuff like that. Boys are this. Girls are that. What do you know? Sound just like my dad, you do. Pompous.'

Then, because Martha loves her grub far more than making a stand, she pulls the plate back to her and starts eating again.

I change the subject. 'When did you stop liking him?' I ask her. 'I mean – was it when your mum—'

It being not-said, of course, makes it doubly said, but I still won't say it. I preserve an almost Victorian horror of the word – in Martha's presence, anyway. She chews for a long time on a piece of naan bread and gazes out of the window behind me. She's always doing this. Makes me wonder if I should repeat myself. But if I do, she'll get shirty. 'I heard you! I'm thinking!' she'll snap. So this time, I wait.

'Did like him once, I think,' she says, very slowly and carefully. 'He's got this terrible back – really bad from when he fell off a digger. One Christmas, he spent the whole time on the floor. And just after I went back to school, he went into hospital. He was there for months. Well it seemed like months. Had to take two buses and a train to visit him 'cos Mum wouldn't drive in the dark.

'Then it must have been spring, 'cos we were making these Easter cards. In class, like. And I brung one home. And Mum was in the kitchen, and she said, you know, there's a surprise for you in the lounge. So I ran in. Thought it was a present or something. She was always giving us brilliant presents. Any time, not just birthdays and that. And the surprise was him. And it really was, you know, like a proper surprise. He had his green jumper on – like yours. You look like a dad in that.'

I pull absently at my frayed sleeves. A little crusty around the edges. 'Funny,' I say. 'This is his jumper. *My* dad's, I mean.'

In a sombre grey suit and a heavy overcoat, my father might look all mysterious and exciting, a little like John Thaw playing Bond. Instead, he favours a look very similar, in fact, to Martha's: sloppy, perforated jumpers and tracksuit bottoms. It's always driven my mother to a frenzy. She is, after all, the first person to point out that Columbo must have been *pretending* to be married, since no real self-respecting Mrs Columbo would ever have let him out of the house in that raincoat.

'He hides things like this,' I tell Martha, 'so my mum doesn't throw them out.'

She nods sagely. 'He's scared of her then,' she says – which with typical Martha-cheek seems every bit as pompous a pronouncement as any of mine. And far less accurate.

It's just not something I've ever considered before. I try, in fact, not to consider my parents too much, because I worry, can't come up with any answers, and it gives me a headache. I once asked my mother why she married him, and she could not provide an answer. Other than that she'd once witnessed him leaping over a gate using no hands, and she thought it was quite cool. Or whatever word they used back in 1788.

But they stay together, and even if they're more inscrutable than Confucius on a very sullen day, I think I can say on fairly good authority that no one scares anyone else. There's a fair amount of exasperation, but they still share a bed. I've even, to my private astonishment, heard it creaking in the night.

'Sweet,' Martha comments. 'But crap. Someone's always scared of someone else. In any relationship.'

'Come off it.' I'm pleased to have drawn an opinion out of her, however screwy it may be. 'What about us? Are you scared of me?'

'We're not having a relationship.' She comes back, quick as a needle.

There's a teensy bit too much of a silence.

'You're just an old romantic, aren't you?' she says.

'No,' I say, pointedly – looking her straight in the eye. She looks away before I do.

A bottle of Bulgarian later and I've forgotten all my resolutions about the things I will and won't say to Martha. I ask her how she manages for money.

'Mum left us some stuff,' she says, shrugging. Her bra-strap appears, black, from beneath the sloppy brown top. 'Got this cottage in Ireland. Get the rent off it. That's how come I met Rory. He was out there, doing his madrigals. Had four of his contraltos kipping in me barn.'

Then the phone rings in the hall.

'I'm not here,' Martha calls automatically, as I go off to answer it. I'm always the one who answers it.

It's just a friend of Rory's. Someone from whom Rory has borrowed a book on Italian church architecture. And who now suspects that I've got that book, and probably Rory, concealed under the floorboards. It takes a fair while to conclude the conversation.

'*Yew kid – ah – perhaps leave it with the – ah – pawters,*' he keeps saying, in spite of the fact that we have no pawters with whom we could leave anything. In the end, I decide the best approach is to pretend I'm just some simple-minded domestic and allow the man to dictate a message to Rory. I pretend I'm copying it all down.

Back in the kitchen, Martha has switched on the fairy lights and she's sat there in the twinkling with the cold air rushing in. She's put a tape on – a home-made one. On one side, the label says *Stop!* and on the reverse it says *Go!* I don't recognise any of the songs – they're not my kind of thing. Hard to see, in fact, whose kind of thing they might have been, other than some dangerously hectic individual.

'A friend made it for me,' she says.

'Didn't know you were friends with any crack-dealers.'

But she doesn't reply. No one – crack-dealers or otherwise – ever rings for Martha and, if they did, she would not talk to them. I ask her why. Again.

'Just don't wanna talk to Dad.' And we're back to her dad. Who doesn't want her to be here, wants her back working for him in Rotherham. Where he can keep an eye on her.

'At least he wants you somewhere,' I offer. But she ignores this – likes to make a conversation go whichever way she wants.

'He has to win every argument we have. Do you know what? He used to make me mum so angry being like that, so you know what she used to do? She used to let him win, and then she'd just go up top and clean behind all the bathroom taps with his toothbrush. She was ace.'

'Didn't he find out?'

'I never told anyone. 'Cept you.'

'I'm honoured.' I mean it.

Then, to interrupt the slightly prickly pause that follows, I go over to the sink and pour hot water and a squirt of Fairy into

56

one of the dirty pans. 'Don't say I never do anything round the house,' I quip over my shoulder. But it doesn't get me a smile. 'I'm sure she must have ... must have loved you a lot,' I say then, trying to think of something nice to say about a dead mother.

Martha brushes all the hair back from her ears. Her brown eyes have darkened a shade in anger. 'She'd never have let him stick me in that place. No way.'

I know she went to boarding school after it happened. But I also know that's not the place she means.

Later, when we're really rotten drunk and feeling a little queasy, Martha thinks it wise to top it all off with a spliff. We've reached those bleak hours, between the end of the mainstream soap run and the start of the cult cheapies. So we sit on the floor in her bedroom and I keep her company while she smokes it. I cannot touch the stuff these days, haven't enjoyed a smoke since the summer of Gibbo and the sand-dunes.

She's got the cheapest room in the flat, looking out on to a bare brick wall. It smells of bergamot and Christmas cake in there, like girls' rooms always seem to – light years away from the nicotinous funkiness of a ripe gentleman. Even the piles of discarded underwear have a certain tastefulness to them. The walls are festooned with photos – chiefly horses and dogs. And lots of leering, red-eye snapshots from teenage parties – all bright, jolly boys and girls, high on their youth and cider.

The scratchy carpet hurts after a while, and I shift on to an old, tatty rug that I haven't seen before.

'Nice eh?' she says. 'Got it a while back, from the shop.'
'What shop?'
'The Spina Bifida shop. When I worked there.'
'I thought it was badgers. You said it was Save the Badgers.'
Martha shrugs. 'Whatever. Seen this?'
She's got a new trick to show me. The tape-eject feature on

her little stereo has a heavily dampened spring and it opens with such mock-hi-tec lethargy that you suspect the manufacturers might be taking the piss. Martha presses it again and again, delightedly. 'It's brill,' she says. 'Like off *Star Trek* or something. So slow.'

Then something occurs to her, and she pitches forward to me, all eager. 'Bet you couldn't take your jumper off and put it on again before it's properly opened.'

I shrug. 'I bet I can't either.'

'*Booooring*,' she groans. 'Give it us. Bet I can.'

She makes me take the jumper off and give it to her. Pulls it over her head impatiently.

'Go on,' she says. 'Press the button for us.'

She does it. Pulls my father's jumper off, turns it inside out and puts it back on again – all before the tape player has finished its ponderous opening rites.

'What d'you reckon?' she demands, breathless. 'Am I ace, or what?'

Anyone who can amuse themselves with their flatmate's father's jumper and a cheap stereo is ace, certainly.

'Bit like the A Team,' I offer.

'What is?'

'They were always building rocket launchers out of a bit of bamboo and some fireworks. That's like you.'

'Is there anything that *doesn't* remind you of something you saw on the telly?'

I am stumped by this one. Have to think about it for a moment.

'Well. There's you. You're not like anything I ever saw on the telly.'

'You just said I *was*. You said I was like the A Team. You're so full of shit, Strange.'

There doesn't seem to be much of an answer to that. I just ask her if I can have my jumper back.

'Did he give you it?' Questions always seem to shoot out of her like a sneeze. Sometimes it's difficult to follow.

'What?'

'This.' She pulls on the sleeve – her sleeve, now, it seems. 'It's the only thing you own that's nice.'

'Naaa.' Briefly talking like Gus – that hard, adopted argot that covers a multitude of wounds. 'I nicked it. Wouldn't give me the steam off their piss, either of them.'

Martha pulls a face. She scratches her chin expansively – the gesture you did in junior school when someone told you they'd met the Bionic Man.

'You're an arsehole,' she says, suddenly. 'D'you know the only thing of my mum's I've got?'

She rummages under her pillow – a small, lace-trimmed thing. Seems a bit Victorian and spinsterish, quite at odds with this robust, tough-mouthed lass. Her hand comes out with a yellow plastic badge that says, in once-bright, red capitals: 'I've got everything'. She thrusts it in my face.

'It come in a little red box that said 'For the mum who has everything'. Haven't even got the box anymore. When she died, me nan come round the next day and threw out all her stuff.' She turns away, putting the badge back under the pillow. Then she turns back.

At first I'm not sure – it's come about so suddenly – but then the light from her bedside lamp glints in the wetness. She's crying – big, fat tears down each cheek, scarcely real, like those scary clown-dolls in French gift shops. In shame, she lets her red hair drop down, like an excusatory curtain, over her face. I wish now I'd said she was ace when she wanted me to, instead of blithering on about the A Team.

'Don't be an arsehole. You're really sweet sometimes. And then you're an arsehole. You always spoil it.'

Girls' grief is like this: close at hand, but no more bearable. Having few other tricks up my sleeve, I reach out and put my hand on hers. Stubby and pink, as if she's just been washing dishes. It's all hot. She pulls it away crossly.

'When they stick you in there, they give you these pills that make everything feel like you're walking through glue. You get spots and you get all fat.'

She isn't fat now. Curvy, certainly, chubby even in a certain light, but not fat. I try saying so.

'That's 'cos I'm not taking them!' she says, almost triumphantly.

I can't say I blame her really.

'Dad met some cock at a Town Hall thing and he said "Oo you want to try her on ECT – it sorted the wife out," and the next thing they've dragged me off for that.'

I know all about the illness, about the huge chunk out of her life, right in the middle of university, and the long time in hospital. But she hasn't told me this before. I didn't even know people still did that to each other. I thought ECT was a monster from the movies, something McCarthy recommended for Marxists.

'Take it it didn't do you much good,' I say, tentatively.

Martha lets out a horsey snort. 'You wake up and it feels like someone stuck this fuck-off big brick in your head. And you can't remember anything – who you are or your phone number or anything. And you just lie there for hours and hours and then it comes back in one go. Like the spins – you know, when you're pissed. You're Martha. And your mam's dead. And they've stuck you in here 'cos they don't like the thoughts you're having and there's nothing anyone can do to get you out.'

She's sobbing now, properly, given up to it completely. I make to pull her close but she turns to face me, letting out one, big, snotty sniff. 'Just promise us something,' she says, in a tiny, clogged-up voice.

'Yes.'

'Don't go away.'

'What?'

'If it happens again, you won't let them do that. Will you? Not if you're here. Just let us go off to Ireland and sit there in my little cottage till it all calms down. Promise?'

'I promise.' She looks down, starts playing with her ring. I hate her crying. 'Just don't cry like that, please.'

'I'm really tired,' she says, ridiculously. She attempts to do something with her hair, and then looks at me, suddenly cross with my presence. 'Just go to bed or something.' Then more gently, 'Please.'

I do not sleep at all well. Thoughts come so vivid they seem like someone else has sent them to me. Somewhere close to dawn, I give up on the World Service. I lie in the silence and remember that sometimes, when I was eleven or twelve, I would walk into a certain classroom, where sixth formers had been doing maths. And I would look at the spiky, unfamiliar symbols on the board and feel a slight terror about the future.

I meant it when I said, 'I promise'. Except Strange is not too hot on promises. Once I made a vow to God: *If you'll make them repeat* Hill Street Blues, *I promise to watch every single episode*. I couldn't even keep that. Not after *Truck Stop* started its final run on the other side.

All my life I've broken things – not just promises, also my mother's ornaments, people's spirits – and legged it. But I am old enough now to look on the dark language of trigonometry and fluid mechanics and not be afraid. Old enough to glimpse, dimly, that some people are drawn to others, not in a bid to change them, but in the hope that they themselves will be changed. I can wear smart clothes, fight for a free inch on the tube, even tell Jo from Minty if I have to. Perhaps that will be enough.

3

There is no need for a manuscript. I have transmitted the necessary truths to you by telepathy.

For the tenth time that morning, like some sickly boy besieging a dinner-lady, I go over to Tara's desk. She's engaged in her favourite occupation – inserting rude words into the on-screen dictionary (a necessary precaution in our business). When I approach, she uncrosses her legs and swivels round on her chair like it still might be fun to do so. She reads the letter I hand her, badly typed on some pre-war museum artefact. I wait by her. She sighs.

'It's *obvious*, darling,' she says. 'Nutter 1, 2 or 3. I've told you all this!'

I go back to my desk to scratch my head for a while. Noakes comes out of his office and stands in the doorway, pulling distractedly at the grey flannel crotch of his trousers. Instinctively, I shift away slightly as he approaches my desk and leans in close – I've noticed everyone else does this too, except Tara, who always belts several feet back with studied violence. There is something ever so slightly distasteful about Noakes, a suggestion that prolonged contact could be physically harmful. I'm reminded of those dubious, smudgy toys in doctors' waiting rooms, covered in a patina of sticky hands and infectious snot.

'Getting on okay?'

'Oh yes,' I say, weakly. He blesses me with a benevolent grin. 'That reminds me,' he says, inexplicably. And he wanders

62

back into his inner sanctum. I wait for a while, but he doesn't come back.

I've done it. Taken Beelzebub's shilling, or eaten the King's goose, or whatever you do, and gone straight to the Pendennis Press this morning. Told Noakes I'd start right away. He was impressed.

'You're a proper keeno,' he said.

But I'm not. The office is hot and stuffy, the seat of my best brown cords feels itchy. I can't quite accept that I'm expected to sit here until the evening comes, and that this is what people, real people, really do. This is what *doing* amounts to, and I'm fighting the Voices, which keep calling me to leg it.

'*Do one*,' they say. '*Leg it.*'

In my bones, and in the blood which boils around them, I've always had these Voices. There is little explanation for them, other than a slightly barmy theory put forward by my mother, shortly after I was born. She was by all accounts quite normal, until I came along. According to Sue, the discovery that she had fallen pregnant at the ripe old age of thirty-nine tampered somewhat with her grasp on reality. I was, as Gus once generously put it, an afterbirth, and for the first six months of my unintended life, my mother, in a deep depression, refused to have anything to do with me, or even give me a name. For provisional purposes, Sue called me after a favoured ex-biology teacher, whose name was Alastair.

My mother, sequestered up in the attic with a stack of *National Geographic*s, found the seeds of her recovery in tales of tribes both extant and extinct, developing a fascination with folklore and magic. After six months, she emerged from hiding, declaring herself a reborn citizen of the cosmos. Her child, she declared, thumping her much-thumbed copy of *The Golden Bough*, was some sort of changeling, sired by ghosts. A suggestion whose effects on my father's ego can only be guessed at.

Further calculations revealed that while my mother was born on May 2nd, the feast of St Sara, patron of all gypsies, I was myself born on the same day as the convening of the first World Conference of Romany Speakers. I was then, so my mother's theory ran, in spite of my pale complexion and precocious fascination with TV, quite clearly a gypsy child, a *chavo*, born to her through some karmic freak of the space-time continuum. She decided to name me *Kalderash* though, as a concession to the rest of my family, she allowed that my second name remain Alastair.

To my father's distress, she started to wear a great deal of jewellery and to claim that she saw and heard secrets in the night sky. Slinging me in some kind of hessian papoose, she spent every spare moment in the Picton library, poring over learned texts on the Romany. She learned a little of the language (so she would understand me when I started to talk). *Gorgio* became her favourite word, the pejorative (and only) term for a non-gypsy, with which she abused everyone from my father, to bus conductors and ugly newsreaders.

My mother never truly recovered, though in time, as I grew into a robustly Anglo-Saxon creature and resolutely failed to understand Romany, her theory held increasingly diminishing quantities of water. She nevertheless continued to spend a fortune on Eastern clothing and made us eat hot, greasy stews with whole archipelagos of paprika floating on the top. I thought, until I went to school, that every kid had one of these hopping mystics at home, prone to bouts of nonsensical reasoning and the waving of amulets.

School at least ensured that I picked up a few of the trappings of normality. I realised that other people had mums who made sense from time to time, in between making them fish fingers and wearing jeans. Rather than enter lengthy explanations, or pass the K off as Kevin, I allowed the world to call me Strange. I disappointed my mother and she withdrew, yet again, though throughout my life she has remained on the margins, like some anthropologist on permanent secondment, watching my every move with fascinated trepidation, as if in the tying of a knot or the yanking of a lock of hair I might reveal myself, at last, to belong to some deeply exotic lineage.

A few traces of my mother's post-natal obsessions remained with me, throughout the time I was growing up and beyond. It was my habit, for instance, to spend practically every Sunday, and the evening before such regular horrors as Hymn Practice and Cross-Country, in a state of near-suicidal boredom and despair, my legs twitching and shuffling of their own accord. 'He's missing his *vardo*,' my mother would announce to my father. A vardo is a caravan. It was a little gag between them – one of those family jokes which are, if anything, even less funny to family members than they are to outsiders.

The gypsy lies dormant in me, in spite of my middle name. I'm a blue-eyed, knock-kneed sort of product with bad feet. Tending to pudginess at the middle, despite having no arse to speak of. I don't resemble some dusky, enigmatic stable-hand in an historical novel. I can't whisper to horses, or charm snakes. I go all blotchy when drunk, and in the presence of beauty. Just two things might suggest a little of the Kalderash: a heaviness of the stubble, which leads people sometimes to accuse me of being Irish. And the compulsion, when under pressure, and expressed as commands from my bowels and kneecaps, to find my *vardo* and leg it. To do *one*, as they say in Merseyside.

'Do *one*.'

This is impossible. How many other editors have ever had to deal with a full-sized Romany Voice Choir in their heads? But I can't walk out of another job. That promise I made changes everything. It has to. So I grit my teeth and force my thoughts downwards to the world of madmen and their MSS. I look up the files Nutter 1, 2 and 3 on the computer, though I know it's hopeless. I've read them already.

'They're hopeless,' I tell Tara, looking over to her window-seat where she sits (and, as Noakes intimated, does indeed stare at builders). 'They all refer to books as if they've been written. There's nothing here that's relevant to someone who's transmitted his manuscript by telepathy.'

'Ballocks,' says Tara, spinning round on her chair again. I have to fight the boyish urge to see up her skirt. 'You'll have to write a special one. Anyway, it's a q. good idea. Once you see one, you usually get a rush of others. They get together, you see, authors. Go to the same loony-bins, probably. Had a whole week of Italian bomb-making manuals once. Dozens of them. V. weird.'

The author's intention – to save the male population of the world from attack by women – is a worthy and noble one. Also exceedingly timely. Unfortunately, being an unenlightened, though concerned mortal, I was not able properly to receive the telepathic transmission of the manuscript. If the author would deign to provide me with a crude, typewritten text, I should be happy to read and evaluate it.

'What d'you reckon?'
Tara nods as she reads it – an elegant, if slightly equine gesture.
'F. good,' she says. 'Remember to sign it.'
I remember. 'Sarah Gaskell.'
'No! He obviously doesn't like women, does he? None of the nutters do.'
'Declan Moon?'
She nods at me. 'And give the file a name.'
'How about Nutter – Utter?' I suggest. She lets out a disturbingly loud laugh, one which brings Noakes scuttling forth from his office like a furious beetle.

'The Chatter Levels,' he says, casting a hooded, threatening eye across the room, 'are beginning to peak.' He says that Tara is on Final Warning.

'What's that?' I whisper to her, when he has stalked off again, this time propping the door to his office open with a box. Tara shrugs, arching a solitary eyebrow.

'Oh I'm always on Final Warning,' she says. As if that explained things.

Nevertheless, I'm cheered up by what Tara said about nutters. Nutters don't like women. I, on the other hand, am pretty certain that I like women. Ergo: not mad. In fact, I don't just like them. I prefer them, immeasurably, to blokes.

I remember the only time I ventured down the road to see Martha in the Pickled Newt. Not a woman in the place, apart from her. And why would there be, when the only entertainment is a pack of grizzly men, hunched around the bar? Nugent, the gaffer, swivelling his great, yeasty, sizzling pan of a face around the bar all night in search of some fresh breach of protocol. Obsessed, all of them, like ancient Israelites, with their secret rules and codes: *to Wilf only shall Wilf's tankard be given; only a puff sits down when there's a free inch at the bar.*

I'm well out of it here. If the work is dull, at least the view is better than the one Martha faces every day. No sight is ghastlier than a bunch of blokes round a bar. What did she say to me the other night? *Don't know why they bother talking. Might as well just wank off and see who shoots the furthest. That's all it amounts to.*

The pile of manuscripts in front of me was, when I broke off to talk to Tara, a hillock, the sort that is maybe known locally, by cyclists and people who drive too fast. Now it's a landmark, featured in the more detailed atlases, a Scafell or a Snowdon. Every fifteen minutes, a scowling Minty clops across and adds a few more to the top. Latterly, she's had to stand on a chair to perch them dangerously up there, and the stack is starting to sway with every footfall. I'm evaluating as fast as I can. Here in my hastily assembled work-outfit – brown cords and moleskin jacket – and with my newly washed hair sticking up like a beaver pelt, I feel very like some pet rodent, a gerbil in a wheel.

My new job at Pendennis is far from hard. It involves sending letters to authors. The letters are designed to make the authors believe: that we have read their books (which we haven't); that we think their books are good (which we never do); that it would be a good idea for them to send us a cheque, so we can publish whatever it is they have written.

The chief agent in all this is the 'Reader's Report', which I churn out in droves, faster than choc-ices. For every kind of manuscript there exists, on the computers, a pre-written report, which praises the work's unique benefits in vague, but glowing *Mail on Sunday* terms: *A rip-roaring, roller-coaster of a read, from start to finish*, and so on.

Of course, you have to be careful you're saying something vaguely appropriate. I nearly told the author of a charmless collection of Christian poetry that her work was *darkly funny*, but luckily Tara spotted the error in time.

I print these letters up, and then I sign them, under any one of a number of handles: Sarah Gaskell for the poets and novelists, Declan Moon for the more chappish stuff – car maintenance and academia – Charlie Watts for sheer, undisguised porn. Charlie Watts is my most convincing signature – it's the one that gets the most practice.

Every now and then, some title emerges whose depths of craziness could never have been foretold, as with the telepathic gynophobe. So then I have to write the report from scratch, adding the models to the database when I finish them. I give them a reference, so I can use them again, and they enter the archive, taking their place among the ranks of Islam.Nut, Smut.Lesbo, Obit.Doggy and, most worryingly, HandBk.N-balm.

'Borrow your ruler, petal?'

I nod, not wanting to lose my place in the latest, very peculiar letter I'm reading.

Tara seems to have much the same job as me, and none of the problems with it. This is largely down to the fact that she doesn't do any work, but is still able to occupy herself, quite happily, for the entire day. In the face of Noakes' perpetually penultimate warnings, she chats freely to everyone else in the office and, when they won't answer, she amuses herself snacking and chewing and borrowing things.

The letter in front of me is on mauve paper and from a very aged theosophist in Bexhill. I'm not at all sure whether I'm even holding it the right way up. I turn to ask Tara what she thinks, and am astonished to find her measuring her nose with my ruler.

'What are you doing?'

She puts the ruler down.

'Geometry. I was just trying to find out why your nose goes up and down in the middle like that. Mine doesn't.'

'It's just a bit buggered up.'

She looks sceptical. 'Of course, darling. Punch-up down the Dock Road, was it?'

I'm used to this from the Southern types. The slightest trace of a Northern accent and they'll accuse you of pretending to be some working-class hero.

'It's always been like that. I was born with it.'

Tara looks sympathetic. 'Sorry. Does it hurt?'

'Of course not. It's just the way it is. Well. I used to get a lot of nosebleeds.'

'Golly,' she says, adjusting her fringe. '*Poor* Strange.'

'When I was little,' I say, warming to my theme, 'my mum used to make me sleep on a plastic groundsheet. You know – when we went to hotels . . .'

I trail off into silence. Tara's staring at me, one dubious eyebrow aloft, and one nostril aquiver.

'That's *actually* just a little bit more than I really wanted to know, darling,' she says, with withering irony. 'But thanks.'

I look down at my desk, duly withered. Reminded, suddenly, of something Martha said to me last night. *You always spoil it.*

At lunchtime – Noakes has made it clear that this is a dispensation, rather than a right – I go off and purchase some reptilian kebab from an outfit of haughty Scythians and wander along the Uxbridge Road in the rain. I'd hoped for a little company, but Tara and the others have brought odd, feminine lunches with them – mysterious pots of calorie-free cous-cous, kiwi-fruit paté and pine needle crisps.

'You can't go out,' Tara had declared clearly, even through a gobful of stewed beanshoots. 'It's raining.'

'I won't melt.' That's one of my father's favourite quips. He despises, even fears umbrellas. Refuses to have them in his sight – though he's never explained why. It perplexes me, but at least the comment earns an unnecessarily loud laugh from Tara.

I catch a few minutes of *Jacaranda Cove* in the window of Radio Rentals, but it's the aftermath of Shoni hiding her still-born child underneath a pile of Lori's laundry. All talk and sod all action. So I wander, greasy-fingered, into the newsagent's next to the tube station in search of a copy of *TV Forum*, which is this obscure, slightly geekish periodical for devotees of TV drama. You might say it has a cult following, since I've never seen an up-to-date copy, nor encountered anyone other than myself who's ever read it. And I've only seen it once myself, on Runcorn station as a matter of fact, and since then, no trace. If I didn't have that one copy stowed under my pillow back at the flat, I might suspect I'd dreamt it.

This newsagent clearly thinks I have. In answer to my question, he just shakes his head nervously, as if I'd asked him if he stocked *The Hitler Diaries*.

Reluctant to head back to the office just yet, I wander into a tiny bookshop, where it occurs to me that I might try and make some amends for upsetting Martha the night before. I choose a book about a man who hypnotises horses on his ranch in California. Sheltering in the doorway, I draw a very bad cartoon horse on the inside cover, and then can't think of anything else to put there. I sign it Strange. I put an X underneath it and then change my mind and make it into a squirly blob. Thinking this now looks a little scruffy, I try to make it into a flower. This having failed, I make it into a bigger, and far scruffier blob.

In the afternoon, I put the horse-book at the side of my in-tray where it remains until Noakes comes out and finds Tara's packet of dry-roasted pumpkin seeds on top of one of the scanners. After his ensuing attack on 'Foreign Objects in the Work Arena', I put the book under my stool and work harder than I've ever worked before.

By three o'clock, at which time Noakes is ensconced with a haunted-looking Nigerian in his office, I have grown heartily sick of the job, or more truthfully, with the great writing public. Mad Muslims on the Jews. Mad Jews, for that matter, on the Muslims. Tiny, frail old Hampshire ladies with intricate blueprints for the extermination of all queer flesh. Not so much Vanity Press as sheer, unexpurgated Depravity.

The final straw is a slim work by a Georgian ex-army officer now living in Highgate, entitled 'Her Cherry Gizzard'. It details, in lurid, specialist terminology, the sexual initiation of a teenager by her lesbian swimming instructor and her Georgian, ex-army officer husband. In Highgate.

After hearing me groan repeatedly in disgust, Tara eventually scoots over on her chair and takes the manuscript off me, promising to write something suitable on my behalf. She makes no moves to do this, however, and every time I look over her way, she's arched skinnily over it, flipping through the pages and chuckling softly as she plays with the tiny jewelled dots in her earlobes. Every now and then, she underlines a word and adds it to the spell-check.

Raised voices start to come from Noakes' office, shortly after Minty breezes in there with the tea. There's a crash, and the Nigerian bowls out at full speed, cursing in some foreign tongue. Noakes is behind, pleading urgently, as they pass out into the little corridor which leads to the stairs. I can hear Noakes bleating something about royalties. That he will pay them, I guess.

'Dis-honest!' This from the Nigerian – as if it was the rudest word he might apply to another man. 'Dis-honest!' Then the door slams and he's gone. Noakes comes back, cherry-red and sweating, sawing violently between his legs. 'Bloody choccoes,' he says. I hate that he picked me to say it to.

I go and hide in the loo for a while – the only place it's safe to do nothing – thinking that I don't want to be anyone's very rudest word, I want to be home, soaking up the dramatic delights of *Shortland Street*. Then thinking, in strict rotation, about Martha. In that place, doing the medication-shuffle, all day, round the same bright, white room. Wondering how anyone could let that happen.

Ten minutes later, I'm back at my desk. Calm and thinly smiling. The bulk of my frustration is being expended on an individual from the top of my pile, a Mr Dan Kane, who quotes an address in Islington and who has written a truly godawful pile of guff.

' "Sing Me Empty" ', writes Mr Kane, is 'the fictional charter of Generation X, a written blueprint of the popular consciousness. Best described as leftfield,' it merges the 'raw heat of Juan Lopez with the icy calm of Theravada Buddhism; the staccato rhythms of street-argot with the formal aesthetics of the Celtic bards.' Not only this, but it tells (according to the synopsis) the tale of a female jazz musician whose love 'for an abused and disturbed man drives her towards a nihilistic act of musical expression which ruins her career'. I'm improving on this quite a bit. I should add that Mr Kane is either trying to do something innovative with language, or he just can't spell.

I go to town on Dan Kane. The existing report for his type of book, Nov.Pretensh, doesn't go nearly far enough. I write a new one in which I declare that I stayed up all night to read Mr Kane's book and, when I got too tired to carry on, I went out and scored some speed to keep me going. I write that 'Sing Me Empty' is nothing short of a cult classic, the 'arid, hoarse and angry voice of a shat-on generation'. I write that Mr Kane's work 'disturbed as it delighted, stung me as it seduced me'. Mr Kane, I conclude, is 'up there with Damien Hirst, *The Face* magazine and ketamine as the founding fathers of a new anti-epoch'.

I feel a lot better when I've finished it – and not in the least bit guilty. Dan Kane strikes me as the very worst sort of tit. And it's not fraud, not really, because, judging by the quality of the manuscript (dot printer, bog-roll paper) there seems little likelihood of him paying to have it published. At worst, Dan Kane will show my report to some dippy tart in a pub on the Essex Road and perhaps get a blow-job.

I, on the other hand, just show it to Tara.

'Dan Kane,' she says, snottily. 'I bet that's made up.'

' 'Spect so. Will it be okay?'

'Mm,' she murmurs, vaguely. 'Didn't know you were into horses.'

'Eh?'

Tara taps the open book in front of her. She's blatantly, shamelessly taken my book from under my chair and is reading it in the middle of the office, in full view of Noakes.

'It's q. good,' she says, looking at me curiously. 'I had a horse once. Well, a pony. Never had you down as the horsey sort.'

'I'm not. It's a present for someone.'

'Oh yes,' she says, pursing her lips in a Carry-on saucy sort of way. 'Who would that be?'

'Girl in my flat,' I say, feeling my ears grow hot. 'Martha.'

Tara flips her head back and strokes her throat with her nails. 'Oh yes,' she says, weightily. 'Rory doesn't seem to like her v. much.'

'But I thought they became friends in Ireland or something.'

'Yes,' she says, carefully. 'But he changed his mind.'

'Well. I don't care. *I* like her.'

Tara just puffs a bit of air out of her nose, a laugh or a snort, I can't tell. She flips the book shut and slides it over the desk to me.

'You've made a right mess of the inside.'

'It's difficult to see precisely why you people need to stand up and chatter in order to work,' a stern voice utters from behind us. I almost jump out of my skin. Turning round, I see Noakes peering out of his doorway. Wordlessly, I sit down at my desk. 'Final Noise,' he says, shaking a finger at Tara, and then slips back inside his office. I glance over at Tara, but she has turned to stare out of the window, so I start working again.

There seems to be some odd sort of telepathic connection between Noakes and Tara. Somehow, Noakes *knows* when Tara's not working. He knows when she's plaiting rubber bands together or gawping at the men on the scaffolding over the road. And Tara knows he knows. He catches her at it, every time, with unfailing accuracy and she makes no attempt to stop it happening. It's like Colt Ceevers, the 'Fall Guy' – stuntman and part-time bounty hunter. Every episode begins with Colt looking forward to a well-earned rest in Tampa, Fla. He's sitting, planning it, in his bath tub, smoking a cigar, when the attorney woman turns up with some new bail-jumper to track down. Colt never thinks about hiding, never thinks he could just fly off to Tampa, Fla. the minute he's done his last movie-stunt and not tell her where he's gone. He *lets* her catch him.

Like Tara. She expects to be caught, demands it. I suspect she'd be offended if Noakes decided to ignore her.

It's about four o'clock. Sitting here, dreaming of Colt Ceevers, a terrible, treacly sort of weariness descends on me, like hands pressing me down toward the floor. It worries me, because I realise this is exactly the same weariness that gives rise to Tara's Chase Me games with Noakes and Minty and Jo's languid indifference. It's not just some quirk of posh girls, or London. It's the universal tiredness of the worker, of the person who habitually stays up too late because they want to have some sort of a life after their job, and hence whose head fills up with sleepy glue mid-afternoon. And it's happening to me.

But five o'clock is the end and, as with even the most ponderous story developments in *Melrose Place*, the end does come. I celebrate its arrival with an inner cheer. Almost expecting a bell to ring, Noakes to beetle out saying, severely, 'That bell is a signal for *me* to end the day. Not for you to start shuffling your bags.'

I hide in toilets, try to look up girls' skirts, get sleepy in the afternoons and perk up at home-time. This is what the working life does to you. By the time you retire, you're practically incontinent. A few years after that, you're sucking puréed apple through a straw.

I'd half expected Tara to shriek as the clock needle struck home, perhaps leg it, aeroplane style, all the way to the bus stop. But instead, when it reaches five, she is the last to stop working (or more precisely, doing the *Daily Mail* crossword) then lurks leggily about the office as everyone else dons their coats. She seems to be waiting for something. I ask her if she's coming.

'I'm waiting for a lift,' she says, shiftily. Which figures. Probably some celebrity flamenco-dancer with his own Jag. That's the way it goes. It'd be stupid to think otherwise.

Just as we're all going, a skull-headed lady, corrugated with age, arrives and produces a hoover from some secret cranny. She stands in her grey coat, waiting by its side, staring at me with gimlet eyes. I fancy she gives a slight curtsey as I pass her on my way out.

My legs want to walk, to celebrate their recaptured liberty, but I'm tired and hungry, so instead I catch the pink line to Hammersmith. From the ticket office, down the stairs, right on to the platform, Minty, Jo and myself are in crocodile, each just a cock-stride ahead of the other. We all know this, but some private agreement dictates that we don't speak. Even worse, the activities of a vast and confused party of Poles mean that Minty and I end up in intimate proximity to one another on the train, so close I can smell her scalp. The electricity given off by two people trying not to acknowledge one another is enormous and disturbing.

'Not a bad day, really,' I say, giving in.

'Sorry?' asks Minty, frostily, meaning I ought to be.

'For a first day,' I explain. 'Not too bad.'

'Oh,' she says, staring ahead of her. The doors open, and she gets out. Ladbroke Grove. I'm travelling in the wrong direction.

I'm excitable and a bit nervous when I finally get back to the flat, clutching my cheer-up gift in one hand, a bottle of headache-red Bulgarian in the other. But I needn't be. Martha is, unusually, not there. I go into her room and sniff the air. Then feeling guilty – because I'm reminded of those men who steal things off washing lines – I go and sit on my own in the kitchen. The flat's so quiet you can hear not just the dripping of the taps, but the fridge's gurgling fight for the right temperature, the walls as they acquire a fresh atomic coat of nicotine. I don't like it. *Why isn't she here?* There hasn't been a half past five yet when she wasn't here.

I put the kettle on, aimlessly, and wait for it to boil before remembering that Martha has broken it and that I want neither tea nor coffee in the first place. Suddenly, after years of managing more or less happily by myself, I find myself at a loss, uncertain whether I can usefully fill an evening alone. The TV, oddly, seems like beggar's choice compared to an evening with Martha. Which, I tell myself sternly, is not good.

Unsure whether the light pressure in my belly is hunger or indigestion, I open the fridge and look for something to eat. I don't think I can face Cheesy Garlic Beans tonight – seems to underline the bleak, monastic character of a Tuesday night alone – so I heat up the rest of the Indian Potato Thing, which, with the innovative addition of some grated Cheddar, now resembles something from the early *Doctor Who* special effects department. I put the telly on and drink the wine.

I remember when three pints of fizzy lager and a couple of fags used to send me reeling home, so gloriously smashed that I stared in defiance at passing police cars. Now I can stick a whole bottle of rot-gut under my belt and emerge with only a dry mouth and a faint desire to hear myself whistle. Something is happening here – soon, I'll be a fully qualified booze-hound, in recovery. Making feeble excuses every time anyone offers me a drink. '*Sorry – I'm on these pills for my joints*', '*Sorry – I just can't bear the smell of pubs these days. So smoky.*'

I can't just have a drink, like some people can. I have to have drinks. One drink, I've worked out, turns to a hangover in one hour. Two drinks, not for two. And so on.

That can of Mirage is still at the back of the fridge. Martha swears it's not hers. Just as I swear the vast brown and cream Y-fronts in the airing cupboard are not mine. *God – it tastes like nail varnish*. Like the smell of nail varnish, mixed in with something spicier, like a tandoori waiter's vest. All over Southport, and Widnes, girls get smashed on this. They're a tough breed up there. Who left it here? If only it could have been Taboo. I wouldn't have minded Taboo. *The drink for daring people.* Much classier.

I cheer up a little, and start watching the soaps on the mingy, crackling, black-and-white set in the kitchen. It's always distressed me that this is the only TV Rory has in his flat – it suggests a flawed character, and that his eventual homecoming might be a lot less than fun. I'm reminded of Jill, who'd always always ring me up in the middle of *Tour of Duty*, as if she didn't know it was happening. An indifference to TV is a sign of a deeper, spiritual bankruptcy.

Channel Four's latest offering, premièred tonight, concerns the struggles of a bunch of pensioners in a condemned tower block in Grozhny. It's only slightly bleaker than *Brookside*. And the cast is more sexy.

Love soaps as I do, I sometimes wonder if all this grim, urban anguish isn't strangling the form beyond repair. The Americans had it right in my view – escapism should be as vital a feature as sharp dialogue. If I was in charge, soaps wouldn't even be set in the present any more. I'd pioneer Britain's first ancient Roman soap. '*Tonight, Agrippa has a vision of the Goddess Minerva. Cassius, meanwhile, unbeknown to Claudia, starts his first day as a professional charioteer . . .*' And there'd be glamour, too. Hold the tower blocks and your greyly lit squares. Retrospective, tropical, this is the key to the telly revolution. Someone should do something mythical. *Paloa-Palua*: an everyday story of prehistoric Hawaiian folk. '*This week, Oa invents the surfboard. Meanwhile, Ua is seduced by a giant tortoise and gives birth to Time.*' I ought to write this down. *TV Forum* would love it.

Now I know why people drink Mirage. It tastes like bubblegum and has a kick like coal gas. A kick which has left me feeling somewhat less than groovy. I decide to take a shower to sober myself up. Only then, rummaging naked through the clutter on my bedroom floor, do I see that I've only got three pairs of socks. I can't reasonably go to work without socks.

Noakes would turn blue. I spent the last of my money on the wine. Which leaves only one option. I call home.

An unexpected, croaky little voice answers the phone. 'Two-six-double-five-oh-three?'

Shite. I've done it again. Rung their old number.

'I'm sorry, Mr Mason. It's me again. Alastair Strange. Keep forgetting.'

The man laughs. 'Ah – the young Master Strange again. You must have a very bad memory. They've moved, you know.'

'I *do* know.'

I have established something of a long-distance friendship with the ancient Mr Mason, who purchased my parents' house, which they exchanged, secretly, during my final year at college, for a one-bedroom flat with ceilings lower than my own head. Back in June I rang to say I was coming home after graduating and got Mr Mason, who said, as I recall, that it was a wonder someone who didn't know his parents' phone number could graduate at all. The move they explained, on being challenged, was for their own safety, a move as befitted those in their declining years, or their early sixties, depending upon your state of confusion. Since they have been there, they have collectively suffered a bruised hip, two sprained ankles and a broken wrist, due to the winning combination of zero space and maximum possessions.

My father answers this time. For his own, perverse amuse-ment, he has decided never to answer the telephone as a normal British telephone-owner would. He just picks it up, holding the phone about eight yards away from his mouth and whispers 'Strange'. It means only a third of potential callers ever get through – most people hang up at this stage, deeply puzzled, never to ring again.

I explain about the socks.

'I'll get your mother,' he says. He is not to be bothered with such tawdry matters as socks. It was ever thus with him. He maintains a carefully engineered impression of dwelling on some distant, ethereal plane, has always taken considerable relish in not remembering birthdays and Christmas, or the names of his children. When I was younger, if I rang to say I'd be staying out late, he used to insist that he thought I was still upstairs in front of the TV.

My mother is slightly tetchy when she comes on the line. She is watching a documentary about hospitals.

'I asked Dad,' I say in my defence. 'About the socks.'

'Yes, well,' my mother says. Which is always her response if you make reference to my father. It is identical to her responses on Bosnia, teenage mothers and other thorny issues. 'He's busy,' she adds. 'He's got the orals this week.'

'Strangeways?'

'Walton.'

My father, for reasons unfathomable, teaches German, conversational, GCSE and A level, to guests of Her Majesty all across the north-west. It isn't lucrative, and nor does he, to my knowledge, enjoy it. On duty, he wears a bullet-proof vest, and clips a rear-view mirror to his blackboard.

'I just need a few pairs.'

'What kind?'

What do you mean what kind? Socks are socks are socks. But I don't say this. I say, 'What?'

'Well what will you be doing in them?'

Mother. 'Wearing shoes, mostly. Walking, sitting. The odd bit of standing,' I say. 'Oh – and maybe some shuffling.' But this is wasted on her.

'I'll send you some of your father's.' She sounds impatient now.

'Gus called me, you know,' I say, trying for some semblance at a normal family conversation. 'About a month back.'

'Who?' A favourite game of my parents. Everyone calls my brother Gus, has done for as long as I can recall, but our parents still insist his name is Jeremy. Just one of the reasons Gus hasn't seen them in ten years and probably never will.

I give in. 'Jeremy.' No more energy for these struggles. 'He's in Borneo or something. He's coming home for a bit. Got to have an operation.'

'What kind?' A touch of concern in her voice – she can't disguise it.

'Oh,' I say, airily, 'nothing big. I don't really know.' Gus' operation is not a subject you'd want to go into with your mother. Or really with anyone. It makes me feel a little queasy.

This launches my mother into an account of the hospital series she is currently watching. It features a woman having a steel probe inserted to measure the pressure in her head. I shut down temporarily. She has a curious fascination with all matters surgical, my mother – knows exactly which women in their block have had their wombs whipped out and which a plastic hip inserted. Strange, when you consider that she used to hide in the toilet till Sue had cleaned my nosebleeds up.

Suddenly she says something that makes me tune in again.

'There was a girlie rang here for you the other day.' She has always called them *girlies* – as if her son's love life is in its way just as cute and endearing as the powder paint pictures he used to bring home from school (always signed under a sobriquet – Lee Majors and Leopard Boy being my favourites). Between the ages of fifteen and twenty, this habit of my mother's made me furious. Nowadays, it does not. There are too few girlies.

'What girlie? I mean who?'

'Oooh,' says my mother, which is a bad sign. 'It began with a W,' she says, with the utmost certainty. 'Or maybe an N. Anyway – I gave her your number. Do you know, I think it could have been a T?'

The conversation degenerates as my mother begins to consider diphthongs and I say my goodbyes. Thus assured of a steady, if not to say probably excessive supply of socks to my new address, I shower, finish off the rest of the booze and, struck by a drunken fancy, I decide to write a long letter to *TV Forum*.

The pages of the magazine scatter round my feet as I pull it out from its hallowed position under my bed. I've really got to find another copy – mine looks increasingly like something unearthed from the ruins of Jericho. And Martha has drawn all over the front and back covers. Not that that really matters, because I know every column-inch by heart, including the seminal essay 'Peak Practice: a Weberian Polemic?' and the classifieds, where the enterprising autist can pick up all 886 episodes of *Albion Market* on Betamax.

All the evidence suggests *TV Forum* folded long ago but, because I'm full of Mirage and the fag-induced palpitations are roughly similar to a kind of excitement, I go so far as to put the letter in an envelope and copy out the address from the back of the magazine. By the time I've finished the letter, which sets out my plans for the prehistoric Hawaiian soap, I've forgotten most of what was in it and, on top of that, I'm conscious that it's probably very similar to the nutty letters I've been reading all day at Pendennis. But I don't care. I feel curiously knackered and happy as I lick the envelope – it's been so long since I wrote anything, however bizarre, on my own initiative. Chuckling to myself, I nick a stamp from Martha's room and go to bed.

Some time after drifting off, I hear the crash of the front door. Sneakily I switch the bedside light on, pick up *TV Forum* and foggily flip through to my favourite page. Martha comes heavily past my door, and goes into the bathroom. She pisses like a bloke – I can hear her let out a long, satisfied sigh as she finishes. I lie very still, hoping. *This way, Martha. This way.* I wish I had a Star Trek tractor beam, to draw her in invisibly.

The plumbing whistles and screams as she flushes – a chorus that, to me, always sounds far more embarrassing than the restrained grunts of an honest evacuation. *Bugger.* She's made straight for the kitchen. She's crashing about in there now, singing some song.

> *Monkey Snax, Monkey Snax,*
> *Cheesy, Beefy, Scampi and Hot.*
> *Lunch-time, dinner-time, home-time snacks,*
> *So mums look out for the Family Packs.*

She must have had an extra shift at the Pickled Newt. Whilst there are Fulham hostelries only yards away whose provender includes salads of roasted goat and distressed basil, the Pickled Newt is a sparse establishment devoted solely to swift intoxication and the only nibbles sold there are Monkey Snax. The good ol' boys there guzzle lorry-loads with every pint.

My hand's raised to switch off the light again when Martha belts down the corridor and thumps on my door with what could well be her head. 'Awake?'

Before I can answer, she has opened the door. She's got the horse book in her hand.

She looks very different. I'm used to Martha in androgynous garb – just a much more kissable version of my father. But tonight she's wearing a sort of floral-print dress with black, woolly stockings. She's even got a bit of make-up on.

'You look nice,' I say, involuntarily. She makes a face and flops next to me on the bed.

'Zit mine?' She waggles her new book at me. She smells of booze and outside and my deodorant. 'I'm too drunk to read it.'

'There's tomorrow.'

'Can I stay here?' And in answer to the obscure gurgle that comes from me – 'I mean—' – she sounds almost apologetic. 'I can't be arsed going back to my bed now.'

'Go on.'

She scrambles under the duvet. She's still got her strappy shoes on and everything. *Oh fuck.* I turn away from her slightly, ashamed – there's a monstrous right-angle in my boxer shorts.

'Mm,' she says, comfortably. Puts her warm face against my shoulder, her arm over mine. 'You've got a very distinctive smell.'

'Mm,' I reply, trying to sound supremely at ease, like some elderly cat on Temazepam. While in my bones and the blood that boils around them, a thousand, muscular P.E. teachers are bellowing: *Kiss her! Stick it in her! Attack, attack, attack!*

'Fuck!' This time, the sound is outside my head. It's Martha. *Don't falter now. You heard the woman!* I turn over to her. She leaps out of bed.

'Me fucking bagels!' she yells, staggering off and yanking the door open. Dark carbon smoke pours thickly in.

4

I love Heathrow. And I hate Goldhawk Road. I love Heathrow because it's where every other fortunate, idiot-grinning bastard seems to be going when I'm on my way to work. Each morning, I filter myself on to one of these silver tubes, packed to the hilt with smiling people and their suitcases, headed for the futuristic hubbub of the airport, then on to places whose sound sets me dreaming. Jammed with my nose glinting in the vinyl of the tube map, I look at Acton and Arnos Grove and all I can hear around me is San Francisco, Moscow, Tokyo. I don't so much want to visit these places as entomb myself in their motels and flop-houses – live on nuts and Bitbürger from the mini-bar as cables feed me forty, fifty channels of hitherto undreamed-of drama, in a babel of bewitching tongues. As we enter the tunnel, the smell of luggage intensifies; we could be thirty seconds from the airport, the threshold of anywhere. And then we arrive at Hammersmith, and I have to get out.

When I was a kid, we used to spend a week in North Wales every summer. They were unfailingly grim weeks, spoiled by the rain and those racist folk of the valleys. But I always forgot this and on the motorway going down there, I used to feel acutely sorry for the people on the other side of the road. They were going home, poor sods, holidays over when mine had just begun. And now it's the other way round. The curious maths of karma. I'm jealous of everyone on the westbound Piccadilly Line.

I hate Goldhawk Road because I always seem to end up

there, despite it being a place with no purpose or meaning. Once or twice, this has been due to my being caught up under the armpit of some jolly Finns and bodily ejected, along with them and their luggage, from the train. More frequently, as with this morning, the tannoy will offer some scratchy murmur about security alerts or passengers under trains (surely you stop being a passenger once you're *under* a train?) and we are forced to get off and wait, yet again, on that wooden frontier-post of Goldhawk Road with the only diversion a gum machine that takes drachmas. Trapped, like a bride on the eve of her wedding, in limbo: not Shepherd's Bush, not Hammersmith; not home, not work.

Still, there are mornings when even Goldhawk Road makes an attractive alternative to work. And I was late anyway. At least I've got a genuine excuse now.

Noakes takes a dim view of the old public transport excuse. He's found out some special hotline you can ring to find out, at any given moment, if someone has fallen under a train at Mudchute, or if some pensioner's shopping trolley is being gleefully exploded by the Transport Police at Perivale. Tara got herself exposed ignominiously yesterday when she arrived – according to Noakes' circa. 1981 digital calculator watch – seventeen and a half minutes late. She said, in her initial defence, that the Central Line was 'all buggered up'. Noakes scuttled off and came back only minutes later to announce, triumphantly, that the Central Line was far from all buggered up and had been running eighty-seven per cent on-target all morning. For a split second, she looked a bit scuppered. Then she just patted her crêpe-de-chine covered abdomen, said 'Got the monthlies' and smirked as Noakes vanished, faster than goose shit sliding down a hot tin bucket. I like Tara more and more.

It's Friday. I've been working nearly a week, which is a record for me. And even if most of the work has become familiar to the point of hypnotic, I'm here today with a skittish sense of excitement. This is because, having confessed, with embellishments, the sorry state of my fortunes to Noakes, he's promised to give me an advance. I'm to approach him at the end of the day, he says, shadily, as if we are arranging some sale of narcotics.

This still means a full day to get through. The sight that first greets me this morning is my In-Pile (the 'Pre-Evals' as Noakes has now lovingly termed them) which, like some dangerous haemorrhoid, has given birth to a number of subsidiary growths, each festooned with yellow garlands of admonitory Post-Its, each rising painfully as the minutes tick on by.

If my heart sank a little at seeing this, it took a bungee-jump when I looked in the side-office and saw that Ben Fielding, the other boss, was back from his holidays. Fielding is a short – in fact, tiny – sandy-haired fellow with a big beak of a nose. If Noakes reminds me of a panda, then his shadowy back-up Fielding is clearly some sort of parrot. In addition to favouring vivid red jackets with a yellow amoeba tie, he has a thick, grey tongue, which flaps somewhere about bollock height in relation to me.

Wee Fielding is bronzed from his latest jaunt abroad, jaunts which, according to Tara, take up the bulk of each working year and send Noakes' blood pressure sky-high. Fielding hates me, because I'm not posh, and several feet taller than him. I hate him for the reverse of these reasons – because he *is* posh, and too small – and because he hates me. He started it. (*Strange: Try and grow up.*)

Fielding's role at the Pendennis Press, whenever he deigns to fulfil it, consists of meeting authors, or speaking to them on the telephone, and lying through his precision-capped teeth. Whereas the dodgy nature of their dealings causes Noakes chest pains, palpitations and an ever-itching scrotum, Fielding takes an undeniable relish in the whole affair. The more furious or paranoid the author, the greater the challenge and, to his eyes, the more golden the reward at the end of it.

This morning, I'm halfway through the learned treatise of a Scarborough GP, who claims to have developed a cure for psychosis using a tincture of turnips, when I hear Fielding talking in tourist-Russian.

The door to their office is still being kept open as an anti-Chatter measure and from my desk – if I strain my neck up and out – I can just see him, perched in his vast leatherette swivel chair, bright blue socks peeping from the bottom of his trousers, looking like a boy visiting his father at work.

'*Kanyechno, da, da, ladno,*' he says again and again. '*Da, da, pazhalusta.*' Then he clears his throat. 'No – ah – not really. Just the rudiments,' he adds, a tad sheepish. Then he listens for a while, wincing, holding the phone away from his ear, as a faint voice barks from the earpiece. 'Oh quite!' Fielding's back in his stride. I watch him greyly lick his lips. 'But we *are* slightly inundated, you see. The bulk of our editorial staff are at the Book Fair. You know the . . . er . . . the . . . Stuttgart Fair. Oh yes. Publishing event of the year and all that.' He chortles at something the caller has just said. 'Oh no doubt, Mr Yelevadze. Who knows? Strange hotels. Away from home. Jacuzzis. Quite.'

After chatting soothingly to the man for another few minutes, Fielding puts the phone down and bellows. 'STRAAANGE!'

He comes rushing out. And those that haven't stopped work already, do so now. The sight of a tiny man angry is far more riveting than a large one. In an instant, I am back in assembly again. Singled out, from among four hundred boys, for wearing a *Coal Not Dole* sticker on my blazer. Now as then, a desert has sprung up around me, a thousand miles in every direction, populated only by tumbleweed and snickering sprites.

'Where's Yele-fucking-vadze?' Fielding rasps, the expletive

twice as effective amid all the Etonian fruit-cake vowels. 'He's waiting for his evaluation.'

I say I'm not quite sure, which turns out to be not quite the right answer. Fielding, sputtering like a mad goblin, starts to ransack the pile of manuscripts on my desk, flinging them all across the floor. The office goes deathly silent. Minty and Jo look straight ahead, smug – like those people who have reserved seats on a Friday night train.

'What's the title?' I ask, in a small voice.

'Cherry Arse Something,' mutters Fielding, now on the floor, doing a little extra damage by pulling manuscripts from their folders and scattering papers all about.

I look over at Tara. She makes a guilty face, sucking her lips in as she pulls the manuscript out of her handbag. All tattered now – a brown mug-stain on the front page. 'Erm – I'm afraid I took it home with me,' she pipes up, sweetly. 'F. – I mean, I'm *awfully* sorry.'

Fielding's little head bobs up above the desk. 'Took it home?'

'Yes.' She does a teeny little gulp and bows her head for added effect. An expert. 'I thought it was those poems I'm editing.' She gives a little sniff. Fielding wipes his brow and stands up.

'Now now,' he says, hoarsely. 'No need for all that. Things happen. Just erm . . . yes.' Then he turns back to me, more sharply again. 'Better clear this up. And make sure that fucking Bolshevik gets his letter today.'

He then announces, running a wee finger around his collar uncomfortably, that he fancies a little stroll.

'Why did you take it home?' I ask Tara, once Fielding has donned an action-man-sized crombie and skipped out of the building. She just shrugs.

'I don't know. I haven't got any books at home.'

'But it's disgusting.'

Tara just looks at me and sucks on her tooth, pityingly.

Best, I resolve, to have as little to do with Fielding as possible. The man's a psychopath. But having nothing to do with Fielding is going to be especially tricky today. Noakes has just announced, with some awkwardness, that he has to go to the 'Clinic' and will be away for much of the afternoon (Tara snickers behind her hand). I picture Noakes in disguise at some Centre for Scrotal Disorders, situated in darkest Dagenham.

I work through lunch, guilty because I am making so little progress. My mind, and other, more tangible parts of me keep returning to Martha. When, after the Tale of the Burning Bagel, she came back in to me. Not wearing the dress now, she stood before me starkers, save for a trace of carbonised crumb at the corner of her red lips.

'Still look nice do I?'

And in imitation of my brother's Salford scallywag, I let drop a solitary eyelid. 'Oh aye.'

In the morning she presented me, solemnly, with a blackened bagel for my breakfast in bed. Then she kissed me, threw a few things into a carrier bag and went off, to visit a cousin in Barnet. The next day she called, said it was awful in Barnet, that she missed me and was coming home. Though apparently not just yet. Enough contact to ensure that I have worked slowly and with no interest ever since. Remembering everything – every new touch – with a curious, patient, autistic recall. I've even stopped videoing *Neighbours*.

Other things distract me from the work I'm doing, too. I've begun to notice that the atmosphere amongst the workers of the Pendennis Press is far from one of harmony. Put more frankly – Minty wouldn't piss on Jo if she were on fire. And vice versa. It seems that in spite of having the greatest deal in common with each other, being both blonde, unutterably posh, and romantically entwined with someone called Hugo, these two like each other the least of any other possible pairing in the office. Even

Tara and Noakes, or me and Fielding. Not only did last Wednesday afternoon see a fledgling dispute concerning the photocopier, in which the lid was demonstratively slammed by Minty, and a pile of Minty's papers vigorously displaced by Jo, but today there is a palpable degree of aggression concerning the sandwich order.

'I can't get alfalfa from Fanucci's,' insists Minty, whose turn it is to fetch the lunches.

'So go to Zanotti,' says Jo, tossing her long flaxen hair, angrily.

'Zanotti's bloody miles away. It's raining!'

'So?'

'You won't melt,' Tara chips in, smirking at me.

And when Minty comes damply back, Jo opens her sandwich fully, like a corpse on the morgue table, and sniffs at the contents.

'That's got rocket in it. Look!' Between a pair of bright red nails, she holds aloft an offending fragment of shrivelled vegetable, like an old, discarded foreskin. 'Why did you make him put rocket in it?'

'I didn't *make* him put rocket in,' says Minty, through a mouthful of pumpkin tabouleh. 'He just always does.'

Shunk! Jo tosses the sandwich in the bin sulkily. 'Well I can't eat it,' she declares, to everyone, folding her arms and lips.

I offer her a placatory Polo mint, which only seems to aggravate her further. Jo most assuredly does not like me, or indeed anyone not called Hugo. Occasionally this week I've answered his calls and Jo has snatched the telephone away from me – as if I might exert some polluting influence on their love.

When the last of the sandwich wrappers has started to smell in the waste-basket, Fielding returns from his 'stroll', which must have taken him to Uxbridge and back, and ensconces himself with the *Times* crossword and a pot of Earl Grey. He says, breezily, to tell anyone who rings that he's out, unless it's his wife, in which case we should say that he's with an author, probably a young blonde one.

'*Dear Lady,*' reads the perfumed, handwritten note attached with sticky tape to the top of the poetry, '*and intelligent woman. Thank you for your kindest words of encouragement. I wish to dedicate this next volume of poems to you, the light which found and nourished me in the darkness of rejection. And also to marry you. I do not mind that you are disfigured and live in darkness. I shall come to London as soon as my father's liver stops working – which is any day now.*'

The note, which carries the musky scent of India, is signed indecipherably and accompanied by an unremarkable anthology of three hundred haikus, typed on a hairy paper still fairly close to wood.

Every day, I encounter something like this, so tragic that I can't face dealing with it straight away – or ever, in fact. I put the folder to one side – on my subsidiary Tragic Pile, which is itself growing to the height of a pit pony.

The remainder of the day passes without event, save for an exclusive first glance at the Rev. Seagram's earth-shattering monograph, 'Did Our Lord Really Visit Cornwall – As Legends Have It In Those Parts?' And, after that, the rare treat of a trip to Ryman's.

On the way back, with a carrier bag full of stationery, I notice a tiny newsagent's shop I've never seen before – tucked in between a dry cleaner's and a Thai restaurant. I decide, in a strange spasm of hopefulness, to give it a try. I do so with mixed feelings, I have to add. Several times over the past couple of days, I have recalled the drunken letter to *TV Forum* and blushed.

The newsagent looks like he might, in the last century, have been one of Mr Barnum's chief crowd-pullers – a tiny, delicate scion of the Andaman Islands with a gigantic gleaming head. The interior of the shop has that familiar newsagent's smell –

egg sandwiches, musty paper and spilt beer – and the selection of papers is poor. Running my eye over a short row of Irish provincial weeklies, the chances of success seem pretty small. But I've come in now. And he's eyeing me hopefully.

'I don't suppose, by any chance, you've got a magazine called *TV Forum* have you?'

I wait for the familiar grimace, the snort of contempt, the wearisome shaking of the head.

'Yes yes!' the man says, delightedly. And he starts to rummage under his counter. I can't believe it. *TV Forum* is alive!

I'm always surprised when I receive a friendly reaction from a stranger in London – where pleasantry seems to be regarded as the first harbinger of rape. Unfair perhaps, but I'm influenced by my first experience when I arrived at Euston station and my watch was at the bottom of my bin-bag. I asked a grizzled old cockney newsvendor type for the time. He wouldn't tell me. Instead, he gave me some advice. 'Buy a *faqin* watch,' he told me.

In contrast, this man practically makes me fall in love with him. In a haze of dread and excitement, I start picturing my letter on the back page of *TV Forum*, jostling for space with the learned theses of the broadcast-nerd community.

The man's luminous head pops up again. He holds aloft one twiggy finger. '*Wet please Juan mints.*' And he scuttles away to the back of the shop.

I look at my watch. I should be getting back to the office. But I can't come this far and walk away empty-handed, can't disappoint this beautiful little egg-headed man.

A queue has started to form behind me. I don't look round, for fear of disapproval, but I can hear the other customers shuffling impatiently, rustling their papers and coughing, wondering which awkward tit has managed to bring business to a grinding halt. An almighty crash comes from the back of the shop – the sound of a thousand magazines landing on someone's head. Then an eerie silence.

'Laaahd!' complains a sonorous Jamaican bass from the ever-lengthening queue behind me. I feel obliged to make a noise myself, to show that I, the culprit, am at least in sympathy. 'Jesus Christ,' I offer, keeping the tone religious.

'He can't help you now,' says a voice behind me, punching me playfully in the back. I turn round.

'What are you doing in here?'

Tara holds up a copy of *Minx*.

'Needed a fix. Actually that's a lie. I just can't bear to be away from you for a minute. What are *you* doing here?'

'Just this magazine I'm after.'

'What magazine?'

At this point, the newsagent returns, wobbly, dust-streaked, with a large open cut on his forehead. I feel a twinge of alarm.

'Look – perhaps I could come back . . .'

He holds up a finger again.

'Please.' And he pulls out a silver, clanking step-ladder at least three times his height and lugs it away into the nether gloom of the shop.

'F'*faq's saike*!' explodes someone behind us. A tiny glance behind reveals the shop, now bursting to the seams with people, like a lorry-load of Central Casting. I feel myself reddening at the ears. Tara edges in alongside me at the counter. 'They'll be wondering what's happened to us.'

She's right. I'm very tempted to leave, but it would seem unfair on the newsagent after all this. And so worth it, so very worth it, if he really has got a copy.

At this point, the religious Jamaican, a chunky man in a creaking leather coat, shoulders his way to the counter. 'Look man – all I want's a packet of Green Orbit. My cab's outside on a double yellow. Just let me in first, eh?' His tone suggests that this could be more than a casual proposal.

I'm just about to move out of his way when the newsagent returns again, breathless and elated. 'I knew, sah!' he cries, placing a dirty, shrink-wrapped magazine on the counter with a flourish. 'I knew, sah. I rimembah.' We stare at it, all three of us – me, Tara and the Jamaican.

TV Foursomes says the title, in lurid, Amsterdam yellow. And below it, a gaggle of pouting Filipino boys, kohl-eyed, in lycra and lace. Tara coughs.

'Cho!' This from the incredulous Jamaican.

'Six pounds and eighty-five,' says the newsagent, rubbing his hands on his shirt.

Outside, lost in misery, I stalk back on my own. Tara catches up with me on the stairs. 'He says to tell you he'll hold on to it.'

'What?'

'Your magazine.'

'Look. Tara. It was a mix-up. Honestly. I'm not like that.'

But she just shoots me a look laden with meaning and nips into the toilet with her *Minx*. Minty, or Jo, looks up as I come in and tells me that my mother just called. A message I find so highly improbable, I ignore it.

Throughout the rest of the afternoon, I notice Tara looking at me out of the corner of her eye trying, it seems, to understand what kind of a monster subscribes to *TV Foursomes*. I give her a weak smile at one point and she just pretends to be staring at the clock above my head. I keep wondering if I should have another go at explaining, but her manner forbids it. She won't believe me. I've blown it. She thinks I'm one of the dirty-raincoat crew. Of whom we know so many.

Five to five. I'm getting very twitchy now, because of the money. There's no sign of Noakes (perhaps they're replacing his fragmented scrotum with a fibre glass prosthesis). Tara is openly applying a fresh coat of Cover Girl at her desk, and no one has said anything about my wages. I reckon I'd rather ask

Captain Hook for a hand-job than approach Fielding, but it seems I'm going to have no choice. I remember the matter of the lovesick Indian poet, and think this might be useful as an opening gambit. I pull the poems back out from the Tragic Pile.

Fielding is 'busy' when I go into his office, having appointed himself a new task for the day. He has announced that we are spending too much on postage, and that, henceforth, he will decide whether a letter is to go out first or second class. He's got Minty standing by the franking machine, and as she passes him a folder, he smells each manuscript inside it, inhaling deeply, as if it were a fine claret.

'First!' he announces. And Minty folds up the editorial report inside an envelope and franks it. 'Pwaagh!' he exclaims, sniffing another. 'Definitely *d.o.l.e.* Second. In fact – no.' He takes another sniff. 'Wait and see if she calls us. I'm not even sure this one's got a letterbox.'

He looks at me. 'What is it?'

He guffaws as he reads the letter I pass him. The braying, confident call of the propertied classes – half hyena, half stockbroker 'Leave it with me,' he says. 'I'll call him up.'

'You *know* him?'

'Christ yes. Done three sodding garage-loads of his books, the little bugger. He's been on about marrying Sarah Gaskell since the mid-eighties. Tara's fault, really. She writes him such bloody good letters.'

'Why does he say she's hideously disfigured?'

'Ah. Little embellishment of my own,' he says, inclining his sandy head modestly. 'Rang me up last summer. Amjit Sammaddi – that's his name. Said he's catching the next available flight from Woggabad or what-have-you. Determined to meet her. So I told him he couldn't. Hideously disfigured, see? Plastic face – burns unit and all that. Refused to meet anyone.' He beams at me. *The fucker.*

'So what are you going to tell him this time?' I ask – one-third wonder, two-thirds disgust. Fielding waves a vague hand about, as if hoping to draw the solution from the air.

'Not sure. I know!' He chuckles drily. 'She's got herself engaged. To the surgeon who rebuilt her face. Got a lovely sense of poetry to it, mm?'

I knew the man was a shit. *But this*. And now I have to ask him, with all utterly undue respect and deference, to help me pay my rent.

Fielding is leafing through his address book, licking his lips in anticipation of the fibbing-fest that awaits him. He looks up. I'm still hovering.

'Why are you still hovering?' he demands. I mention the money. 'I *see*,' he murmurs, pointedly, lifting an eyebrow – as if he'd just caught me having a leg wax in my lunch hour. 'Well, I'm afraid Noakesy doesn't let me sign the cheques these days. Can't you manage till Monday?'

'I'm afraid not.'

Fielding – *oh, what a man* – looks quizzical, cannot quite get his tiny nut around the idea that there might be people on the planet without vast reserves of ancient ancestral trust fund and swindled cash to rely on. Then he picks up his little bulging beige briefcase – made, I expect, from baby badger-skin. He draws forth a pile of cash money – thicker than the most drunken sandwich – and counts out some notes. 'This do you?' He tosses a wedge of them over to me. I look at the notes. 'You don't mind dong, I take it?'

I've nothing against dong. It used to be my history teacher's favourite question. Number thirty, to round off every test. 'Where does a Vietnamese man keep his dong?' We all knew the answer, even John Thomas Longfellow-Lamb. In his wallet.

That's one of the few fringe benefits to Shepherd's Bush. You can change your dong in the kebab shops.

5

Opening the door to the flat, I meet Martha. We almost bang into each other in fact – which I think I'd quite like right now – but at the last instant we hop aside like dancers. She's wearing my coat again. 'You're back,' I say, stooping slightly to kiss her, but she just offers me an ear, which I nudge clumsily with my lips. 'My coat,' I mumble, as I lick the faint bitterness of ear-wax from my mouth.

She pulls it apart, like a flasher. She's wearing the flowery dress from That Night. But she's cut the skirt off clumsily, with something like a nail file. It's just a tattered vest, now, over her black leggings.

'Why did you do that?' I ask, pointing at the remnant of her dress. She looks down. Frowns, as if I'd just pointed out that her flies were open. She seems genuinely puzzled.

'Can't think,' she says. Then she just passes by me on her way out of the door, like any random flatmate might. 'Got to go to the chemist,' she said.

'Why? What's up?'

'They'll be closing.' The answer floats up as she dashes away down the stairs below me.

I feel a bit puzzled. More than that, dejected. I'm worried that That Night might turn into a buried bonk. Just an uncomfortable glitch of the storyline. Meaning only that, when the script-writers remember, we are tense around each other from now on. And in ten years, maybe I make an arse of myself at her wedding. Or don't even get an invite. I had hoped

Martha would be around to share my dong-advance – perhaps might want to head over to White City with me, which I still imagine, staring at the tube map every day, might be some iridescent Moorish citadel.

As a deliberate act of abandon, I take all my clothes off and wander stark naked down the hall into the shower – which is a little cupboard next to Martha's room. Turning the water on and waiting for it to grow warm, I stare at myself in the mirrors. I am not a vain bloke, quite the opposite, but I've always found my own body strangely fascinating. I watch it often, compelled in spite of myself, almost horror-struck, like some *Guardian* telly critic with a soap he professes to abhor.

It's still skinny, like a boy's, at the ribs. But its thighs are a lumpen girl's. No wonder my family used to view me with such suspicion. How can a man have a bulging belly and then practically no arse? I suppose in the same way that even skeletal women can have vast bums. But it can't be right. I wonder what Martha made of it – if maybe that's the reason why she fled and that night has now become That Night and no further night has come after it. She just didn't like it much.

But then, who could possibly predict what they like and don't like? They're not like us – girls. Tara and her builders: '*I love the way he just, sort of, leans up against things when he's having his break.*' Or: '*I know he looks like a football hooligan, but you must surely have noticed that underneath it he's just like a frightened bunny rabbit. And he's got lovely ears.*' I'll never understand. What can this speckled root have meant to Martha?

You shit-house! You dozy bloody shit-house!

A line ricochets around my head, telegraphed in, it seems, from the outside. In shock, I repeat it breathlessly. In front of me, the mirror-image of my flaccid, work-weary tackle, behind me, Martha going to the chemist. And in the middle, inside me, the connection. Martha offering me a cold ear to kiss, all reticent. *The chemist!* I should be down there with her. Paying for the test kit. It's my fault. *She's up the bloody spout.*

I run back down the hall – an odd feeling to be running naked – to where my clothes sit in a pile outside my bedroom door. There's a strange, new smell in the air – sharp and musty, of fags and things unwashed. I should put new socks on I think, absurdly. Mustn't stink at key moments like this. I have a strange, disturbing vision of Martha, older now, divorced, saying conspiratorially, to our son: *'Then your father came down the street after me – followed me right into the chemist. Feet stank like a Polish supermarket. Typical . . .'*

The parcel came yesterday. Twelve pairs of my father's old Wolsey socks. Along with, for no apparent reason, a set of twenty plastic knives and forks. I don't know where, or how, my mother imagines I'm living at present. In some sort of marquee? *Socks, shit-house, hurry up.* I push my bedroom door open.

'Naah then kid,' says Gus, who is lying under my duvet. He shifts a little to greet me and then suddenly contracts with a terrible wince. He lets some air out very slowly through his teeth, like a truck brake. His russet forehead is dappled with sweat.

Gus. With brilliant timing, as ever. But far from his usual swashbuckling self, he looks – quivering under my duvet – more like some gassed subaltern from the trenches at Mons, gaunt and seedy.

'What's up?'

'The cruellest cut of all,' he grunts, and gives a hollow laugh. 'Gorra fag?'

This is pure Gus. He told me, sure enough, when he called long-distance from Borneo, sounding like a tiny man lost in the vast emptiness of a cocoa tin, that he was coming home for a while, that some fiendish tropical boggart had bitten him on what he fondly called his 'old feller' and that he might need some sort of operation. But that he was coming home so soon, and intended to recover from the operation in my flat, my bed, that had remained strangely irrelevant to the conversation.

'How'd you get here?' Instantly I wonder why I asked. Pointless, trivial – the sort of question your parents substitute for silence.

'Gorra taxi from the clinic,' he tells me staccato-style, through gritted teeth. 'Streatham. Cost a fuckin' mint.'

Which gives me a wry smile. My brother, who thinks nothing of covering a continent in a fortnight, angry because Streatham turns out to be a fair step from Fulham and because someone expected him to pay them to take him there.

'Dunno what I'd have done if that bird hadn't been in,' he muses. Then a fresh thought seems to grip him. 'Ey – she's alright, kid.'

She is, I want to say, far from alright, but just then, my brother turns sheet-white, his mouth droops open in horror. He starts scrabbling around, all panicky, underneath the duvet.

'Wassa matter?'

'Jesus,' he says, finally, relaxing, and bringing forth from the rumpled depths of the duvet a long bloodstained tube of bandage. 'Thought me whole knob had come off then.'

I need a break from this. I'm out of cigarettes. There are some dry ones in the drawer – I rummage for them while Gus repositions the pillows behind his head. He takes one from me automatically, without thanks, like a ticket inspector. He has assumed the hue of a toad – a green pallor visible behind the brown. Very sickly.

I sit in the only chair and look down at my great bony brother, his legs stretching a full foot beyond the end of the bed.

'You're skinny,' he observes, having inhaled half the cigarette down to his toes in one, grateful gulp.

Am I? Does Gus even remember what I looked like the last time he saw me? I look down at myself. I'm still stark bollock naked. Gus doesn't appear to find this unusual. Quickly, I grab something, a T-shirt off the floor. 'Aye well,' I say, pulling on some further clothes as I speak. 'I move around a lot.'

'Wow,' he says, pointlessly. Evidently some new fad among the drivers. 'How's our mother?'

'Alright,' I say. 'Doing a course.'

'In what? Pixies?'

'Geology.'

We laugh about this for a moment. Rocks and stones fascinate our mother almost as much as the supernatural. The old house, which she adored, resembled an abandoned quarry, with samples of everything – pyrites, trilobites, purple quartzite and plain old shit from the beach – strewn across every mantelpiece and shelf, regardless of size or aesthetic appeal. One New Year, after Gus left, she announced that she intended to see an active volcano before she died and has gone on to see several. One a year. Always on her own.

'And what about the killer? Someone done him with an ice-pick yet?' A nasty edge to his voice, which makes me feel uneasy. I have never quite understood the depths of Gus' hatred for our father. It seems like hating some far-off and obscure figure from the history books: Isambard Kingdom Brunel – or Trotsky, for that matter. Where's the point?

'Why d'you always call him that? Killer.'

Gus just sighs. He attempts a roll on to his side, panics a little and gives up. 'Going to Nepal next,' he says. 'Soon as I'm up and running. "Roof of the World Trip" they call it. In the brochure. "Shag A Yak" we call it – the drivers.'

'Why?'

''Cos the birds what go on it are all trolls. Vegans and that. Buddhists. They fart like . . .' He searches for an appropriately flatulent simile from the animal kingdom and fails. 'They're dog ugly anyhow.'

I open the window. Whatever Gus thinks of Vegan travellers,

his own odour is fairly unwelcoming at this point in time, underpinned as it is with the faintly urinal tang of TCP.

Leg it. Do one.

The Voices are coming on strong, accompanied by strange twitches down my shins, and I'm tempted. Leave Gus and leg it after Martha. But now I'm trapped – he's launched into an account of a girl on his last trip who was miserable, didn't eat and refused to take part in any of the group activities.

He's just concluding this inspiring anecdote, in which Gus, or a specific part of Gus, sought out the root of the unhappy girl's problems and cured them in a hammock, when the front door slams. *Martha.*

She comes into the room. With a most worrying-looking paper bag from the chemist. She opens it. As at live birth footage, I steel myself to look. She pulls a flat, navy-blue box from the bag.

'Cheers doll.'

It's some heavy-duty painkillers for Gus. As Gus struggles to open them, I blush fiercely, recalling in that instant sufficient 'O' level biology to understand that I am a fool to have even suspected it. Nevertheless, I am overjoyed to see that Gus, and not I, was the cause of her going to the chemist. And barely mind that she goes and sits on the edge of his bed. Which is *my* bed.

'I'd hardly know you were brothers,' she says. I don't much care for the way she says it. I watch her, popping two Co-Codamol into Gus' outstretched, callused palm.

6

Jill has insisted I meet her on the other side of the cosmos – in some very crowded bar in Islington. West London is 'full of arseholes', she said when we spoke on the telephone, and finally revealed her identity as the nameless girlie who had so perplexed my mother.

Jill isn't entirely wrong about West London. The off-licence opposite my flat does special offers on Pimms, and the pavements are acne'd with shrunken jeeps. Standing with her in the Islington crush, however – sandwiched between a pair of polo-necked existentialists with narrow strips of bleached hair down the centre of their chins and geekishly cool spectacles – it seems to me it might be fairer if we said the capital's arseholes are not restricted to any one region.

I hate this cool thing that everyone up here does. At least West London Sloanes, the *rahs*, for all their faults, don't profess to be cool. They are High Tories, most of them, and undeservingly dim in relation to their riches but, as with even the smelliest of dogs, you can find a certain endearing quality to their artlessness. They are cheerfully cheesy. You know that all rahs like doing is getting drunk and going off to Dorset. You know that when those frosty pearl-necklace girls get drunk they will start talking about willies. And when their boyfriends reach, a few drinks later, that same stage of inebriation, they will feel an urge to bare their arses and sing along to 'Deacon Blue'. They are not ashamed.

Not like this Izzie crowd. It took the barman around twenty

minutes to serve us. Not, in fact, because he was busy. But because he didn't want anyone to think he was too eager. He was being cool. Which means what? A studied, uptight, offhand rudeness. Using no words and a pained tremor of an eyebrow, when a couple of friendly phrases might do. And that, of course, is the paradox of it all. To act as if you really don't care about anything, you actually have, secretly, to care a great deal, and be more insecure and anal than a coachload of Scrabble champions. This is one of the *falsest* places in the universe.

I'm careful not to say any of this to Jill, though. She's always said I'm intolerant. It annoyed her enormously when we were going out together, as did the rather camp way I sat – and still sit – on barstools, my passionate defence of *Copter Cops*, the fact that I smoked Rothmans, and never worked as hard as she did. In the end the list grew so big that even Jill began to forget some of the items on it, at which point – the first summer we came back from our respective universities – we decided to call it a day. We are now that thing we call good friends, meaning we have abandoned any intimacy in favour of a few awkward meetings every year.

We were, it's true, once intimate, though a part of me was always afraid I might break something, so neat and pixie-like was her body. And she always favoured the sort of haircut worn by five-year-old boys. In bed, under, above or just chastely at the side of her, Jill made me feel a little like some depraved vicar.

After Jill, I have always sought out girls who come closer to my own dimensions, whilst still looking like girls. Perhaps I narrowed the field a little too much. Between Jill and That Night, there has been absolutely no one. I have trodden the sexual desert – unless you count a certain Norwegian anthropologist who attempted to attract my affections by puking in my bin.

Meetings with Jill follow roughly the same pattern every

time. After polite, and pointless enquiries about each other's activities (I always make something up), Jill will tell me about her latest boyfriend and then accuse me of making faces. I will respond that I always look like this, to which Jill will intimate, in one way or another, that this, the face-making, is the main reason she ceased to find me at all attractive. Too angry to speak, she will then start chewing at her tiny fingernails – a habit that makes me shiver. (I once revered those teensy hands of hers; they aroused in me the same squishy reaction as a kitten's paws.) After the biting begins, we get drunk in bitter silence, swap addresses and go home separately, sometimes even on the same bus or train.

It did seem like a good idea to meet her tonight, though. It's Saturday. Gus is still in my flat, doping himself with the codeine and stinking up Rory's carefully gutted bedchamber after I forced him to limp across the landing and do his suffering in there. I pretended the bed in there was longer, and by the time Gus had laid down in it and seen that it wasn't, he was too weak to move.

Martha got shirty about me moving Gus. Relieved after the pregnancy-scare-thing and subsequently smashed on neat Scotch and a couple of Gus' painkillers, I attempted to gain entrance to her room. And, looking all damp and inviting in her dressing-gown, she shooed me away like a mangy dog. 'You chucked Gus out of your bed. So go sleep in it,' she told me, and closed her door in my face. Rather than look too deeply into the cause of this, I did what men do in such circumstances and told myself that all women were plain weird and that many a sharper mind had failed to fathom them. But I can't help thinking it's not that. More likely something I either did, said, or didn't.

And then before I got the chance to sort anything out, Martha started a full day of shifts at the Pickled Newt. I know this – her working and probably being knackered as well

– is a perfectly acceptable reason for us slowing down. But I just can't help feeling that Gus has a part (albeit an injured one) to play in it all. We never battled over the number of baked beans on our plates, never fought for the boot or the boat in Monopoly. All Gus has done since arriving is smoke cruel-smelling clove cigarettes from the bottom of his kitbag and murmur some drugged-up story about poisoned darts. But I'm bugged by his presence nonetheless – it makes me uneasy.

So when Jill called me up, I was surprisingly keen to meet up with her. So keen, in fact, that I suspect she might have the wrong end of the stick.

As if by way of a stiff reminder, she announces within minutes of our meeting, that she's given up on boyfriends. A very nutty proposal: neither practical nor predictable. She's the sort of person who goes barking mad if left alone for more than an hour and thus always needs someone around, even if they're not particularly pleasant. I know she's even toyed with women when men are in scant supply. And she is very beautiful. Other people have said so.

'I'm living with this guy,' she says, as we squeeze ourselves, in a most unpopular move, on to a bench full of linen-suited broadcasting folk. 'But it's not what you think.'

'Just friends?'

Jill gives an enigmatic waggle of the head, which I take to be a Yes.

Better friends, I hope, than we are, Jill. I tell her a bit about Martha.

'I think I quite like her,' I conclude, passionately.

'Have you done anything?'

Done anything. Not what you think. Instead of some short expression of excitement, or even love, sex for Jill was always rather akin to a Biblical circumcision, a covenantal act of immense formality.

I say that things have cooled off somewhat. I want, almost, to be like our barman here – sound like it's all cool, doesn't bother me. *Plenty more where that came from* and so on. But I don't. For a start, I am, patently, very bothered. And second, it's always best to be truthful with Jill. She has this way of wheedling it out of you, painfully, crumb by crumb, as you might do with an old Christmas walnut at Easter. Always reminds me of the smug Rita Fairclough on *Corrie Street*, with her little nods to camera and her prophetic glances of impending doom.

'Cooled off,' she comments. 'Meaning what I wonder?'

The kind of remark which takes me back right to the first time we went to bed together. Her brother and his girlfriend humping operatically in the room next door. The fried-onion smell of her sweat as she pulled me to her. (It put me off, I remember. I knew so little about girls, then. Even less than I do now. Didn't think she would sweat, or if she did, it would smell like – I didn't know what – like ylang-ylang or fresh-cut grass. I thought they pissed pure mineral water.) The feathery, spooky sensation of the speed I'd sniffed before, in the bogs at the Saracen's Head, pulling me a foot beyond the crown of my head and pushing my pulse to a horse race. And Jill, smashed on vodka, snapping like a maths teacher from the depths of the duvet. 'Come ON! The first time doesn't hurt for boys.'

But things got better then, for a while, as they do tonight. After being frosty and curly-lipped for ten minutes, Jill confides to me that she wants to get drunk. A good sign: normally she frowns on booze in favour of the supposedly more sophisticated toxins, the kind that insert a screwdriver into your brain and convince you the resultant damage is some kind of enlightenment.

So Jill and I get smashed together, whittling our way through my dong-advance. We're doing that pint-of-cider-pint-of-lager trick, which cheats the barman into believing you haven't had a bellyful of snakebite on his premises.

'Why can't you get snakebite down here?' Jill muses, taking a long swig from her cider.

'They think it makes people violent.' This is true. Martha told me. Seems like typical Southern reasoning to me. Up North, at least they accept that most people have plans of extreme violence festering just beneath their skins and, whether they drink sweet sherry or cactus wine, it's going to come out. You may as well ban pubs, or for that matter, people.

'Are you just going to stare at the sodding barmaids all night?'

Jill has finished her cider and is looking irked.

'It's your round,' I tell her. Even though it's not.

As we get drunk, I'm noticing more and more that Jill is different. Not just the renouncing of boyfriends or the absence of jewellery. She is less nervy. Kind of certain. She appears to have some new agenda or Five-Year Plan, beyond all the others – the jobs and the courses – something more transcendent. Keeps looking at me with a kooky half-smile on her face, like a bored god watching some tiny human struggle. I say and do all the things I know will annoy her – like pretending it's not my round – and none of them produces the reaction I've come to expect.

That's one thing about Jill – she always reminded me of my friends' little sisters. So easy to wind up, and with such gratifying results, that you could hardly resist it. It was always a dangerous game and I used to tell myself not to do it. Until it was too late. And now, even though we haven't seen each other in months, I find myself slipping into the same old habit. I hate London, I pretend. I knew even before I came here that all I wanted to do was leave. The response: a tolerant shrug. Southerners, I say, don't understand jokes. Or even those little notes of irony which a Northerner slips in purely as a matter of grammar. I stood at a bus stop only the other day, I tell her, and it started to rain. So I smiled at the man next to me and said,

'Just what we need, eh?' And the man edged away from me warily, saying, 'Naaa. It's not what we *faqin* need at all!' Jill listens to this in total silence, unmoved. This beer, I start, scornfully, on another tack. *Staropramen*. Who thought that was a good name for beer? I long (I don't), I say, for the beer in the old Arts Centre. Ice-cold Higgies. And Jill's reply? Nothing more than a serene smile.

The broadcasters around us, meanwhile, have an argument. Some of them want to eat sushi. Others want to share a taxi to the Buzz Bar. Another sniffs, ostentatiously, to remind us all that there are costly drugs up his nose. They split up, bitterly. We stretch out a little, for about ten seconds, before a posse of off-duty DJs sidles up to our table.

'Anyone, like, er, sitting . . . here?' the spokesman enquires, as if he wouldn't really mind sitting in a hole, but thought he would just, like, ask.

'Yeah. Sorry. Our mates. Just . . .' I motion towards the bar, vaguely. But Jill has lifted our coats off and motioned them all in.

'Cool,' says the spokesman. Surprisingly. Jill glares at me. I feel relieved. We go quiet for a bit.

'Still got your harp?' I ask, to break the silence. I used to tease her about her harp, an enormous concert-hall thing. When Jill played it, the overall view resembled a head-louse attempting to screw the Severn Bridge.

She shakes her head. 'Sold it.'

'Why?'

'Don't earn much.' This is true. The owner of a starred first in music, Jill is now working in a slightly up-its-arse coffee-house on Upper Street. 'Need the money for things,' she adds, pulling at her ear distractedly.

What things? Because Jill, in all the years I've known her, has never once given an answer like that – deliberately vague and misleading. When we split up, Jill didn't opt for cellophane

110

lines like: *It's not you, it's me – I've changed*. She said, loud and clear after the quiz night in the Saracen's Head, as the compère marked the answer sheets: *I really don't like you much any more*. And by the time we had been declared the winners (the prize: three quid and a six-pack of Skol), she'd gone.

What 'things'? Nobody can blame me for being worried. I have, after all, known others of Jill's ilk – the kind who unfailingly did their homework, held down paper-rounds – who are now half-sleeping in vile, pissy squats, in Kirby, and Dingle and Tuebrook. Sticking themselves with needles in a tiresome bid to offend their parents. But not Jill. She was super-organised about everything – even drugs. *I will smoke Pot when I have done my essays and washed my smalls. I will take Ecstasy when there is cause for ecstasy: birthday or new boyfriend.* Jill saw the adverts in the eighties (Skin Care by Heroin) and shuddered. Watched Zammo's decline on *Grange Hill*, believed it and wept.

Not scag, then. Not even fashionably. *So what?* Why does Jill need money 'for things'? I'm speechless with confusion.

'Baaaa!'

Jill looks up sharply. 'Why did you say that?'

'Dunno.'

Because I am drunk. Because, even drunk, I cannot think of anything to say to you.

Things degenerate. Jill starts the biting of the fingernails. And we go.

'Do you want a coffee?' she asks. Courteous to the last. I remember now how, two weeks after we split and loathing me still, she rang to put my next term's address in her little book. Now she wants to give me coffee.

We're standing, uncertainly, outside Angel tube. It's getting colder, now. Then, before I can answer, she changes her mind. 'Better not. John'll be asleep. It's only a small flat.'

'Have to be, round here,' I say. 'John? John Flatmate?'

'He's from home, actually,' she says. 'He knows you.'

I don't know any Johns. Not in real life anyway. I must be the only person in the world, but I don't.

'Yes you do,' Jill says, leaving me to go under. 'John Lamb.'

7

'Am I all blotchy?' Martha demands. She is on my bed, swaddled in my coat, sitting in the dark.

She frightens me. What I'd intended to do was get into bed and have a very long worry about a great number of things. I turn the light on and rub my eyes, still stinging from the smoky pub. Martha looks like a school pudding – all swollen up, wet smears of pink and make-up. She sniffs.

No, Jesus. I've told you before. I can't do crying. 'What's the matter?' I ask, sitting down on the bed – gently lifting her boots and her scribble-pad out of the way. She just shrugs.

'Why weren't you in?' she demands, suddenly, hugging the pillow to her breast. 'You were the only one I wanted to be in and you weren't.'

'Gus is here.'

'He fell asleep.'

Some nasty portion of me is glad she says this. I don't like the idea of them sitting up all chummy, talking together, while I'm not here. Even, yes – even when she needs someone, I'm glad it wasn't Gus.

'He's ace, isn't he?' she adds. I deserved that.

'He's alright,' I concede, generously. 'Thought you weren't going to do any more crying.'

She gives me a wan little smile. 'I know.'

'Why then? Was it Gus? Did he upset you?'

'No. Don't be stupid. I just . . .' I can see her struggling, word-constipated, and then become annoyed when nothing

113

comes. 'Girls get weepy sometimes, alright? They just do.' She rolls away from me and faces the wall. 'You'd know that if you'd ever had a *proper* girlfriend.'

'Cheers for that.'

She rolls back to me – so suddenly that I think for a second she might hit me – sits up, tosses her hair back in fury.

'I just want it all to *stop*. I don't want it to be me. Why did I have to be ill and weird?'

'Maybe it's stopped,' I say, surprised at my own optimism – as if I'd just spat out a painted egg or string of flags. 'Maybe it won't happen to you again.'

She shakes her head, pitying me rather than herself. 'Doesn't work like that, Strange. Doesn't just go. I'm fucked. Up down, high, low, in, out – that's all it is. Forever. I was walking under the scaffolding today, you know outside the Newt? And I thought – why can't something just drop on me, a big massive-like bit of iron and just kill me? And I stood there for ages. And I thought, I really, really, don't care, you know, what happens to me. I *want* something to happen. I don't care.'

'Please don't say that. *I* care.'

'Oh – you *care*,' she says. All the unfettered sarcasm of a thirteen-year-old. Which is, of course, where Martha still is. Thirteen – stopped in time when her mum died.

'Well I bloody do care.'

'So I have to stay alive, because all these people care? My dad. The doctors. You all care. That's really fair on me.'

'Come off it. Don't stick me in with them.'

Martha just goes silent, picking at a stray thread on her leggings. It makes me feel impatient – watching her suddenly irritates me. I don't know what to say.

'What's that smell?' There is a fruity, citrus smell in the room. Martha gives her hair a shake.

'I just washed it,' she says.

'Smells nicer than usual.'

114

'I'm not dyeing it any more.'

'Good.'

She makes a cynical gesture, then falls quiet again for a moment, before asking, quietly, 'Do you really like me?'

'Of *course* I do. I mean. What about the other night?'

She laughs. 'You have to *like* someone before you'll sleep with them?'

'Well. Mostly. Don't you?'

She shrugs. 'Dunno. I never done it with anyone else.'

'Shit.' She frowns, looks troubled, uncertain of my meaning. 'I mean. Why didn't you tell me?'

She sighs. ''Cos you'd have done that thing.'

'What thing?'

'That thing you do. Being all careful with me. Can't even say Dead or Mental Hospital. Can you?' She laughs. 'Thought Virgin would've finished you off.'

'That's just nasty.'

'Yeah well I am. And you're *stupid*. You're stupid 'cos you think you'll be a better person if you sit round holding my hand.'

'You *asked* me to. Remember? You said "Don't go".'

'Yeah well. I wanted a – I wanted a bloke. Not a shrink. Just summat normal. Like other people have.'

'With *me*? Normal?'

'You *are* normal,' she mutters, looking down. 'Compared to me you are.'

I cannot work out if she is saying we are over or that we never were. Either way, the knowledge is depressing.

'I'm going to make a drink.' Tea: the great British let-out clause. What do they do in those dark regions where there is no tea? Face their problems, maybe even solve them? Surely not.

'No!' she says, urgently. 'Don't go in the kitchen.' Suddenly more Northern in her agitation. *Naw. Dawnt gaw.*

'Why not?'

115

'Just stay in here.'

I am still very drunk. I need some liquid. Martha is being just a touch difficult.

'Not from the kitchen,' she insists. 'From the bathroom.'

When I come back with the water in a cloudy toothmug, she's up from the bed, and rummaging through the drawer on my bedside table.

'You're made up,' she accuses me, turning round and sitting back on the bed. 'You've no pictures of anyone or you or anything.'

True, almost. I have, not a picture of a fish, but an actual one, fossilised, in a chunk of rock: *Knightia*, eighty-five million years old. And in a Woolworth's frame, a black and white I tore from a book, Meyer Lansky, I think, or Bugsy Siegel. I am nostalgic, it would seem, for any era I never lived in. But as for public pictures of me, or my family, Martha's right.

You only keep pictures, I think, if your parents kept pictures. According to Sue, our parents were married for twenty-one years before I came along, but there is no record of this event, nor of her and Gus' births, or the twenty-one years of marriage. The time before I appeared is an historical enigma. No one, not even Sue, can tell me anything of consequence, except that our father had travelled a lot. Sue was born in Cheltenham. Gus was born, a year after that, in Berlin (West). She knows another thing: that our father is the man who discovered Bulgarian wine and, knowing it to be cheap and nasty enough for the British palate, began to import it. Then one day, all that stopped and he was home, and home became an obscure corner of Merseyside. Where I made my ill-timed entrance.

I do not ask questions any more. When I was younger, I tried to ascertain why the attic was locked. Why my father never let me sit at his desk – went ballistic when I did. And the response was always the same. Silence, followed by diversion. A dropped cup or a burst of song. In time, I gave up.

There seems no point explaining any of this to Martha. Not now, at least. I've got a picture of Sue – a tiny passport square which I keep in my wallet. I show it to her.

'She's big,' she says, dismissively. Then she bites the top of her hand, looks guilty, like a kid who really, really didn't mean to swear. 'I'm sorry. Things just come out.'

Sue is good, actually, sharp, warm, nosey and, undeniably, quite big. On her first day at the cake shop on Bispham Road, they said that she could eat as many cakes as she liked. Then on her second day, they said she could no longer eat as many cakes as she liked.

Martha laughs when I tell her that.

'Nice to see I can still make you laugh.'

She stops laughing, brushes the hair out of her eyes. 'You can still do all sorts,' she says.

'Not so normal then, am I?'

She smiles, wanly. 'I don't want you to be. Not really.' She kicks me gently in the back with her boots. 'Stand up,' she says. As I stand up, she's clambered under the duvet, and wrapped it round herself, a plump, mascara-stained chrysalis.

'Oh you're staying, are you?'

'Yeah. I'm keeping me coat on.' She speaks down to the mattress.

'You'll be hot.'

'Don't care. Me mum used to keep her coat on round the house all day, you know.'

'Was it cold?'

She ignores me. 'When we were next to the yard. 'Cos people were always coming round, knocking on the door. So if she liked them, she could say she'd been out and she'd just got in. See?'

'Aha.'

Martha never seems to trust that I'll understand her. Not

entirely unreasonable, I suppose. Given some of the stuff she comes out with. But I do.

''Nif she didn't like them, she could say she was just off out.'

'And what about when she went to bed?' I say, trying to wrestle a fraction of the duvet from under her.

But she won't answer, just wriggles down into her cocoon a little further, making cartoon noises of contentment. I turn the light off, take my boots off in the dark.

8

Who put these knots in my head? A rusty cord is scraping against the edges of my skull, filling the cavity with ferruginous muck. I will think nicer thoughts. I must – before my head falls off. *I am made of dandruff and the sweepings from a chiropodist's floor. I am very ill. I will always feel like this.*

I'm awake at exactly 6.13 in the morning, mouth sticky, filled with gluey fumes, heart banging like a trapped bird and my head full of these nutty, obsessive thoughts. This is the true hangover – Strange-style.

Kicking sideways under the covers, my feet meet space. Martha isn't here any more. Just me, and a whole host of regrets which have waited for this moment for weeks. All the crimes I ever committed – the lies, the absences and rudeness to others – saved up for times like this, lingering at the back of my skull, gathering power until I'm sick with the sauce, then charging at full tilt, smack into my forehead like suicide-bomber-bees.

I turn the pillows again and again, in search of a little coolness to sleep on, but everything has become suffused with a damp, tropical heat. As I shift about, scratching under the duvet, little gusts of Gus' unwashed odour come out from the folds, disgusting me further as I touch my itchy, booze-distended belly. The thick, lemony smell of Martha has gone from the bed.

But she's been here, certainly. Impossible to forget that. First there was That Night. Now there is That Other Night.

119

She was nothing like Jill at all. Not just because she was soft and welcoming and there was lots of her, all smelling like a Danish pastry, plump and warm as we clung to each other, shedding our clothes into the tangle of the bed. With Martha, there was something else. A sense of everything being ... *appropriate*. Fitting together, settling into place just right. We found each other's mouths, not because we were trying to find each other's mouths, and each had some rough idea, with our eyes shut, where the other's might be. But because this was where our mouths went. Together. And the hotter, aching parts of ourselves, the same. Together. Like those Israelites put it: *one flesh*.

Israelites? The remembered rush of blood abruptly dies as I wonder what it means when this brand of teenage toss comes freely into your head, as easy as making a shopping list. Love? But what if you've always had a head full of nonsense? Does that mean you're not in love? Or just more likely to fall in love, a faulty circuit, like those kids who always have a skin rash or a nosebleed? And where is she, anyway? What was she up to before I came in?

Then, naturally enough, I start wondering what I was up to before I came in. And, because I wasn't that drunk, I remember: Jill. *And Lamb!*

There's no point trying to escape it, putting on the radio or reading a book. *Sometimes*, Gus had said to me that summer we shared the house, on the subject of the mortal hangover, *ye can just clear it off with a right good wank*. But not now. A wanker needs few resources, it's true, but he needs to concentrate. Scant chance of that with your thoughts crashing in like waves.

Normally, these little poisoned sessions are confined to my most recent misdemeanours – pissing out of the window, or moments of regrettably drunken candour. Whatever I did the night before.

But this morning, my mind skips over those harrowing moments with Martha when it seemed we were destined to become enemies. Instead, this morning, everything is focused way back, on my most wicked, smelliest days, the days of jerking off into a rugby sock and slicing off my spots with a razor. When I took my new grey duffel-coat back to Shawcliffe's, and spent the refund on crisps, and an Oxfam jacket which I had to hide in a bin-bag in the garden. Every act, spread out over years, at once, like Inca-time – no line, no gaps of goodness in between them, just all at once, a roundabout of wrong-doing.

And I know why all these are coming back now. Because of what Jill told me, when I said I didn't know any Johns.

Yes you do. John Lamb.

John Thomas Longfellow-Lamb. Or John Lamb, as he has apparently become now. Unlike the others, I never gave him dead arms, or stole his shoes, or went for his slender arse with a compass point, that porridge-coloured boy with the feather-thin bowl of black hair. I was better at it than the rest. I invented the cry of 'Laaamb, baaa-lamb, baaa!' which in time came to echo round the draughty corridors of St Mungo's like a school song.

It was Strange, A.K., secreting the comedy of his own initials, who first noted the irony of the name John Thomas Longfellow-Lamb. For even into our final year, his dick remained a lamb's, tiny and neglected, never reaching beyond his balls. With girlish modesty, he always wrapped a pale blue towel around himself to cover his shame. Someone always whipped it off him. *Maggot-dick. Shortfellow-Lamb.* In seven years, as my own squeaking became a growl and even the most Nordic boys began to sprout seedy moustaches, not a dark hair surfaced on the form of Lamb, not on a wasted leg, a skeletal arm, or between his haunting, pale-pink, slightly bulbous nipples. Whole crowds of boys, from those ever-shrinking first years to the haughty literati of the sixth form, used to crowd in at the windows of the swimming pool, simply to behold, and

121

condemn the spectacle of John Thomas Longfellow-Lamb getting changed.

I was alone there in lacking team spirit and a passion for exercise, but I was wedded to my fellow-inmates in the hatred of Lamb. Sensing – from the first time we heard him hawking snot into his Kleenex, smelt that curious talcum-powder smell – that something alien was in our midst, we damned him with the heartiest helping of school spirit ever seen since the last king died.

I always thought, after that chilly encounter in the market café, that he must be dead. Either that, or on medication so strong he wouldn't know when he'd shat himself. But he's alive and probably well and living in Islington, not in some random mildewed attic, but with Jill. My first, my only girlfriend.

I picture them meeting through an advert in the back pages of some specialist magazine. If there's one for connoisseurs of lardy TV drama, then there's surely another one for damaged souls: *'Has this man ruined you? Apply in strictest confidence – Survivors of Strange, PO Box 38 . . .'*

I feel angry at the idea of them together. Like a jilted lover. But not jealous – I'm afraid of it. Afraid they spend their evenings swapping Strange-stories, building up a dossier of dislikes, perhaps even fashioning some straw Strange-doll on which to project their diverse, and justified angers.

Why do we do this – clamp our eyes shut and stay in bed beyond the point where sleep could ever venture? I'm not merely awake now, I'm hyper-awake – the force of my thoughts alone could power a small food processor. There's nothing else for it . . .

I make my shaky path to the bathroom, wash with my eyes shut and go into the kitchen. As I shut the door behind me, a large, tropical bird screeches, swoops down at me and deposits a warm swab of grey guano on my left ear. Martha, smoking by the window, shouts too.

'Shut the fucking door. Can't you read?'

She has tacked a piece of envelope on to the glass panel: *Shut The Fucking Door*. I slam it shut and sit down on the floor, this all being a little too much.

There is a parakeet flying around our kitchen.

Its shit lies in tiny, clay parcels all across the cork-tiled floor. The same shit which is now dribbling down the lobe of my ear. I look up malevolently at the bird – it is loudly-coloured, the totemic spirit of Fielding – green and red, with a smear of blue on its head.

'Isn't she beautiful?'

'Where did you get her?' When our brains grow numb with experience, these are the sort of dull, crappy queries that remain.

'Found her last night,' she says, brimming over with ecstasy. 'On the bus station. She's called Deirdre.'

Martha lets out a little sigh, a heave of the bosom, as if it contains feelings too great for her to bear. I don't like it. But I understand now why she forbade me from the kitchen last night. I look more closely at the bird, perching now on the pelmet and pecking at her scaly little feet. *Deirdre?*

'How do you know she's called Deirdre?' I ask, wearily.

' 'Cos I was *meant* to find her last night. It was the date me mum died.'

I suddenly feel sorry. She hadn't said a word about it, I'm certain.

'Was that her name?'

'Deirdre Deirdre! Deirdre!' Martha calls, ignoring my question. And in answer to each one of her cries, the bird cheeps lovingly back.

I squint at Martha in her blue zip-up cardigan and frayed jeans. Absolutely no trace of the previous night's distress about her now, she is a different woman, joyous to the point of preoccupation. But not that shiny-eyed, dreamy state that

Cagney and Lacey employ to suggest they've had a damn good rogering the night before. Something else, distracted, given over to otherness.

'She loved parrots,' Martha says, looking over at me. 'But me dad wouldn't let her have one. Said they had diseases.'

I say nothing, wondering suddenly if she even remembers last night, the painful questions we asked and the gentle, wordless answers with which we silenced them. The sunlight from the windows is bright, revealing the squiggly surface of my eyeballs – a virus in a microscope. I stand up slowly and still I feel dizzy.

At which point the kitchen door swings open, knocking me aside, to reveal Gus, in a long, striped, biblical sort of garment. He waddles in like a bow-legged Canaanite and shuts the door. Flips me a sly wink.

'See you met Deirdre then,' he says. Then he passes the item in his hand to Martha – a rough fragment of coarsely dyed hessian. 'You can keep that,' he says. 'They stick that over the *kullu*,' he informs us, 'when it's boiled.'

'Wow,' Martha says, receiving it reverentially.

Kullu? I don't think I can be bothered to ask.

'Been up long?' I enquire, airily.

'Oh ages,' Martha says. She sits down at the table for a second and then stands up again.

'Up wiv the sun mate,' Gus says, predictably. The bird lets out a series of mocking calls.

'She'll be good for Gus, as well,' Martha says. 'Make him feel at home.' Then she sits down again, unzips her cardigan. Her pointless movements begin to bug me; I realise we have not even touched each other yet.

I give her my first ever stern look and say I wasn't aware that Gus had ever made his home in the Amazon.

I endure a tense breakfast, in which Gus consumes three bowls of sugary porridge and an entire loaf – a feat which somehow impresses Martha. After he has finished eating, he constructs a large joint, crumbling something like a pound of black, sticky hashish into half a fag's worth of tobacco.

'Better than Ready Brek,' he says, passing the completed product to Martha. I watch her smoking it. She catches me, and I look away. Gus watches this closely.

'Wassup?' he asks.

'Nothing,' says Martha, coldly, taking a deep drag. 'Ooh,' she adds, almost sensually, as the smoke enters her. Gus grins. 'Nepalese.'

And he begins a lengthy lecture on the other delights he plans to savour in Nepal. Though I notice he leaves out the 'Shag a Yak' part.

'I wish I could go,' Martha says, with another wistful sigh, as she pushes a slice of barely nibbled toast away from her.

Gus, who has got me to lug his kitbag in, and is now spreading an array of ethnic curiosities across the floor, looks up. 'Ye can do, luv,' he says. 'They never fill up, the Nepal trips.'

Not an unusual response from Gus, who always does his best to tout for fresh clients for the firm. Anyone who in conversation expresses the vaguest desire to visit Sarawak or Surinam, from nonagenarian newsagents to nursing mothers, is promptly bombarded with brochures. But I don't like it. 'Costs a lot,' I say, hastily. 'Doesn't it?'

Gus gives a very emphatic shrug. 'Not overly much, like.'

'Wow,' Martha says. Again. She moves over to the sink, stepping over me with exaggerated care. I wonder when, exactly, Gus is planning to go to Nepal. Some time before fucking lunch, I hope.

Deirdre chooses this juncture to land on Gus' shoulder, as if acknowledging a kindred soul. Gus, very coolly, doesn't move a muscle. 'Long as ye lay us an egg, love,' he quips, 'ye can stay.'

Later, Gus pronounces himself well enough to brave the world. Ever the pragmatist, he has cut the end off a long cardboard tray which had contained mushrooms, fashioning a sort of cricket-box to ram inside his Thai fisherman's trousers and thereby guard against chafing. On our way down the steps of our building, we run into the peculiar Sikh from downstairs, who, in spite of being peculiar, is unloading a top-of-the-range, four-head Nicam stereo digital VCR from the back of his Merc. He's a vast bloke with a long beard and a big belly. And painfully shy. Normally, he scuttles away, eyes down at the ground if you run into him. But this time he gives us an odd stare as we go past – a small package, the batteries for the remote, or a wall bracket, drops from his pocket but he doesn't make to pick it up. Just stares at us, this ambivalent, neither friendly nor nasty gaze.

'Weird bloke,' says Gus when we're out of earshot. ' 'E know you or summat?'

'No. Not really. He just lives downstairs.'

'Nutter,' Gus pronounces, expertly. And I suppose he is right. But great taste in videos.

Mad as he is, the Sikh had pretty good reason to stare at me and my huge, waddling brother making our ponderous progress down the street. The anti-chafing device means Gus has to walk very slowly and carefully, like one who suspects every paving-stone to conceal a sea-urchin. I notice all sorts of people giving us peculiar looks and it's nearly a relief when we make it to an Irish pub just over the other side of the road.

I say 'nearly' because this pub is not one of those modern Finnegan O'Mulligan's establishments, such as you might encounter in the pleasanter reaches of Fulham, where the Gaelic charm consists of a great deal of green paint, pipe music and an extra ten pence on the Guinness. This is the Duke of Kildare, a pub so genuinely Irish that there is a certain authentic nastiness to the English drinkers who wander in, despite an overall willingness to take their cash. The licensees would like us to believe there is Semtex in the cellar, even though there is not.

'I'll bring 'em over,' says the fierce-looking landlady.

'What?' I say, anxiously, wondering what, exactly, she intends to bring over. Her two strapping sons, perhaps, armed with shillelaghs. She nods maternally at Gus, who is at my side.

'Sure, the poor lad can hardly stand.'

'Cheers doll.' Gus, limping away back to his seat, gives her a wink, and her barnacled face dimples up, girlishly.

One thing still truly endears me to Gus. He can't hold his ale. A vast man of matching appetites, he spends months at a time away from drinkable alcohol. In addition to this, even when he hasn't just been circumcised, his system – ravaged by malaria, amoebic dysentery, bilharzia, beri-beri and the like – is nearly always full of quinine or penicillin or something that takes umbrage with the booze. After a single pint, Gus generally gets sincere, sometimes maudlin. After two, he gets roaring drunk. The third induces coma. It happens much that way today. We're only halfway through our first drinks when Gus tells me thickly that, sometimes, he gets a bit sick of his job. I'm truly surprised. I get sick of Gus' job, certainly, but that's because it's not mine.

'You almost hardly never get to meet no one,' he explains. 'Not properly, like, I mean.'

When I bring the next round over, he has shifted himself to lie lengthways on a bench and he says that most blokes his age are settled down by now and have families. 'I'm not saying I want that, kid. But when people are on holiday – birds, like – they're different. They act all different, I mean. More . . . *freer*.'

He must believe it worth the effort. He has a black book the size of a Welshman's bible, stuffed with the names and addresses of his conquests. On his rare trips back to Britain, he spends the whole time travelling between places like Plymouth and Carlisle, dropping in on all the girls who have shown promise. I point this out.

'And it's always shite,' Gus responds, bitterly. 'You get to the door and their faces drop. And you get inside and they make you take your boots off 'cos they've just had new carpets in and then you make a pounce and you find they're engaged to the anal twat who arranged the mortgage for 'em.'

It's a heartfelt, passionate speech, delivered with a little too much volume and I suddenly become aware that Gus' words have echoed round the half-empty place in an unexpected pocket of silence. Everyone – a handful of Sunday lunchtime boozers – is staring. It reminds me of that school trip back from Stratford, in the service station, the time when mine was the only voice to be heard giving a beery rendition of the school song to an audience of squaddies and truck-drivers. They hadn't taken it too well, as I recall.

I shrink a little into my jacket. But Gus doesn't seem to care. 'It never seems to work out,' he carries on, just as loud, wincing slightly as he shifts himself to a sitting position again. 'I never seem to meet birds like me. Who don't give a shit. You know what I mean?'

I nod. I sort of do know what he means. Or did, at least, until I met Martha.

Gus takes a deep breath. 'I's gonna to ask you. That bird.'
'What bird?'

He tells me what bird.

There are, to my knowledge, only two drinks that have the power to transmogrify in the mouth of the drinker. There is the Bloody Mary. A fine drink, in good company. But let one of your fellow tipplers lean across and tell you that all Chinese girls have horizontal twats, let some girl you have patiently plied with coffees until this awesome moment when she will take a drink with you, let her lean across and confess her ten-year obsession with David Hasselhoff and the magic is gone. Suddenly you are drinking cold tomato soup. Which someone has put a tiny bit of vodka in.

Guinness is the other drink. As Gus says *Marfa*, it turns to bitter black coffee in my mouth. 'What about her?'

Gus gulps off the remainder of his pint at one pull. He'll be sick. I hope.

'Has she said owt about us?' He narrows up his eyes like a hero in a Western. As do I.

'Like what exactly?'

'I mean – you know, does she fancy us?'

I make a face.

'I don't mean just a shag like,' he adds, respectfully. 'Couldn't anyway, could I? Not right now. I mean – she's alright. Different. I been talking to her loads. She's brilliant. Reckon she might come on the trip, like – if I sort of pushed her? She gorr'any money?'

Quivering, my hangover returned in a trice, I light a cigarette. If we were Chester and Dale, the twins on *Pacific Reach*, I'd have hospitalised him by now. But I check myself. *Strange: Nothing too hasty.* This is just Gus: lumbering, artless, crashing in with his hobnail boots and assuming always he's the first white man there. I won't get angry. He just doesn't realise. 'She's with me, Gus,' I say, quietly.

Again, the spotlight is on us, surrounded by a watchful hush, as people sip their pints and suck on their crisps to avoid making a sound, missing a fragment of what we say.

'You?'

'Yes,' I say, a little testily.

He makes a philosophical sort of gesture, perhaps copied off some Burmese peasant whose fields have just been trampled by white oxen. It suggests that the mysteries of the world are innumerable. ''Eck,' he says.

We're silent for a while. I look around the pub. There's a tangible sense of relief about the place – some have returned to their drinks, others gone to the lavatory. Then Gus thinks of something. I can see the electrical impulses, one by one, making their slow progress through his mind, leaving shadows on his burnished face. These merge to form a happy smirk. 'Dun't stop her goin' on 'oliday though, does it?'

I try explaining to Gus that Martha is trying to sort out a few difficulties in her life, and now would not be an ideal time for her to take to the Himalayas in his truck, but he doesn't really absorb it. I try reminding him of the Canadian woman, the one who was found half-naked and gibbering in Kathmandhu – but Gus claims not to remember the story. I even try, as a last resort, to beat him at his own game, saying in a low, serious voice, that there are things that Gus would be better off not delving into and that he should trust me. None of which works at all.

'Don't hold your pint like that,' he says, by way of a reply. I freeze.

'Like what?'

'Two hands. Like it's a mugga soup or summat. Just don't.'

Wearily, I put my glass down without a word. We've been here before. It's started again – this criticism, this scrutiny of my tiniest movements, when deeper points are at issue. I may as well never have left home.

Gus makes me tell him where the Pickled Newt is and then, after we leave the Duke of Kildare, he staggers over there, like some ruptured sea-captain full of rum. To see Martha. I'm not going to go over there after him. To sit at the bar all jealous and anxious and make a prick of myself trying to make sure everything I say is funnier, wiser and more interesting than anything my brother could dredge up.

Back at the flat, the foundling bird is going psychotic – transforming our kind old kitchen into a perpetual maelstrom of feathers and shite. I run the gauntlet of her vicious squawks and pellets in order to lug the TV into my bedroom, but the reception is a mockery. I buy Chicken Tikka slices from the corner shop and eat them in my bedroom, churning things around and imagining every tiny creak is Martha's footfall, every click of the window-panes her key in the door. But neither Gus, nor Martha show up that evening.

While we have been out, there is a very confused message on the answer-machine. It is from my mother. *I am*, she announces, haughtily, as if to an errant footman, *the mother of Alastair Strange*. Then a long pause. *Allie. It's Mum.* And then, as if this was not quite clear enough, *Your mother. Can you call please? We've got a new number.* And she gives the old number.

Once when I was at university, just before finals, my father left a series of similarly vague messages. I had no phone, and the porters left half a dozen yellow slips of paper in my pigeonhole. *Your father called./Call your father./Ring your dad, you idle bugger* – this from the nicer, white-haired codger who was nearly retired – */Ring home*. Then he, my father, turned up unexpectedly one evening, and gave me a cheque for a hundred pounds. Because, he said, he had never been an awfully good father. Very odd. One of the few times he ever tried to convey something personal, or truthful to me. He vanished after one cup of coffee. Things to do in London, he said, old friends he had to see. His *people*. Except he doesn't have any friends. Especially not in London.

I do as I'm bidden this time and call home, but there's no answer. I am worried. Not because of the message, exactly. I expect my mother to leave messages like this, answerphones being to her in roughly the same realm as cyberporn. I am worried because of the last thing she said – just as the tape ran out. She asked if Gus was staying with me. Not Jeremy. *Gus.* She corrected herself almost as soon as she did it, but the sound was unmistakable. *G—Jeremy.*

In the matter of worries, there are the chefs and there are the librarians. Some people can be a librarian with their worries. Tag them, give them a file reference, and stick them away for later. Not me. I could try not to worry that my mother has said *G—Jeremy*, but I am a chef. I make a big worry-soup and it swills around my head. Each ingredient feeds off and into the other, spiced with extra paranoia, bubbling away till I boil myself dry.

I'm worrying, for instance, now, about the fact that Martha has brought a parakeet into our kitchen, which she seems to believe is her mother. That there is something distinctly odd about her, and that this distinct oddness has emerged almost directly after sleeping with me. Then I am worrying about my mother's message. Messages. In three years at university, she never called me once. In all my weeks in London, again, never once. Now twice – I remember the other day at Pendennis. I can go on like this for hours. I'm the Masterchef of the Northern Counties.

It gets to about eight o'clock, and I've got the Sunday sickness. The end of *Last of the Summer Wine* brings it on. A sense of unfinished homework, an apprehension of specially chilled rugby pitches – it never leaves you. Even on the dole, when one day is utterly undifferent from all its fellows, the Sunday sickness creeps as ever into your bones. It's even worse when you've got worries.

The phone rings. I have taken to ignoring it these days. So often it's some condescending toff for Rory. The phone is a big white, pelvis-shaped thing with an answer-machine and a fax at its outer flanges. I think of it as a granny's hip, some kind of great, aching bone, that never stops troubling us. But tonight, I bolt for it. Perhaps thinking it'll be my mother.

It's Martha's dad. I had expected some sort of military ogre, but his voice sounds warm. Often, you can pick up a telephone and from the three or four words a person says, know that they are quite dead inside – dumb and nasty, like everyone that ever called for Rory. But this man doesn't sound like that at all.

'I haven't seen her,' I say.

'She come home last night?' he asks, more sharply. I pause, the silence split only by a banshee-scream from the bird.

'Don't know,' I say. Why say that? Perhaps because telling him the truth seems like reporting on her. Betrayal, congress with the enemy.

'I don't even know if *I* came home last night,' I say. He laughs. I take the initiative. 'I think maybe she was a bit upset last night. You know – because of it being . . .' I shouldn't have started it. I can't say the word. But I want him to know, in spite of what she's told me about him, that she's with people who are looking out for her.

'Because of what?'

I take a deep breath. 'Because of it being the day her mum died.'

There's a long, empty silence. Then he speaks.

'Her mum died in June,' he says, icily. 'Anyway. Tell her I called. To say Happy Birthday.'

9

The next few days pass as badly as they do slowly. I can't even bring myself to watch *The Flying Boats*, even though it's the concluding part of Lt Ciapucci's court-martial and even though I've heard the theme tune booming through the building from someone else's flat. I think I've not felt quite so depressed since the summer of Gibbo and the girl in the sand-dunes. One large, hairy factor links these two particular epiodes of darkness in my life. It is nearly seven feet tall and it goes by the name of Gus.

I've begun to recall, with steady, nit-picking accuracy, all the other things Gus has ruined. Family Christmases when Gus stayed out all night and stole the electric motor from my battery-operated Starsky and Hutch car, threw my banjo, à la Mick Jagger, through the gable window. When it was shut. Gus just buggers things up, somehow. Sticks his famous knob, his size 88 boots and his great oily spanners into everything and spoils it. If Gus got himself kidnapped by Chechen guerrillas, they'd hand him back within a week, with a scribbled note round his neck. *Have the fucker back. He's smoked all our fags and eaten our chickens.*

Just as well then that on the Monday morning Gus calls head office and learns that they want him up in Corby for a few days, to look over the truck he'll be taking to Nepal. He goes, calling me at work to tell me this, bidding me ingraciously to *mek sure nowt 'appens* to his stuff and leaving Rory's bedroom smelling like Bangkok. He leaves Martha a big road map of Nepal.

And I hope, pathetically – like a kid who has opened every

birthday present, every packet of handkerchiefs and improving book and still believes there might be one big, frivolous thing hidden in the garage – that Gus' going might allow things to settle down. Martha pulls away from me in every sense of the word. It begins on Monday evening, when I apologise for missing her birthday and suggest we go out and do something groovy – as soon as *Corrie Street* is over, anyway. Martha spares me just a second from stroking Deirdre's eczematous beak, to say over a bared shoulder that she isn't bothered. I have given her *too much* anyway, she says.

It is a ghastly evening. We only spend a few minutes together in the kitchen before Martha goes off, but they are enough for me to notice, to my dismay, that we have started getting on each other's nerves. Every remark I make brings a swift, crushing response and she will not keep still, fidgets constantly with her hair and her rings as if my presence has started to make her uneasy too.

Gus didn't just leave her the map. He has also left his stash with her, and she is smoking her way through it steadily, defiantly.

'You gonna tell me I can't?' she says, as she catches me watching on. I shrug. 'I could've smacked you the other day. Couldn't wait to blow it, could you?'

'Blow what?'

'That I'm a nutter. Not safe with drugs. *A danger to herself and others.*'

My heart beats fast in anger, indignant. I thought we had sorted this out. 'I never said a word about it. Honestly.'

She looks like she wants to believe me. 'Yeh well don't. Don't want everybody knowing. They always go weird on you once they know. Start hiding all the knives. *Should you really be having another drink, Martha?* Arseholes.'

'I never went weird on you. I was just trying to look out for you. I care about you.'

'Oh,' she said, diffidently. 'That one again. *We all care about you, Martha.*' And she took the spliff away into her bedroom.

I'm reminded, not of anything from my own experience, but of the things you hear men say about women. And things I've witnessed in my own little televisual universe. When Sister Dawes, on *Young Doctors*, decided to dump Dr Creevy and elope with Dennis the cleaner. She trashed the Doc's car and forgot his birthday.

Because this is how girls, the ones not so blunt as Jill, like to end things – they make you dislike them, so that it feels like you're the one ending it, not them. But how can it all have come about so quickly? A whole relationship, only the second one in my life, telescoped, played, as some celestial joke, in fast-forward. Before it's even really started.

This morning, she was at the bathroom sink in her underwear, brushing her teeth, and I came in to fetch something from the airing cupboard. She back-kicked the bathroom door shut in my face. And I stood outside the bathroom – seething – waiting for her to come out. Seeing me, she pulled her green towel across her chest. She looked rough, I thought – pasty and tired.

'What's going on?' I said. 'I thought we were . . .'

'What?' she snapped.

'Thought we were friends.'

She gave me a blank look, scary, and padded off towards her room. I followed on behind.

'We *are* friends,' she said, turning round at her door to face me. 'But that doesn't mean we have to talk about it all the time. Just – I don't know.' I watched her again, biting her lips as if to make them bleed the right term. 'Back off for a bit.' And she slammed another door in my face.

The flat no longer seems like home at all. The kitchen is unbearable – the windows locked shut to prevent the bird from escaping, the floor all covered in pellets of crap. Deirdre and I are not on easy terms and she makes a great deal of noise every time I pass into her territory. I'm beginning to wonder if she *is* the reincarnation of Martha's mum, choosing her daughter's boyfriends from beyond the grave.

So I'm spending more and more time at Pendennis. Just like those lugubrious gits who crowd the bar at the Pickled Newt every night, who know it's crap there but not quite so vile as going home to their bitter wives and their angry sons.

When I arrive at work in the mornings, only the desiccated cleaning lady whose name, I have discovered, is Asuncion, is in the office, rubbing every available surface with her damp J-cloth, including the insides of the cardboard folders and the screens of the computers. Asuncion has this very disconcerting habit of freezing every time you go near her, rooted to the spot like some animal caught in the glare of headlights, waiting for you to pass. She seems to suspect that, if you were to catch her moving about, you might justifiably seek to strike her with a rope end or some blackjack. 'Sorry, sorry,' she murmurs demurely this morning as I pass by her to get to my desk. 'I no suppose be here. I go.'

I say there's no need. She ignores me.

'I coming only because Mister Nowaak ring me – is problem in toilet. Much water.'

I know about the problem in the toilet. We've had the plumbers in already. They said they'd fixed it, as you rather might expect plumbers to say.

'I think the cistern might have ruptured,' I say.

Asuncion's eyes suddenly shine with interest. She wets her lips. 'Jour sister? Is ruptured?'

I try to explain, but Asuncion starts to go off at a tangent. With relish, she tells me that her brother's wife had herself ruptured. There had been a great deal of mess. 'Washed in blood' are her exact words. I wait for some redeeming feature of the fable to present itself. I wait a long time. It doesn't come. Eventually, Asuncion's sister-in-law just bled to death.

'I go now,' she says, reluctantly, when this inspiring epic has reached its close. She pulls on her grey coat, which looks as if it was fashioned from a Crimean-era army blanket. 'Much working. Always berry tire.'

'I know. But—' I cast a defeated palm upwards. 'Things aren't so good at home, you see, and . . .'

Asuncion is shaking her head. Interrupts me. 'I clean in many places. I go next Gol' Hawk Road. Cleaning hotel. Then big house in Bal-ham.'

Always berry tire. *Strange: She was talking about herself. Bozo.*

'Jour sista okay?'

Why this strange concern for my sister? Sue is not ruptured. Sue is fine. Sue is always fine. How could someone as big as Sue not be fine? Have the Liver Birds ever suffered so much as a stray zit?

'She's fine.'

But Asuncion looks doubtful. 'Maybe. Maybe no. When jour fam-billy many miles away. Never can say fine, no fine. Never knowing.'

And she scuttles off into the gloom of the morning – cheered only by the prospect of some fresh trail of human misery.

I'm not alone for long, thankfully. Two loud bangs shake the building as the steel-reinforced front door opens and shuts, forcing me to stop whatever I'm about to start worrying about. Noakes and Tara arrive together. I hear his characteristic twittering passing from the porch outside into the hallway and up the stairs. The subject, I gather, as they come up into the office and the sounds become clearer, is the shaky relationship of Tara to her job.

'Certainly NOT,' Noakes states, as he stows his Gore-Tex anorak on the brass hooks by the coffee machine. 'If you've got a choice, then you take the later one. Tell them you'll take the 5.30.'

'But I really sort of need to take the three o'clock,' Tara says, slinging her bag in a practised gesture across the room, over my head, to land on her chair.

'Why do you really sort of need to?'

She sighs, irritated at this intrusion of Noakes into her affairs. 'I've got a cocktail party in Chiswick at 6.30. If I take the 5.30, I won't be ready in time.'

Noakes loses it, big-time. He says, again, that Tara is on Final Warning. He says, waving a Mars Bar around like a pistol, that she needs to sort her priorities out and that if, in the process of that sorting-out, she discovers that the attendance at cocktail parties in Chiswick turns out to be a superior concern to the demands of her job, then there might be a strong case for her, and the Pendennis Press, parting company for ever.

He then says he is very busy. There are two authors coming in, and he isn't prepared to waste any more time arguing.

As he shuts the door to his office, Tara pulls out her tongue, and hops up and down, flicking a V-sign with her left hand, and the one-finger-salute with the right. 'Old Panda-face git,' she says. And sits down at her desk, swivelling round violently a few times on her chair because Noakes has told her it damages the bearings. From her bag, she pulls out a glossy magazine devoted – according to the cover – entirely to the orgasm, and with an air of defiance, she starts reading it very slowly, her tongue poking out of the corner of her mouth.

Still eager to prove to Tara that I'm not some dysfunctional devotee of Far Eastern boy-flesh, I fetch her a hot orange from the drinks machine, which she accepts quite warmly. 'What was all that about?' I ask her.

She sighs. It emerges that she approached Noakes with the option of two dental appointments, one at three and one at 5.30, and she'd been hoping to take the earlier one, and then have the afternoon off. She's going to some famous restaurant in the evening, she says, and needs time to prepare.

'You shouldn't have mentioned the cocktail party,' I point out. 'That was what lost it.'

'But I made that bit up!' she wails. 'I thought it would *persuade* him.'

I turn away from Tara and switch on my machine. There doesn't seem to be much I can do to help. Tara, however, keeps up a series of dark, resentful mutterings to herself, the import of which is that this is a smelly old job and the management of Pendennis Press ought to be *f. grateful* that she deigns to work there.

Four more bangs, and my box of elastic bands falls off my desk. Minty and Jo arrive within seconds of one another. Their mutual loathing has doubled and thickened in the night like dough. There is a more definite sternness about the lips, a coldness in the eyes, a studied deliberation in the way they ignore and avoid each other as they take off their identical navy pea-coats and head for the vending machine. Minty, I notice, looks truly awful – quite like Martha did this morning, pale and red-eyed. Tara – now bored of her magazine and her muttering – notices it too. 'Okay Mints?' she asks.

Minty turns to us, twisting the silver ring on her finger. 'I would be,' she says, through gritted teeth, 'if SOMEONE hadn't completely totally like ruined my whole life.'

I'm wondering which one of us is going to ask her what she means, when Jo slams the door to the toilet with alarming force, causing a framed picture of Paris to fall off the wall and break. And by the time this accident has been dealt with, Noakes and Fielding are bustling about the office, disturbing everything. Minty and Jo settle into a smouldering silence alongside each other, taking great pains to slam, smash, crash and wallop everything within their working remit, from boxes of paperclips to the static-free screen-wipes.

One of Tara's folders is missing from her desk. She rummages everywhere. Starts to look over to me. 'Have you got Pook, darling?'

'What?'

' "Home Surgery On A Shoestring".'

Her look dares me to say something smart. I'm not in the mood. 'Sorry. Haven't seen it.'

She looks puzzled. Pats a space on her desk.

'It was here last night. Couldn't face doing it.'

I shrug. 'Maybe Noakes took it.'

'No. He left with me. And he gave me a lift last night, so it can't have been.'

A lift? Noakes and Tara in a car. Together? I'm temporarily knocked asunder by this idea. Meanwhile, Tara's on her knees under her desk. Crawls out again, backwards, all pink-faced.

'Arses! You didn't see Thingy moving it did you?'

'Thingy?'

'El Morbido. The cleaner.'

'Nope. Sorry.'

'Oh you boys. F. useless,' she says.

The idea of El Morbido at least makes me smile. Asuncion. Our own little Galician Grim Reaper. 'How long has she been here?' I ask Tara.

She shivers slightly. 'Since for ever,' she says. 'You should have seen her during the Waco siege.'

We can't find Pook anywhere. But at least, in the search, the atmosphere between us seems to have improved a little. I take a deep breath. 'Look. Tara. About that magazine.'

She swivels round and gives me a patient, understanding smile. 'It's alright, darling. You don't have to explain. I'm v. broad-minded.'

'No, no. There's nothing to be broad-minded about. It was a mix-up.'

'How so?'

141

I tell her the whole story of *TV Forum*: our first tryst on Runcorn station, my painful, nationwide search for another copy, my drunken letter, my boundless joy when the newsagent said he stocked it.

'You mean you *actually* like that sort of thing?' she asks, plainly astonished. 'I mean *Emmerdale* and that stuff?'

'Well. I don't so much like it. I sort of. Need it.'

Tara shakes her head.

'Golly. I mean. Well – I don't mean to be rude . . .'

'What *do* you mean?'

She shudders faintly. 'I just never had you down as one of *them*.' And she goes back to her magazine.

Before I can answer her, Fielding breezes past and, quite out of character, taps me playfully on the head with his *F.T.* 'Cheer up!' he exclaims. And when I don't respond, he leans in closer to me. 'There's only two things in life which are certain. Know what they are?'

I shake my head.

'Death,' he says, barely able to contain himself. 'And an actress.'

He is repellently jubilant this morning – humming little ditties to himself, and stalking about the office with his yellow check scarf tossed carefully over one shoulder, and his grey briefcase stashed under one arm. He has some Nazi forced-labour song on his brain, to which he has invented his own, faintly racist words. '*Beady wop mop mop wop – beady mop. Beady WOG! Weedy WOP!*' He breaks off from the song after its eleventh, or twelfth refrain. 'Meeting Helen at lunchtime,' he remarks loudly. This is addressed to Noakes, who, purple with exertion, is attempting to fit a new cartridge into the photocopier. 'Helen *Mirren*, that is,' he adds. Noakes slides out anxiously from under the photocopier.

Possibly the 'clinic' have sternly warned Noakes to leave his tattered old scrotum alone and find a new object for his

142

frustrations. This morning, it's his pendulous earlobes, which he has taken to stretching out to outrageous angles – like blobs of bubblegum. 'You ARE planning on being around today aren't you?' he enquires, tentatively, yanking away. 'We've got authors in for their briefings. Dan Kane and that Russian.'

'What Russian? Seems to me we've got something of a rash of Russians at the moment, old chap.'

'The army fellow. Leved . . . yellev—' Noakes stops, staring at Fielding for a moment. 'What are you doing with my bloody briefcase, Ben?'

Fielding glances down in astonishment at the thing under his arm, as if he, too, is surprised to find that he is carrying it. 'No, no. This is mine, old fellow. Had it for years.'

Noakes staggers to his feet. 'But I've—' he says, weakly. Then he lunges for the low sliding cupboard just by Tara's dark-stockinged knees. She yelps in alarm, scooting away on the wheels of her chair. Noakes tosses the contents of the cupboard aside – stacks of paper and an industrial quantity of staples – to withdraw an identical, soft grey briefcase. 'This is mine,' he says, weakly, all dazed, as if gripping the ark of the covenant. 'From Vivien.'

Fielding suddenly acquires a perplexingly large amount of phlegm in his throat – a development which requires his sole attention, and a great deal of coughing and snorting. At length, just as one of us is about to call an ambulance, he says he'd better just pop down to the chemist. Noakes stands in the centre of the office, staring after him, fondling his empty briefcase. 'I don't use it,' he remarks to me, vaguely. 'Always preferred carrier bags.'

The first of the day's authors arrives at 11.30 sharp, for what Noakes has lavishly termed his 'briefing'. This meeting marks the first and only face-to-face contact an author will have with our organisation, and only occurs once a non-refundable, twenty per cent deposit is nestling safely in the Pendennis coffers. The briefing begins with coffee and biscuits with Noakes and Fielding and ends, ideally, with the payment of the remaining eighty per cent.

A military man – not a second late or early – Lev Yelevadze, author of the romantic classic, 'Her Cherry Gizzard', is ushered through to the back office by an unctuous Fielding. Yelevadze is a sinewy fellow with Tartarously high cheekbones. When he took his camel coat off, I saw for a chilly moment the ripples of his arms underneath his starched white shirt – arms for overpowering people, pinning them to bunk-beds, enacting the scenes so lovingly described in his novel. He stared at Tara for a long time – Fielding had to call him twice before he went into the little office.

After half an hour of hearty, chappish laughter, Yelevadze comes out again. This time, before Fielding or Noakes can see him towards the door, he stalks over to Tara like a puma, leans down across her desk, starts talking to her, not in Russian, but some wilder, Turkic tongue – with the aspirants of the hill-tribes, men who drink the blood of their horses. And not because they particularly need to. '*Yeremy lie Turk ooh Dan Gus gay Lou – Larry's Ma,*' he says. Or something like that.

'Sorry?' Tara says, politely.

The slender, nut-brown fanny-hound grins, showing a parade of gold teeth. He straightens up and turns to Noakes, who is hovering protectively behind him. 'Your lady,' says Yelevadze, bowing stiffly, 'is like apple blossom.'

After Yelevadze has gone, Noakes comes back up. Says very sternly to Tara that flirting with authors is the kind of thing that gets a girl the sack.

'I was just sitting here!' she protests. 'I wasn't doing anything. If someone wants to call me apple blossom, there isn't an f. lot I can do about it, is there?'

Noakes says that he's going to introduce a dress code. I wonder if this includes me.

'Dad's a real prick,' Tara murmurs to me out of the corner of her mouth as Noakes bumbles off to devise some sort of office purdah. I stop typing, in mid-fib.

'Who?'

'Dad,' she says again, quite plainly. 'I hate him.'

Never. *Not even in* Falcon Crest, is the phrase that comes to mind. I shake my head, stare down at the page in front of me, and watch the words turn to shapes, like road signs when we are drunk. *The idea of it!* They are so utterly unalike. Good, funny, bold, *nice* (even with the v's and the f's and the q's). Versus bad, boring, cowardly, ugly. Slim and certain. Fat and unsure. Not possible. Never. They hate each other.

But then – what would you call the cocktail of doubt and weariness that seeps through me when I think my father's name? Love? But nor is it hate – not like Gus. Noakes stands as an awesome reminder of the sort of parent I could have had. I'm aware, suddenly, of feeling just a little bit grateful and – even if she does think I'm a deviant – a lot sorry for Tara. 'I'd never have known,' I say to Tara, with evident sympathy. She shrugs.

'You haven't met Mummy,' she says.

I'm reminded of my own mother, who ended up with someone equally improbable. Who's left another message on the answerphone at the flat (6.30 in the morning, if you please) and rung the office again. Keeps missing me. As she has done all my life, with her gifts of rowing tops and pen-knives. Every time I call back, there's just no answer. But something makes me keep on trying.

Later on, at lunch, I try to think of a birthday present for Martha, but I can find no inspiration in the supermarkets and ethno-trash outlets of the Shepherd's Bush Road.

Ethno-trash perplexes me. I wonder if, somewhere, there's a huge warehouse of the stuff. And all the mock-hippy stallholders and shop-owners just come and buy it by the yard. Like

145

offcuts – beads, rings, Ecuadorian goat-hair ponchos, Yin-Yang dope-boxes, Ganesh-shaped soapstone joss-stick holders, anything to fill a shop and fleece a few unknowing students. Is it the same in Asia? Do *their* suckers buy *our* trash, as a neat sort of trade-off? Picture the scene at the University of Uttar Pradesh: 'Hey, Ashok. Love the shellsuit.' And Ashok looks all off-hand and says, 'Yeah – just a little something I picked up in my year off. I went trekking in Merseyside.' I must ask Gus. If he ever comes back.

I'm walking past the bookshop again, and wonder if I should maybe buy her a book as a belated birthday present. But I've already bought her one, and she hasn't read it. It's under her pillow, and none of the pages has been turned. Unlike Gus' map of Nepal, which she has opened out and stuck to the wall above her head.

The only vaguely groovy thing I see is a small suitcase, covered in some Friesian cow-print fabric. But a suitcase is the last thing I'm going to buy Martha . . .

Back in the office, I call home again. Still no answer. I'm surprised to find myself doing all this. Why am I so bothered about returning a few dozen calls from my parents? I'm not, regrettably, but understandably, like those sturdy Cockney souls on *EastEnders* who grunt continually about the merits of 'family'. I haven't truly worried about 'family' since I was five and we were told at school that you had to believe in the baby Jesus to get to heaven. Which I knew none of my family did. Just as they regard themselves above normal human relations, so have I grown to think them beyond my concern. The cause of headaches. Donors and darners of socks. Spinners of weirdness and mystery. And not a lot more.

But now I'm not so sure. Why do they want to speak to me now – after twenty-three years of speaking only in riddles? Why did my mother call Gus Gus? Are they mellowing with age? Or are they merely tying up the loose ends, in the manner of those who know the end is coming? They're not young. I don't actually know how old they are, but it's old. They say *wireless*, after all. My father even talks about the *Light Programme*, instead of Radio Two. In a bid to appear a little continental, that same father has smoked Gitanes for most of his life – or at least, for as long as I have known him. And my mother has just that sort of dippy, objectless intelligence which turns to Alzheimer's when the kids are gone and grown. I'm beginning to picture some sort of gruesome deathbed confession.

Gitanes – the thought of them makes my chest ache. I want a cigarette now. I'm such a sucker, a born addict. Even the soupy beer they drink on *Emmerdale* makes me crave a pint. Gitanes were, not surprisingly, the first fags I ever stole and smoked myself. And what fags. The polar opposite of a gentle introduction to the world of tobacco. Most days, I'm fine. I can gun a couple down on the way to work, one at lunchtime, perhaps a sly one with Tara mid-afternoon. And then once six o'clock comes, I'm free to choke myself to death until bedtime. I can handle it. But if I encounter one reference to a cigarette in a manuscript. Or look out of the window and see one of Tara's builders lighting up. Or just think about it myself. Then I'm scuppered. *Strange: Have a fag.*

Noakes is down at the computer shop, purchasing some costly and unreliable addition to the office paraphernalia. Fielding, so he would have us believe, has met Helen Mirren, and is now having a little snooze (post-Armagnac, I hope, rather than post-coitus) on the couch in his office. The coast is clear.

When he first caught me smoking, my father's sole response was a weary nod. I was on the wall outside the post office and he cycled up, unseen. I stubbed it out on the wall – but the butt caught in the folds of my overcoat and sat there, smouldering. Then when I came home, a hole in the side of my coat the size of a duck's egg, no one said a word. But two days later, I was over at Sue's house and she was very stern about the whole affair. 'It's drugs next,' she said. And Billy nodded, grimly. 'That's the road you're on.' And I skitted them both – inwardly.

Now I'm standing over the little sink next to the toilets, carefully blowing my smoke out through the air vents, and thinking they weren't far wrong. The smoker, like the scaghead, has a million methods of hiding his habit from public scorn. And from himself. Take my route home. I walk an extra ten minutes a day, so as not to have to handle the steep ascent to the Talgarth Bridge. Or the matter of dropped money. Even skint, there is a hierarchy of coins I will and will not stoop to pick up. 20p, or more, is worth feeling sick and dizzy. Anything below that, forget it. I am tab-governed, certainly, like the junkie by his powders. Sue and Billy were right.

I'm exactly four drags in, when a tall, expensive-looking woman comes clicking up the stairs and stands at the door. I yelp in fright, and push the cigarette out of the vent. My heart's banging painfully. It's hardly a relaxant, the sly fag. The woman is in her forties, I'd guess, with long dark hair. She's smiling. At least, I think that's what she's doing. She has that taut *Knots Landing* brand of beauty which can only come from a thousand face-lifts. I suspect she finds it quite hard to blink. And God knows what a sudden fart might do.

'They said there was a Young Man here,' she murmurs, patting the top of her hair carefully, as if some sore nubbin of spare tissue might rest there. 'Vivien,' she adds, holding out a limp, sculpted hand.

'I'm Strange,' I say. And her eyes widen like two carnivorous flowers.

'I don't think so,' she breathes, weightily. 'Not at all.'

I explain. She lets out a silly laugh.

'Well hello Stranger,' she says, with a glancing pat on my arm. I try and muster a smile. If you can think of a joke about a person's name, you can pretty much guarantee they've grown quite sick of it already.

What does she want? She carries on standing there, moving fragrantly a little further into the tiny room. My back is now jammed up against the immersion heater and I'm just beginning to shuffle, awkwardly, when Tara appears behind the woman, with a number of teaspoons. (Noakes has very rigid views concerning teaspoons and their proper siting in the work arena.)

'Leave him alone, Mummy.'

The woman turns round to face Tara. They kiss in that cold manner that women have perfected amongst themselves. Tara's mum. Talk about Meet The Family. All in one day. I wonder if Asuncion is about to be shepherded in from the hoover cupboard and introduced as a younger sister.

Tara's just a few inches taller than her mother. From the deliberate gap between them, and the way they stand, arms folded, it's clear they have been in competition for a number of years. 'Are you coming to Fabio's?' says Tara's mother, ignoring me now, and reaching for a strand of her daughter's ebony hair. 'Don't wear black, darling, promise me. It shows off your . . . lumpy bits.'

Tara, upon whom there are fewer lumpy bits than a sheet of glass, pulls away and glares, replacing the strand of hair behind her ear. 'Dad won't let me out anyway. I tried. I even made up a cocktail party, but he wouldn't let me. He's being an f. shit.'

'Hey—' admonishes the mother, holding up a sharp red fingernail of restraint. 'Now no. Have you asked Ben?'

'Why would I?'

Her mother links arms with her girlishly. I see their hands together – identical, thin assemblies of chopsticks.

'Let's just ask him. Come on.'

And she leads her off, towards the main office. I watch them clop away together, two-headed, intersecting at the elbows like a single, glamorous gorgon. Tara returns, briefly – hands me the clutch of teaspoons. 'Be a sweetie,' she says.

And sure enough, about an hour later, and before Noakes has come back, Tara is swathing herself in fake fur and making ready to leave.

'Where are you off?'

'Dentist's,' she says.

'But Noakes – your dad said—' I have just about assimilated this surreal fact by now.

'Oh Ben says it's okay,' she says, airily. And like that, cheery as a lord's bastard, Tara gathers up her bag and waltzes away. She turns back, though, just before she goes out of the door. 'Mummy thinks you're a *doll*,' she says.

The news does nothing to cheer me up. What can Vivien know? She married *Noakes* for Christ's sake.

I remember the first time I kissed Jill – Lower Sixth, the end of lunchtime, outside the Girls' gate. And my pleasure, that first time anyway, wasn't so much in the kiss – we'd been in the park smoking John Player Specials and our mouths tasted like a pub carpet. It was more that there were other people kissing there, all the strong, tough, flirty-eyed boys from my year and the year above, and their glamorous girlfriends, the kind who managed to look like women, even in their Sixth Form blazers. And I thought – *Hey. I'm here. Part of this.*

But that feeling passed away with the rising knowledge that Jill took a certain, slightly mawkish relish in the exotic, and that, far from being any sort of doll, I represented simply another item in the collection, alongside the Mormons and the stammerers and the women and the married men.

I became resigned, after we split, to the knowledge that, whenever a child went missing in my street, I would be the Nasty Squad's first port of call. *Not got a girlfriend, have we, Alastair?*

150

Martha made me certain I was wrong. And then, it seemed, just changed her mind. And why? She didn't mind that I knew about her being ill. I never pushed her to talk about it. It all went wrong after Gus came. If Gus hadn't put all that rubbish about Nepal into her head, it'd still be like it was before.

Forget it Gus. I mean JEREMY. Go stir things somewhere else.

That's what I should've said. I should've chucked him out of my flat when he was still unable to put on a pair of underpants, let alone resist.

Get lost Jeremy. Take your kitbag and do one.

'Sorry?'

Minty is standing in front of my desk, proffering a sheet of paper which has fallen from the folder I'm working on. A sheepish warmth spreads out from my ears.

'Nothingsorrythankyou,' I say.

They have removed me from evaluations for a while, and put me on editing. I'm handling the pitiful account of a Mr Tullis, from the town of Rome, Ga., whose work 'I WAS ABOARD THE ALIEN SHIP' is cast entirely in capitals, giving the impression of something screamed (loud being, in Tullis' ever-ignored universe, on a par with true). It is accompanied by a number of entirely pointless, blurred black and white photographs. Each photograph, despite having a different caption, is indistinct from its fellows, featuring only a large, whitish smudge, against a background of grey, like swabs of semen spat at some breeze-block wall.

Tullis has apparently approached various worthies for their comments upon the manuscript.

'I look forward to reading it,' Senator Bob Dole has said. No mention is made of his opinions after reading it. Perhaps he hadn't realised that this collection of cum-shots and four typewritten pages *was* the manuscript.

I concentrate hard on the text, determined not to be caught

muttering out loud again. The atmosphere in the office has grown charged and heavy, like the beginnings of a bad storm, or a queasy trip. My stomach feels fluttery and light as Minty and Jo crash and smash their way through the day, in the chilly combat of women's silence.

But gradually, as the gestures and the resolute refusal to answer one another's phones lose their insultative potency, words are beginning to creep in. I keep catching little *sotto voce* sounds above the hum of the machines, brief, curt exchanges which, the instant I look up, become silence again.

'*SPACE CRAFT*' bellows the caption to Blob Number One. '*IT CAN GO AT WART FACTOR NINE. I WAS ABOARD THIS.*'

'Can you move?' Minty says, waspishly. I look up. Minty is trying to get back to her desk with an armful of papers. Jo, seated on her swivel chair, blocks her path. They face each other off, like a pair of blonde bulls in a paddock.

'Yes?' says Jo, finally, wheeling forwards on her chair just an inch so that Minty still has to squeeze her way through. A subtle means, I suspect, on Jo's part, of suggesting that Minty is a bit fat.

'What?' snaps Minty, glaring over at me. I duck back to the typescript.

'*SPACE GIRL*'. The caption to Blob Two. '*ON THE SHIP. SPACE GIRLS ARE NOT LIKE U.S.A. GIRLS.*' And here, Tullis adopts a more furtive, intimate tone: '*Space girls see inside.*'

I take a hunt through the file to find the author photo, take one look at his duck lips and his bottle-bottom glasses and feel incurably bad. I'm the *same* as these people, for Christ's sake. Obsessed with my TV-reality, unable to form lasting relationships in the non-soap world. Full of shite and fuzzy dreams. The *same* as all the people I'm ripping off. I sit still for a moment. Put my hands over my face and feel for a delicious instant the cool balm of my damp palms. I rub my eyes, which only has the effect of making everything twice as blurred. The day's little shocks and buffets, instead of making me wish, as usual, to retreat to the warmth and safety of my bed, are making me feel careless, full of abandon. I pop over the road for a can of Lilt.

When I return a few minutes later, there's a hissing coming from the toilet on the stairs. The ruptured cistern again? But as I go closer to investigate, I realise the sound is an argument, being conducted in hot whispers.

'I didn't KNOW?' protests a slightly quizzical voice. 'I thought it was my one!?'

'You've fucked it all up,' says the other voice. 'He's got to have steel pins in his hip now. He's been dropped from the water-polo team.' Minty's voice.

'It's not my fault?' Torn between statement and interrogation – this can only be Jo.

'And we've had to cancel skiing. Do you know what you've done? I've lost my arsing deposit.'

It all begins to come clear as the row rages on – I piece it together, like an archaeologist, from the fragments which float from under the door. It seems that Minty's Hugo, he of the steel hip-pins, telephoned the office on Tuesday night, but as a result of lackadaisical office procedures and the fact that he sounds exactly the same as Jo's Hugo, he got transferred through to Jo. Now Jo, having waited three hours in a grisly Fulham wine bar for her own Hugo the night before, gave the caller a piece of her mind, and declared the relationship at an end. Minty's Hugo, his world having collapsed, went home to Buckinghamshire, drank himself into a semi-coma, and drove his brother's Isuzu into a tree. He is now in plaster from head to foot, and facing a decade of surgery.

As this sorry tale unfolds, the whispers turn into full-blown shouts.

'What do you mean I can have yours? I don't want yours. Yours has got pointy teeth.'

'How fucking dare you? Yours has got ear-hair?!'

A blow – not a slap so much as the sickening thud of bone on bone. Then, through the glass door leading into our office, I see Noakes pacing about, looking under all the desks, as if hunting for his missing workforce.

'Why are there no girls?' he demands, as I come back in hastily. Hitching my trousers as if I've just been in the loo. I shrug. I don't think I could explain if I wanted to.

Noakes scratches his head repeatedly. A little shower of necrotic flakes descends from his scalp. 'Jeepers,' he observes. 'We need some tea for Dan Kane.'

'He's here?'

'Yep,' Noakes says. 'Strangest bloody Dan Kane you ever saw, I'll wager you.'

He ponders on this for a moment and then glances at me, almost shyly. His hand strays back to his scrotum for an instant, before he snatches it away. 'Can you – could *you* make the tea?' he says – as if it might be an unlikely, or even a rather offensive thing to ask of a bloke. I say – a touch haughtily – that I've mastered the rudiments of tea-making.

'Good on yer,' he says. 'Three. No milk for me – I've got some special . . .' His voice trails off. He looks embarrassed – shuffling from foot to foot. Sucks some stray scrap of sugariness from his index finger. 'I'm terribly sorry,' he confesses suddenly.

I wonder what I'm supposed to say. 'It's quite alright.'

It might have been quite alright. Were it not for the fact that, when I go into the office with the teacups balanced on a round wooden tray, I drop them. I drop them because, sitting all elfin and expectant in the guest seat between Noakes and Fielding, is Jill.

At university, when my room was filled with droning, toking drugs-bores, I used to wander round the college searching for vacant rooms. Sleeping on couches and floors. Or sometimes just walking round the town all night long, fuelled on samosas and Diet Coke from the all-night garage. Last night, as if in nostalgia, I walked around West London from 6 p.m. until 9 o'clock the next morning. I tried, in fact, to walk to Heathrow, but gave up at Acton. I saw White City, or rather, I learned what it was not. I sat on benches, in bus stops and on walls, throughout those dead, orange-lit hours which somehow seemed exciting when I was a kid and never got to see them. I walked past the Pickled Newt when all the lights were off – looking up at the scaffolding outside, creaking slightly in the breeze like a gallows. I walked past our block too, several times, but couldn't face going in. Wishing I could sit in the warmth of the kitchen with Martha, but knowing full well there would be no warmth there. I watched the blue flickering of a TV from the front room of the Sikh's flat at three, and at four, and again at ten past five. He must have similar viewing habits to me. Which only demonstrates how very, very peculiar I am.

The whole night's been like some prolonged acid-trip in reverse, beginning with eleven hours of come-down, and then, as the dawn finally comes, leading off into unwelcome weirdness. Finally, groggy and cold, I'm mounting the stairs to our flat. I'm supposed to be in work, but I can't bring myself to care any more. I pick up the mail from the flap in the lobby.

There's some dreary thing with a window in it for me. On the first landing, I notice the door to the mad Sikh's flat is open a crack and a dark, sorrowful eye is watching me go up. But I'm not even bothered about that.

Martha is nowhere to be seen. Maybe it's just that I'm tired, but everything looks new and strange now – not my flat at all. I know every coffee-stain on the hall-carpet, every fleck of fag-ash in the saucer under the rubber-plant. But they're not the same. On the answerphone are two messages. One's from Martha's father. 'Wish you could see the garden, love,' he says, sounding as awkward as all fathers at leaving his voice on record. 'It's lovely with all the leaves. Perhaps maybe come back up for the weekend?' And then a breathless message from Rory Rolfe, either on a mobile or calling from the epicentre of some fierce interstellar battle. 'Tour's over,' he's saying. 'Can't WAIT to see you all!'

This is all about as much as I can stand without a cup of tea. I kick the hatstand and go into the kitchen. Deirdre makes a few earsplitting protests and then contents herself with removing large flakes of paintwork from the wall above the washing machine. I think I'd like to know what parakeet tastes like, picture Deirdre with a couple of garlic cloves up her bum and a sprig of rosemary for a hat.

On the table, next to a pair of Martha's socks, is a letter on thick paper. It's addressed to her, from a firm of Estate Agents in Drogheda, Ireland. It says they look forward to doing business with her. To a smooth and swift sale. I bolt straight into her room – but everything's as normal. Except that, with one of my editing pens, she has now traced a rather self-defeating zig-zag route across the map of Nepal. I sit down on the bed.

She's selling the cottage. Going to Nepal. With Gus. Unless I do something to stop it. But how can I? This is pure jealousy, Jacob and Esau. The hatred of brothers. However nobly I might dress it up as concern, I just don't *want* her to go. I want her to stay here with me. I thought she wanted the same thing. That was why I promised her, took that beastly little job in the first place, and ended up defrauding Jill.

The look of utter bewilderment on her face as I walked into the office and dropped the tea. Jill in her khaki interview-suit, all hopeful with her notebook and her little folder, trying to look grown-up. Her astonishment, fading swiftly to anger as she sensed that all was not as it should be. Why do I have to hurt everyone, ruin *everything* I touch?

The front door to the flat slams, and I hear someone dump a large number of bags in the hallway. Gus? Then I hear a voice calling 'Hallo'. A man's voice – refined and none too pleased. The calls grow louder as he approaches. I dash into Martha's room and hide behind the door, keeping very, very still. Breathing through my nose. Hoping, ridiculously, that perhaps he might just go away.

I hear him open the door to my room, and then close it again. There's a lengthy, chilling silence.

'Alastair?' His voice, a profound theatrical bass, has an edge of agitation to it. 'Martha?'

I hear a pair of squeaky shoes march determinedly down the corridor, past the telephone, towards the room I'm in. Not for the first time, I admit belief in an utterly malevolent God whose sole concern is me. Then the bird gives a whistle.

Rory Rolfe may well become a world-famous impresario of medieval music. Perhaps, one day, in certain choral circles, his arrival at a party will be greeted with the hushed fever that precedes a Liam Gallagher or a Larry Hagman in more plebeian company today. Whatever becomes of him, I'll always remember my first sight of him, as I nervously peep out of Martha's door towards the kitchen, and see him standing there, in a tailored tweed suit, wiping shit off his jaw as a tropical bird swoops and pecks at his hair.

'This is a little peculiar,' he remarks, knitting heavy blond eyebrows into a V. He must be all of thirty, but his manner is pure headmaster.

I try apologising. Try explaining that the bird is only a temporary tenant – rescued by Martha from the bus-station – but it does little good. The mention of Martha only makes the furious glint in his eyes that little bit brighter. Stepping gingerly through the seed husks and slippery guano that festoon the cork floor, I offer him a cup of tea, shouting over the jungle squawks and whistles of the bird. But Rory doesn't want tea. He doesn't drink tea. It makes him agitated, he says.

The most alarming thing about Rory is that, in spite of being livid (his hands are permanently trembling with the buttons of his waistcoat) he insists on an outlandish pretence of charm. As Deirdre mounts one feathery assault after another upon his person and Rory shoots away from her with pure terror, he nevertheless tries to convince me that he's overjoyed at our meeting. 'Tara says you're a FANTASTICALLY talented person,' he enthuses. *Note: must be a fraud.* 'I can't WAIT to have a really good talk!' Then he tries to say, above the birdhouse-din, that he's planning on having some friends – a sculptor and some Czech mime artists – over to dinner this evening. 'Perhaps you'd caah to join us?'

I think I would not caah. Not at all. To avoid replying, I say I'm trying to sort out the bird situation.

'Oh no, no, no,' he declares, with all the veracity of an Argos jewellery salesman – and glaring murderously at the airborne creature as he says it. 'I don't mind one bit. It's all quite bohemian.'

And as if in defiance of this statement, Deirdre skilfully scores a direct hit on Rory's tie.

It turns out that, at the back of the kitchen cupboard, Rory has several rolls of netting, left over from an attempt to create a garden out on the balcony. I craft this netting into a vast, floppy cage and with Rory's assistance manage to fling it over the bird. We drag the whole affair into Martha's bedroom – avoiding little more than frayed nerves and nipped fingers. But still Rory isn't happy. He makes himself an artistic snack of star-fruit and figs, arranged on the last remaining plate, with a glass of lemon juice. Then he sits stiffly at the table, rubbing imaginary spots of dirt with his fingers, and radiating the kind of disapproval you could feel in a darkened room. I hover, smoking cigarettes, which are quite evidently adding further fuel to Rory's nark.

'Did you have a good journey?' I ask him.

'No,' he says, screwing up his face into a mime artist's parody of distaste. 'People kept smoking.'

I put it out under the tap.

'Oh no, no, no,' Rory cries, horror-struck, devastated that I might have thought that he was implying something rude – which, of course, he was. 'PLEASE feel free. If this is how you people want to live . . .'

And, after suggesting that I call him 'Roo' (I could no sooner call him Sugar Ray Robinson) Rory stalks down towards his bedroom, leaving me with a dustpan and brush wondering, weakly, where I should start – if anywhere.

A few moments later, he's back in there with me. This time, he just beckons me with a single, commanding finger. I follow him to the doorway of his bedroom. Gus has unpacked the contents of at least three kitbags and left them strewn across every spare cubit of Rory's room. A pair of mud-crusted boots rests at the foot of the futon, next to some kind of aged tribal oatcake, wrapped in grease-proof paper. There are spanners, wrenches, and rusty fragments of truck-machinery stacked up like a mini-scrapyard on the writing table. Some skimpy trunks are dried out, stiff as a board, on the radiator. Everywhere across the room, like little captured clouds, are wispy swabs of cotton wool. 'And this,' Rory says, coldly, 'was in my bed.'

Between finger and thumb, as if it were a dead hen, he holds up one of Martha's bras.

11

The process of looking for Martha would not exactly score high marks for form, or content. No pack of bloodhounds, no stopping of passers-by. My head's filled with sickening visions of opium dens and neon-lit doorways, but I don't know where those kind of places are and I doubt Martha does either. Though nothing would surprise about her now. I'm going to the only place I suspect she could be.

Not that I know what I'm going to say when I find her. Part of me wants to push her under a tube train, another to stick her to the floor with Superglue until she talks, tells me what turns a friend, *a lover*, in the middle of the night, from a warm, nice, funny sort of lass into a cheating bitch. I'm not angry at Gus at all any more. I turn, fuming, up the Baron's Court Road, past Gandhi's old house and bank upon bank of seedy doorbells and realise I almost feel sorry for him. Gus is just a fool, loin-counselled, swaggering and dim. It will never be any different.

Then I cross the road and see the Pickled Newt. I start to feel dizzy and afraid, as if approaching the battlefield. Or a rugby pitch. From a catalogue of regrettable moments in the pubs of Southport, I've come to believe that I have the sort of face that makes hard men angry. Some mystical daubing, like the mark of Cain, which subliminally instructs anyone who is good at fighting to have a go at me, who is not.

I must be angry. I'm really going in there.

And Martha's told me some fairly prohibitive tales about the Pickled Newt. About the landlord, Nugent Carr, who spends all night alone in the cellar watching judo videos. The thieves and the hired bruisers who get drunk in there. The builders, who've been ostensibly doing the renovations for six months, but instead spend every afternoon stoned in the beer garden at the back.

A small party of men is gathered on the tables outside as I pass into the pub. They dog-eye me. I try to ignore them. One of the men softly murmurs something that sounds like 'wully-bully'. They do this a lot in London. We may assume it means nothing supportive. Inside the pub, it is dark and cold. The decor is strictly Glaswegian Minimalist – tiled surfaces that can be hosed down with ease, furniture that is hard to fling. The bar is a long polygon of mahogany, like the panels from an old train. Upon it, men have scratched atavistic designs with their keys – a crude fox or dog, the word 'Chelsea'. As if in defiance of the fact that this is the grimmest corner of England, they've got Tito Puente playing on the jukebox.

At the bar, a surly leprechaun ignores me for as long as he can. I prop myself up, the sweat cooling on my back in the dank, stony air. The lager-chiller makes Gothic-dungeon sounds. *Strange: Don't listen to your heart. It'll only make it faster.* I listen instead to the men next to me, plasterers – like a pair of corpses from Pompeii, they're both covered in a fine grey dust which scatters all around them with every move.

'So he says he can't pay,' one of the cadavers is saying, quietly. 'And I says I've got four chippies and a plarsterer coming up from Plaarstow and what'm I telling them? So he says – oi. Don't start giving it. He says – look. I'll be straight with you. I'm skint. He says – you can have me dog if you want.'

His companion sucks in disbelief, causing himself to inhale a lethal quantity of dust. The door leading from the Ladies opens. *Martha!*

Except it isn't. My instincts must be amongst the worst in the universe. It's a fat, coughing woman in a velour jumpsuit. She's at least fifty.

'So I says what dog is it?'

'*Wully-bully.*'

'And he says she's a pit bull. I says, you know, let's see it then. And he brings it out.'

A bitter, knowing laugh from the companion.

'An' it's just some kinda shaggin' poodle, yeah?'

There's a long, tricky sort of pause. The man who's been telling the tale looks pained and upset. It's all been pointless, no man understands another. He wipes a patch of pink into view on his brow. 'Naa mate,' he says, puzzled, glancing up to the darker reaches of the pub. ''S a proper pitbull. 'Kin yooge it is.'

'Cunt,' observes the other, following his workmate's gaze to a solitary figure reading his paper at the far end of the bar. He pronounces the word lovingly – *q'ant* – only a Tuareg goatherd could have bettered him on the glottal stop. I suddenly feel a long, long way away from anything familiar.

The leprechaun finally ambles over, polishing a glass. 'Yip?'

I ask him if Martha's working today. He snorts. Calls to the landlord. And the man at the end of the bar – the object of the plasterers' anger – puts his paper down, slides from his stool in the shadows and comes across to me. Dressed in jeans and an open shellsuit top. Unshaven and going bald. Indistinguishable from the punters, which as Annie Walker always said on *Corrie Street*, suggests a pub on its uppers.

With a little more than innocent interest, he asks me why I want to know about Martha.

'I'm a friend,' I say. *What a joke.*

''S your tough shit, innit?' he says, compassionately.

Then he walks off back to his seat, and takes a sip from his pint. 'She legged it last Saturday,' he calls back to me. 'Said she saw a rat come out of the cupboard an' run up her arm.' Settling himself back upon his stool, the landlord remembers something. He wags his newspaper in my direction. 'If you see her, tell her I want my *faqin* parrot back.'

'You should just move out,' Jill tells me. We're sat in the Café Sandanista on Upper Street and she's watching me as I pour another helping of 'Stag' whisky into my cappuccino, still trembling. 'You're just making her unhappy. She probably wishes she'd never told you.'

Which is Jill all over. Full of practical, yet impossible advice, like an agony aunt or careers teacher. But I always knew that. Someone has inserted a giant spoon into my life and whipped it into a fracas. And in the midst of all this chaos, I had to go somewhere, to the last person in London who speaks sense. Even if she hates me. Which, she freely admits, she does.

'You said you were working for a bloodstock merchant. *A fucking horse dealer!* That's what I mind. Not the fact that you've swindled me out of a grand. Not the book. It's the lying, Strange, *the lying*.'

Jill is a big fan of The Truth. Once I asked her, when we still had our hands in one another's pockets, if I could commit any crime so heinous that she wouldn't come and visit me in jail. She said espionage. Because it was 'all about lying all over the place'.

I'm truthfully penitent now. And, having come to her after the Pickled Newt, bursting into her coffee shop near to blubbering, I seem to have at least softened her anger to a hearty resentment.

'But how can you not have read my book?' She's still utterly baffled – trickery like this is, to Jill, like the apprehension of eternity.

I try, once again. 'We never read them. We just sort of say what we know the authors want to hear. It's – well, I suppose you could say it's quite clever, in a way.'

164

Jill does a very familiar look which defies me to continue in that particular vein.

'They just kept on giving me the work. Said I was good at it. What could I do? Everyone needs a job, Jill.'

'Come off it! You? You were always happiest sitting on your arse watching Polish bloody soap operas. Since when did the Protestant work ethic suddenly start to plague you?'

I am silent, thinking. Since Martha. Since I met someone who was actually a lot better than Polish soap operas and I made her the first promise I really thought I could keep.

'So what if "Sing Me Empty" does actually turn out to be a bestseller. What then?'

Wearily, I look up, and take Jill patiently through the finer details of vanity publishing.

'Jesus!' she says, sitting back in her distressed iron chair when I've finished. 'So I'm never going to make any money?'

'You'll get royalties,' I say. 'For a couple of years, they'll send you a cheque – maybe a tenner or something – they just make it up. No one buys the books. They can't, really. They're all just in this big warehouse in Dagenham. You'd have to really go out of your way to buy one. There aren't any bookshops want them.'

I'm telling her the truth, but this only seems to make her more cross. 'It's FRAUD,' she claims, sternly and loud, banging a spoon down on the table. People look up from their cups and stare.

'It's partnership publishing,' I counter, minus any sort of conviction. 'It gives people a chance to publish books that wouldn't normally get published.'

'*Why* wouldn't they?'

'Because they're crap,' I say, too quickly, and watch Jill's lips tighten into a neat funnel of fury. 'I mean most – some of them are.'

'And you tell them they're not. That's your *job*?'

I nod, looking away.

'How the hell could you go into a job like that with your eyes open? You're a bad man.'

She always had that talent for the biblical, Jill. A finite number of categories for everything and everyone. Esau: *an hairy man*. *A good man*: anyone else. *A bad man*: me.

'I'm not,' I say. 'Really I'm not.'

She chooses not to take this point further. Just mashes her fork down into her abandoned slice of Italian cake – some kind of eggy bread soaked in neat alcohol.

'Still say you could've found yourself something better.'

'Pendennis Press was the only job going.' That's practically true. On the train down from Runcorn I went through the paper cover to cover and, apart from an editorial opening on that popular quarterly *Food Packaging Digest: Asia*, Pendennis' was the only *Guardian* ad I read that called for people with neither qualifications, experience or bags of team spirit.

I'm suddenly aware that, for probably the first time in my life, I'm being honest with Jill. And it does feel better, or at least less painful than letting her pick out all the embarrassing, ignominious indignities herself, piece by piece. Jill's looking at me almost fondly, shaking her head. 'It's not surprising really. The way you've ended up. Considering your family.'

Jill never warmed to my family much, nor they to her. She said my mother, and her paprika stews, made her dizzy. We ate dinner at mine the day after I first slept with Jill, and she swore blind that she saw my mother *sniff* me. Jill's opening gambit with Sue, just a few days later, was that her parents had a sofa upholstered in exactly the same fabric as the dress Sue was wearing. Thereafter, Sue referred to Jill as 'the harpie' and once, memorably, gave her a roll-on deodorant for Christmas.

I shrug. 'I'm really sorry,' I offer. 'About the book. It must be awful – you know – to have a vision of something. And then just find out it's all been a con.'

166

Jill bristles, like a cat stroked the wrong way. 'It wasn't a *sodding* "vision", Strange. I just thought we could make some money.'

'We?'

'Me and John,' she says. 'It's his story, really. The profits are – *were* for him. He needs the money.'

Panic on panic. What ghoulish vices has Longfellow-Lamb adopted in order to survive, after the seven years of Strange-torture? *I need the money* she'd said, that night we met in the bar. *For things*. What things?

Jill laughs, pityingly. 'He's having the operation.'

'What operation?' Penis enlargement, rhinoplasty? A new head? I picture anything. Anything but the truth that she tells me:

'He's having a sex change,' she says. 'He's a woman. Well, he should be.'

I end up spending that night on their floor – a surgically tidy flat, the size of a first-aid kit, just off Rosebery Avenue. Far from assailing me with a knife or gun, as he once promised to do, John Thomas Longfellow-Lamb is gentle and decent with me. He makes up a bed with the sofa cushions – even goes to the Seven-Eleven for Nurofen when the Stag turns bad on me.

Even in my state, I can see that he is – will be – a beautiful woman. The parka and the lisp have gone. As has the perpetual snotty cough. He moves well nowadays (or at least, the manner of his moving is no longer so freakish in its surroundings) silently in bare feet about the flat. All slim and graceful, with these dark, elliptical eyes. Eyes that almost watered when Jill explained to him about Martha.

'I've got to find her,' I say, when Jill voices for the fifteenth time the sensitive opinion that I've doubtless stuffed it up for ever with Martha by trying, like a *typical bloody male*, to run her bloody life. 'I've got to.'

'But why?' Jill demands. 'You said it yourself. She hates you now.'

I look helpless. Lamb gives a shy little cough, pleads permission to speak: 'You don't really think that though, do you?'

I shake my head miserably. Jill tuts.

'Well what *do* you think?' She is relentless.

'I don't know. I just. I just don't see how you can change overnight.'

'Maybe she's always hated you, deep down. I should know.'

'What?'

'You've got this *way*,' she says, gathering a rather unsettling momentum, 'of just winding people up. You can be quite cute, in a boring sort of way. And then you come out with these . . . these really nasty things that are supposed to be jokes and then when you realise you're not funny, you hover about looking all pained and concerned, trying to make up for it, so it's like having a cross between Bernard Manning and some bloody social worker on your back that you just want to *strangle*.' She takes a deep draught of tea.

'Finished?'

'No.' She swallows. 'You're pretty crap in bed as well. You make love like you'd rather be watching telly.'

'Thanks,' I say. 'Turn you down for the Samaritans, did they?'

'Maybe,' Lamb interrupts, hastily, 'maybe if a person can change that quickly, then – well, then they're not actually very well.'

Jill looks scornful. 'What do you mean "not very well"? Trying to say it's just some women's bloody hormonal thing?'

'Well hardly.' Lamb motions to me. 'Strange said it before. I mean – she looks ill. Tired all the time. Keeps thinking she's seen rats when she can't have done. Steals a parakeet. That's right, isn't it?'

Eager nods from me.

'Well then. I mean – I'm not saying I know anything about it. But it's possible, isn't it? She's unwell. This is the manic bit.'

'Right,' says Jill, firmly, like she is closing a book shut. 'Problem solved. Get her to a doctor.'

Get her to a doctor. Fill a cup with water. It's all that simple, in Jill's universe. Flatmate needs a sex change? Fine! Sell his novel.

'How can you get someone to a doctor when you don't know where they are? She wouldn't come anyway. I know she wouldn't.'

'She got any family?'

'A dad. Up in Rotherham.'

'Well tell him then. It's his business.'

But it isn't his business – I know what he'll do if I tell him. I know where he'll take her.

'I can't do that.'

'Why not?'

'Because I still might be wrong. I might just be being jealous. Because of Gus. And anyway, I promised her things.'

'What "things"? Is this more of your sodding tortured liberal "good man" bollocks?'

I make a sound, then. Not so much a cry or a shout, nothing so recognisable as that. More a choked-up bellow from the bones like a thing trapped.

'I think we should let you get some sleep,' Lamb says, gently.

My God, Lamb, I think, as he starts to tidy up the room. How did you get so good? He's still an odd fellow – vague and dreamy, prone to delivering huge, groundless grins during the middle of a conversation, as if he's just been illuminated by some sudden shaft of glory. But so seemingly right about everything.

'I'm really sorry about this,' I say, as Lamb and Jill make ready to go to bed.

'Don't be silly,' Lamb says. 'Anyway – we've got to get an early one too. Got a long day tomorrow.' They glance at each other.

'What are you doing?' I ask.

Another glance between them. Lamb coughs nervously again, rubs his top lip with a finger.

'He's got to give a sperm sample,' Jill says. 'Actually.'

I ask her to repeat this. It doesn't make any sense. Why would a man like Lamb, who has eaten shit since playschool, now want future Lambs to suffer in this world? Particularly now, when he's about to wave goodbye to maggot-hood, to transform into a woman. What use, to anyone, is the seed of Lamb?

'I'm going to have his baby,' says Jill, defiantly. 'Later. When we're more secure.'

'When . . .' I look from Lamb to Jill and back again.

'When I'm a woman. Yes.' Lamb says.

'Got a problem with that?' Jill asks, evidently hoping that I have. So if I do (and it's only with the mathematics of it all, not the morals) I'm determined not to let her see it.

I wish them luck. I said they never needed the Pendennis Press in the first place. The *News of the World* would probably give them enough to raise a whole family on their own Pacific island.

'Oh Christ!' Jill exclaims, angrily. '*Strange!*'

And she storms off to bed. Lamb looks apologetic. 'Bit of a sore point, I'm afraid.'

When he turns out the light, leaving me to fret the dark hours away, Lamb pauses for a moment by the door. 'I think you've just got to – you know – look into yourself a bit.'

'Look into myself?'

'I know that sounds a bit hippy. I mean – *I* don't think you're a jealous sort of person. I don't know you, really. But I don't think so. You've got to decide.'

'Oh good,' I say.

170

Lamb gives a soft laugh. 'It'll work out,' he says.

'How do you know?'

Another soft sound. 'Just a feeling. Feminine intuition, call it. Must be the pills. G'night.'

'G'night.'

And he leaves me.

God only knows what sort of a person I am. Back home, one of the local papers used to run a regular feature. Merseymart Hero of the Week. *Plucky pub landlord Denny Cork (67) saw off three viscous* [sic] *thugs with a stuffed swordfish/Big-hearted waiter Sotiris Papophitis (21) rescued a swan from rush-hour traffic.* And, because I had 'A' levels, I used to laugh at them. But I also used to wonder – what am I? And then, round about the time of that girl in the sand-dunes, I looked into myself about as much as I dared. And ever since then, I've known what I am. Just as Onka would tell you. I am Merseymart Shitehawk of the Week. Every week.

But Lamb made so much sense, in all other respects. He knew exactly what I was trying to say, saw straight through all the self-pity and the hysteria, through all the agitation caused by Jill's quick-fire interrogation, and said the one bare-arse, blatantly obvious thing I've been trying to avoid thinking about. The one worry I *have* stored away, *have* kept right at the back of my mind, haven't taken out and looked at because I've been too bloody wrapped up in being jealous. *It's happening to her again. She's going crazy. It's not me. Not Gus, even. Not her, either. She's ill.*

So is it true? Or am I just angry with her – jealous, seeking revenge? Filing under Madness all the evidence that really only says She Doesn't Like You Now, You Know. Lamb thinks not. For some unfathomable reason, Lamb doesn't think I'm a bad lot. He doesn't blame me for what I did to him at all. Even though I was the one who broke him, the one who brought about the terrible day, in the Fifth Form, that sent John Thomas

Longfellow-Lamb shrieking into the dark folds of his parka anorak, never to return to our world.

We all had medicals in the Fifth Form. They took us in groups of three, down to a secret room in the bowels of the school. Boys came back swapping ghoulish tales of spontaneous hard-ons and spatulas up the rectum. They took us at random as well – no earthly rules of alphabet, age or shoe-size governed the selection. A sixth former came round the classes and called out names. You followed the flapping back of his blazer past the statue of the founder, under the portrait of the Queen, by the wretched stink of the toilets, up to the kitchens. Then down stairs and other stairs, round corners, blinded by lights – as if they were trying to disorientate us.

Three of us were in a little room I'd never seen before. Me and Lamb and a Chinese called Caesar Wong. A mannish, though female nurse told us to take our clothes off and wait. I don't remember saying anything to Lamb – there was no point, I suppose, if no one was around to hear how funny and shitty I could be. Caesar Wong didn't count. He spent every spare moment in the computer room or playing mental chess.

Lamb had no towel to hide behind now. He tried to wrap his blazer round his waist like a sarong. They took me in first. No hard-ons, no gloved fingers, just questions, a sugar lump with some venom on it and lights shone in some of the less noxious crevices. I got the feeling that the undressing was a publicity stunt – performed just to subdue us, instil us, at that lariest of ages, with some sense of awe for the system.

When I came out, the nurse followed me and called Lamb in. She looked at him, shuffling towards her, holding his blazer at his waist like a tattered kilt. 'Don't be silly,' she barked. 'I've seen it all before.' And she held out a hand for his blazer. Lamb had to give it her. I was pulling on my trousers by then but stopped, let them fall back round my feet. Caesar Wong stared.

172

The nurse stared too. I suspect she was wrong – she had not seen this before. *Lamb was wearing women's underwear*.

And did I keep quiet? Trusting that Caesar Wong would inscrutably return to his theoretical chess board and his computers, did I maintain a tactful adult silence? Or did I run full-pelt into the library at lunchtime, and, ignoring the birth-marked librarian, announce the fact to over a hundred rowdy boys that John Thomas Longfellow-Lamb was wearing knickers?

I wasn't among those that lynched him behind the cricket pavilion. I had no desire to grope inside his trousers for his lace-trimmed underthings, or to parade the shredded garment later round the library like a Cheyenne scalp. But I sent him over the edge. Truthfully, that was me. Merseymart, for short.

And now, truthfully, as I lie here on Lamb's floor, I run over all these events in my head, as I have done a million times before. But something fresh keeps coming up to me, like a toothpaste-burp at lunchtime. That I haven't ruined Lamb. Not even Lamb thinks I ruined Lamb. And if that's true, then maybe I'm not just a bad lot, preordained to suffer for all the badnesses I unavoidably commit. It isn't like that at all. Maybe I can change things.

12

I'm receiving the kind of bollocking nobody beyond the age of fifteen experiences. Standing in Noakes' office, in front of his desk. The door is open, so that everyone else can hear. My head is bowed. Every now and then, I give it a little deferential shake, as if to say 'Yes, I agree. It isn't good enough, is it? Can't think what came over me, Sir.' Every one of my features is fixed into the mask of one who sees he has done wrong and wishes only to pay for it with his balls.

Noakes is saying that the Pendennis Press is shortly to witness an event nothing short of a Cultural Revolution. My own unaccounted-for absence yesterday has been but a symptom of the rot. There has been universal backsliding, he says, moral lapses, missing files, errors in the typescripts and a general lack of respect. Chattering, he adds, has increased to epidemic proportions, along with illicit use of the telephones.

I care more about the grey matter at the corner of Noakes' lips – wondering what its chief component is: sugar, spittle or skin. I don't think, in fact, that a bollocking has ever seemed quite so infinitesimally unimportant.

'I'm getting builders in,' Noakes promises, proudly banging his fist on the table, as if announcing his intention to deport the intelligentsia to some distant rice-fields. 'I'm going to install sound-proof screens around each work-station and scanning port. I'm going to have a red light and a green light outside this office, so you can't just come barging in here like a hoon, upsetting the authors. What is it?'

174

He looks crossly at the doorway, where Asuncion has materialised, attempting a complex mixture of bow, curtsey and forelock-tug. She approaches, glancing fearfully at me. Behind her she trails a tartan shopping basket on wheels. 'I go now Mister Nowaak,' she says.

Noakes waves an angry hand of dismissal. 'Yes – yes. Very good,' he said. Then he calls her back as she trundles away. 'Hey! Asuns – Asoo. You!'

She freezes. 'Si?'

'You've got an em ess ess in your – in that thing.' He points. On the top of Asuncion's little trolley is one of our yellow folders. She smiles, creepily. 'I find on stairs, Mister Nowaak,' she says, handing him the folder. 'I am forget.'

When things have settled a little bit (Noakes made me count every yellow folder on the shelves twice) I ring home again. I don't care about Noakes' New Order. There are things on my mind. Martha and the theoretical rats. My family. I call my parents' home, but it's the arsing, stinking, pointless answer-phone again. I think about hanging up, but instead, I try to leave a message. 'It's Alastair,' I say. 'But you know that. I mean – well, you don't, but it is.' Down the phone I hear the squeak of the tape as it travels round the machine.

'You rang. And this is me. Ringing back. Erm.' Out of the corner of my eye, I notice Noakes in his doorway, unwrapping an oblong of butterscotch. He's looking directly at me. 'Yes, Mr, er . . .' *Oh God. Mister What? Think!* 'Mr Butterscotch,' I say soothingly into the phone. 'We *have* received the manu-script. It's with our submissions department.'

'Who were you calling?' Noakes demands, sternly.

I blush. 'An author.'

'An author called Butterscotch?'

'Yes,' I say, desperately. 'Well – it's Batterscott, really. But it's a sort of joke between us. I call him Butterscotch. And he calls me Stranger.'

Noakes swallows his current dose of confectionery and walks over to my desk.

'I've never heard of him. Where's his folder?'

I look down at my desk with an expression of calm, deliberate enquiry. Corrosive sweat springs out all across my back.

'He's probably in your office or something.'

Noakes smiles, nastily. He waves a hand towards his office. 'Show me.'

As I walk, trembling into his office, a small, smug, adult voice within comments that I have been here a thousand times before. Condemned by my own fibbery into ever more desperate charades. I will persist with this, I know, until Noakes either gives up, or I break down and throw myself upon the mercy of my confessor.

Fielding frowns as I walk in and start to scan the shelves for an item that we all know is not there. Noakes stands in the doorway, hands on hips, waiting. This is ridiculous.

'Think I know the name,' comments Fielding. 'What's his bag exactly?'

'His *bag*?' I ask, in utter confusion.

'His thing. What's he written?'

I stare, helplessly. Noakes lets out a long, cynical sigh and is about to speak. But his words, reproof or release, never reach me, because at that moment, Jo bursts in beside him and interrupts. 'Mr Sammaddi's here?' she says, or queries.

Noakes gapes at her in alarm.

'Who's he?'

Fielding clears his throat.

'Some sort of Indian I suspect.'

And he suspects right. Jo is shouldered out of the way at that moment by an elephantine posy of red roses, behind which is a young, handsome Indian, with neatly parted hair, and a princely moustache across his cheeks. He flings the bouquet on to the table.

'Do not tell me I cannot see her!' he commands, majestically. 'I must see Miss Gaskell. Where is the darkened room?'

We all look at Fielding, who gives what is, for an ugly man, quite a disarming grin.

Before I can do myself any further damage, I am summarily ushered out of the office. The door slams behind me and almost as soon as it does, a series of howls begins to issue forth. I kick the door in frustration, then turn around, to face the quizzical gaze of Minty and Jo. Sweat springs out on my back.

I sit, shuffling in limbo at my desk, as Mr Sammaddi wails and sobs and screams for a full ten minutes behind that door. Tea is taken in to him, but neither it, nor the Garibaldi biscuits which Jo compassionately offers, do anything to abate his grief-stricken cries. Everyone looks up as the door opens, and they show Mr Sammaddi out, still clutching his bunch of roses – all tear-streaked and puffy-eyed. He sniffs, drawing himself up to his full height, attempting a pitiful semblance of nobility. He fixes his eyes straight ahead of him and passes through the office. But by my desk, he falters and stops. 'Would it be possible,' he asks, stiffly, with a tremor, 'to place a small tribute on the Lady's desk?'

'Oh by all means,' says Fielding, warmly. 'She works – worked here.'

He motions to my desk. Mr Sammaddi fixes me with a hateful glance.

'Couldn't you have waited!?' he asks me. I am just signing a letter in the name of Sarah Gaskell. Fielding snatches it from me before Sammaddi can see.

'He's just a temp,' he says, urgently. 'We had to do something.'

Sammaddi nods sadly. He places a single red rose on top of my monitor. He clasps his hands together, looks at the floor in a pious attitude, the floor which he imagines her gracious feet to have rubbed and scuffed and trodden gum into. 'Dear Sarah. May the next life be sweeter,' he says, with another, almighty sniff.

And he leaves. Noakes and Fielding congratulate one another, ignoring me completely, and retreat back into their lair to celebrate with some more tea. I breathe a sigh of relief, and sit for a moment or two with my head in my hands.

I'm here, today, for one reason. I am trying to make myself cold, clear, free of emotion. I know I have to go to the flat, I have to find Martha, find out whether she is ill or not. The thought that she might be anywhere gives me a headache. But Rory Rolfe will be in and out of my room, alternately inviting me to private viewings at art galleries and being cross about the pubic-hair-spiders in the plugholes. And when I find Martha, all the feelings I have about her – love and lust and anger and jealousy and hurt – will surge up the minute I see something familiar, like a jumper she wore on a particularly ace day we had together, or a bared bra-strap I got into the habit of pinging against her smooth shoulders. And I won't do the right thing.

Work is getting harder and harder. I'm listening to the gathering breeze outside, and gazing at the clock every five minutes – Noakes has clearly tampered with it, the Revolution has included a revision of time: each minute, henceforth, to last three. And there are no diversions – I can't talk to Tara, or even watch her crossing and uncrossing her legs all day. This, I should add, is nothing to do with any fear or respect for Noakes' New Order. Tara has simply not turned up.

Later on, I have a query concerning some illustrations for a book entitled 'Smiles After Piles'. This book is, in fact, of no informative value whatsoever, being the detailed, lyrical (even anal) account of one man's stay in hospital for a haemorrhoid-ectomy. Noakes has put a Post-It on the folder. 'Strange:' it

178

says, in Noakes' patent administrative cypher, 'Ill./Cover ill.? Pls. deal.' I go into his office. Fielding has his tiny zip-up Chelsea boots up on the desk, polishing them with a soft rag.

'What kind of cover can you do for a book like this?' I ask. Fielding says he has a few suggestions. Almost choking on his own wit. Noakes and I ignore him.

'Tara's good at covers,' I suggest. Noakes stiffens. 'That young lady,' he says, grandly, 'is no longer an employee of this company.'

Fielding stops polishing. His rheumy eyes are shining brightly. 'Sacked Tara?' he says, hoarsely. Noakes looks defiant.

'I have appointed myself Human Resources Manager for the Press,' he declares, jabbing a short, thick finger at his chest. 'I hire and I fire.'

Then the newly appointed Human Resources Manager turns back to me. 'Give it to . . . one of those other girls.' I go out. 'And shut the door!'

At least some kind of ceasefire has been negotiated between Minty and Jo. The mood between them, though not exactly friendly, has at least lost its more violent elements. When Minty passed Jo the stapler earlier on, her response bordered on the cordial.

'Have you heard about Tara?' I ask them, encouraged by this fresh spirit of amity. Together, they shoot me a withering, Chelsea-blue glance. 'Of *course* we have,' says Jo.

'Oh,' I say. A little deflated.

Tara. Whose company has been one of the chief antidotes to all the other horrors of this workplace. And she liked me, too, it seemed. She never called anyone else *darling*, never called on them to rummage in her handbag. Never followed them to the shops. When she uncovered my secret passion for TV drama, her disgust was precisely because she'd thought better of me – she was odd, but she was my friend.

As a distraction, or more to prevent myself from sticking my fingers in the nearest welcoming socket, I start designing a cover for the Piles book – an abstract design, pure white with a deep red circle spreading out from the centre. It is not nice, I admit, when I finish – but no nastier than the contents of the book. And it's better than any of the other suggestions. Jo wants a tube of Anusol and a seated, smiling man. And Minty only came up with a blue ice cube, the title written inside it.

I'm just putting the Piles file away when the door downstairs slams and a cold gust from outside rushes through the building. There is a tuneless humming and a rustling, becoming louder. Then the inner door opens and there, before me, stands Tara.

'Morning darling,' she says, cheerily, slinging her bag across the room. 'Gosh. I'm absolutely shagged.' She stops on her way over to her desk, pauses and looks suspiciously around her. 'Why are you all staring at me?'

She doesn't know.

'I thought you'd . . .' my words trail away. But I'm saved the task of telling her what I thought she'd . . . because at that moment, Noakes scurries out from his office, armed with a roll of bright orange tape.

'Stop there!' he commands. 'Don't approach your work-station.' Tara stands, rooted to the spot while Noakes approaches her desk with the tape and begins to pull off a long strip from the roll.

'What are you doing?' Tara asks.

Noakes looks up. 'Your work-station is being sealed, young lady. You are not welcome on these premises.'

Tara goes even paler. She swallows. 'Why?'

'Files have gone missing.'

'But why's that my fault?' she asks, querulously. All her former assurance has vanished in the face of Noakes' almost surgical efficiency.

'I'm not prepared to discuss this. You've got three minutes to leave or I'm calling security.'

Tara gives me a hopeless look.

'We don't *have* any security, old chap.' This from Fielding, who has appeared in the doorway of his office.

Noakes looks unconcerned. 'Then I'll carry her out myself. She's had her final Final Warning, Ben, and that's that.' A strip of the tape adheres to the hairy fibres of Noakes' tie, and he busies himself with that for a moment. Minty and Jo stare at Tara, unabashed, as Fielding moves further into the room.

'Can't we at least discuss this Noakesy?'

Noakes looks up, reddening.

'What's there to discuss? She's a quisling. I don't need proof. I raised the little bleeder. I know what she's capable of. I remember one time, she got her sister's oboe and she . . .'

'But to just *sack* her . . .'

'I can sack who I like Ben. She's MY daughter.'

Fielding reddens – the heat of his mounting anger broadcasts the costly scent of his aftershave across the room.

In the silence, a dustbin outside is knocked over by the winds and clatters down the street. There is a distant shout.

'Sure about that?' asks Fielding calmly. Tara lets out a short gasp.

'You know she is,' Noakes insists. 'Vivien promised me.'

Fielding snorts. 'You and I both know the sorts of things Vivien promises. Just remember Paris.'

At that point, Tara gives a little cry and sits down on the floor. Feeling a stab of pity, I cross over and place a hand on her trembling shoulder.

'You're not authorised to sit on my floor, young lady,' says Noakes coldly.

'I don't FUCKING CARE!' she screams. 'You miserable old panda!'

At this cry, Fielding, motivated by some rush of paternal

feeling, comes across to us and kneels on the floor by Tara. His knees give off twin clicks within seconds of each other. 'Tara,' he whispers, urgently, as if trying to calm some agitated beast, 'it's alright.' He reaches for one of her ivory hands and holds it, limp in his own. 'I AM your father. I really am. I can prove it. Just look at your ears.'

'My WHAT?'

He points. 'Your earlobes. Tiny. Like mine. And your eyebrows. You can do this, can't you?' And he raises one sandy eyebrow aloft. 'No one else can.' He glances around the room as, unconsciously, everyone else present tries and fails to raise one eyebrow. Except the tear-stained Tara. She blows out a lungful of air in defeat and then looks fearfully up at Noakes, who has now wrapped the entire desk in adhesive tape.

'Is it true?' she asks, in a tiny voice.

'Proves nothing,' says Noakes, ignoring her. '*I* paid the school fees. The ballet lessons. Kept her in shoes and flats and bloody cocktail dresses. What did *you* do?'

Fielding clears his throat. 'Should've thought that was obvious, old thing. *I* loved her mother.'

Tara begins a fresh burst of sobbing at this. The phone rings, ignored by all. Fielding leans in and, uncertainly, rubs a horny little hand up and down her arm.

'There there,' he says, soothingly. 'There's no need to cry. Look on the bright side.'

'WHAT fucking bright side?' Tara wails.

'Well,' says Fielding. 'At least it means you're not Australian.'

Noakes has had enough. He throws the tape in the bin and knocks the still-trilling phone off Minty's desk. 'Listen to me Ben,' he declares, quivering with indignation. 'You can take your briefcase. And your bloody pommie Rupert-the-Bear scarf and all the other things my wife has given you over the years. And you can – you can stick them somewhere dark!'

182

And Fielding, no doubt confused by all the high emotion, says that nothing would give him greater pleasure.

13

Back to the flat in the early afternoon with a sodden and miserable Tara at my side. Fielding gave me a tenner to take her home. But Tara wouldn't go anywhere near her home, or her dad's, or Fielding's, in case she ran into Vivien. I had, by that stage, realised that things were not going to become clearer or calmer wherever I went, and was twitching to get home. But there was something so lost and forlorn about Tara that I felt I could not leave her on the Shepherd's Bush Road. So I took her into a pub and sat and fidgeted as she drank glass after glass of Chardonnay and cried herself into a more stable frame of mind. 'I think I always knew,' she kept saying. 'The way he used to look at me. When he picked me up from school. And every term, it was like he hated coming there just a little bit more. He'd start on me the minute I was in the back of the car. I wasn't working hard enough, I was too thin or I looked like a hussy.'

'What about your mum? Didn't she say anything?'

'She just said I had to make more of an effort, said it was difficult when daughters grow up. And now we know why, don't we? I remember the first year he stopped coming. It was the Lower Fifth. He just sent the train fare. And I thought – it's because I've got tits at last. The dirty old bastard just hates me because I've got tits. I was *so* wrong. It was just because I must have looked less and less like him. And more and more like . . .'

'Like Fielding.'

'That sneaky little *parrot*. Ugh!' She shudders. 'How *could* she?'

We sat there for a full two hours, as the rain started to batter the windows outside. In the end, I suggested she come to my place, not because we were too drunk – give any human a crisis and they can sink more booze than a roustabout on shore leave – but because the landlady and her two barmaids were growing shirty, having clearly decided that Tara's tears were the product of my own cheating heart. Every turn at the bar brought a slightly icier welcome. By two o'clock it seemed likely that one, or all of them, might subject me to some impromptu surgery on the pool table. Besides, the more insoluble Tara's dilemma seems, the more I have begun to twitch and shuffle and worry about Martha. Tara keeps saying how glad she is I'm listening, how glad she is I'm here. But most of me is not.

It's a real pig of a day. The *Evening Standard* headline at West Kensington said, a little ambitiously, 'Tail End of Hurricane Greg Lashes Britain'. But it's not far off the truth. There's a tree down at the bottom of the Baron's Court Road and a dirty old poster has followed us all the way from the tube station. Maybe this is what the gods have arranged – got their little story in such a tangle that nothing short of finishing half the cast off in an air crash or typhoon can sort it out.

The Sikh from the flat below us is shouting at a man of about my age, who is standing on the steps to our block, as I lead Tara up. The Sikh, I've noticed, has started spending the greater part of every day standing at his window, or in his doorway, watching out for something. Probably the nameless goblins inside his head. 'You are not a resident. I've never seen you before,' he is shouting down. 'Go away. Go bugger off.'

The man looks embarrassed. I give him a sympathetic look as I put my key in the door. Tara hides her tear-stained face.

'Friendly people yur,' he says. A Welshman.

I turn and look at him – all storm-spattered in his new jeans and a mauve sweater that says 'Active!' He has a small, tightly packed sports holdall with him and that friendly, eager manner which says Straight Off The Bus. I feel for him. What a night to arrive.

'Yur, mate – are you eleven?' he asks.

'Hardly.'

'I mean number eleven.' He pulls a scrap of paper out of his jeans pocket. 'I've come about the room, see.'

I take my key out of the door and let it swing shut on us. Tara, growing impatient at my side, sniffs loudly.

'What room?'

The Welshman jerks his thumb back down the road towards the station. 'There's a card in the off-licence. Are you the bloke?'

'You've got it wrong,' I say. 'There's no room.'

He shows me the scrap of paper on which he's copied down the details.

'I'm sorry,' I say, 'there's been a mistake.' And I open the door again. Tara pushes her way through, but the man just tries to follow me in, assuming an eager, bleating voice.

'I'll be out most of the time,' he says. 'Working. I'm very quiet. I mean – not *too* quiet, like. I like a laugh.'

I say once more – looking anxiously at Tara's retreating back as she disappears into the gloom of the hallway – that I'm sorry.

'I don't smoke,' he throws in, desperately.

'Then you won't like it here.' Slamming the door on him. A shitty thing to do. But how many people can I care about?

So she's going. Advertising her room. It's all happening so fast. Like her hectic-music tape. *Stop! Go!* I start to feel dizzy and distant with trepidation.

On the first landing, the Sikh is standing in his open doorway – he's a huge bloke – with glasses on and a sheaf of papers in his hand. Probably some exhaustive list of rules and regulations.

186

'Hey YOU! Number eleven,' he says, excitedly, stabbing a finger at me.

Not now. Distressed colleagues and barmy flatmates are one thing. Angry neighbours is just one step too far.

'Not now. Really. I mean it. Not now,' I say, very firmly. And before he can come up with some fresh outburst, I run up the stairs past him. Tara's already by the door, wiping her nose bright red with some crumpled scrap of tissue. She gives me a weak smile.

Rory greets us in the hallway. As soon as we come through the door, he darts sprite-like out of the shadows in our hall, puts a finger on his lips, and eases us back out on to the public landing. 'Tars!' he cries, delightedly. 'How SUPER!' And he kisses a region of air near her left ear. 'What are you doing here?'

'I've—— ' she says. And then gives up. Rory looks at me quizzically.

'She's a bit upset,' I say. 'Can't we go in?'

Rory shakes his head. 'Martha's come back,' he hisses, theatrically.

'Good,' I say, though I'm not even sure I mean that. Rory's shaking his head gravely. 'Not good?'

He combs one of his eyebrows with his fingers. 'She came crashing in last night. I had a few friends over – the mime people, you know. I'm afraid she must have been absolutely *spifflicated*.'

I have to fight the urge to laugh. 'Spifflicated?'

Rory nods in utter seriousness. 'Yes. Stank of the stuff. Anyway – I simply asked if she was okay and she . . .' Here he takes a deep breath and wipes his brow, as if wringing some fearful confession from himself. 'She said an Oath. She told me to' – and here he drops his voice another notch, so that he's just mouthing the words – 'eff-you-see-kay off.'

'Where is she now?' I ask.

'Asleep.'

I make him admit, then, that standing outside our own flat is taking things a tiny bit far. We all go back inside. Tara runs straight to the bathroom and turns all the taps on.

Rory, as well as heaping all of Gus' travel-cornucopia into a huge pile and sticking it in my bedroom, has packed a small, tailored holdall for himself. It's in the hall by the potted plant. He's going to stay with Saffron, his fiancée, for a short while. 'There's nothing else for it,' he tells me, grimly. I'm not sure which he fears most – going out in the storm or spending the night with Saffron.

I mention the man on the steps outside, tell Rory I saw him off.

'Well I just think you should know,' he says, formally, as he's about to leave. 'She's got to go. I'm sorry. I expect you were friends, but she can't stay. Don't see anyone else off. Show them the room.'

So Rory's chucking her out. And if he does that – she'll have no choice. She really will go. Still – we've got some time. Martha's room, I know, is looking more and more as if the Rolling Stones have invited some teenage groupies over for a weekend of cocaine. It'd be a strong-hearted tenant who took delivery of such a room, particularly with Martha lying asleep at the eye of the storm.

But when I creep along and push her door open slightly, she looks anything but the agent of chaos and destruction. She has my overcoat flung over her, so that just a corner of her sleeping face is visible. She has attacked her luxuriant hair with scissors at random, but the effect, though disturbing, is not ugly. She looks like a sleeping gosling, sparsely feathered and vulnerable. A leg kicks out and a part of the coat slips away. She stirs slightly, murmurs as the colder air reacts with the bare skin of her ankle. Tentatively, I replace the coat over her leg and creep back out.

The bathroom door opens and Tara emerges, looking a little, though not a lot better. 'Roo,' she says, hoarsely. 'Is it alright if I stay for a while?'

Rory's got his bags in his hand and is on his way out. He looks torn. 'I'm off to Saffron's. I've sort of promised.' A thought strikes him. 'But you could come too. We could have supper . . .'

Tara shudders – again I'm not sure if this is at Saffron or the thought of supper. She shakes her head. 'I won't darling.'

Once Rory is gone, we stand awkwardly in the hallway, unsure of the next step. Tara seems quite embarrassed to be here now. It's that little twist that life's editors tack on to the end of a catastrophe. When someone's seen you at your lowest ebb, you can either go on and let them see the rest of you. Or you can just walk away. And Tara doesn't know which way to take it.

'Do you know Saffron?' I ask her. She nods.

'Bit of a tartar,' she admits. 'She's from somewhere queer. Like Leicester.'

We laugh about that for a second and then start to speak at the same time.

'You first,' she says, after a further round of false starts.

'I was just going to say we could have some coffee. That's all.'

Tara shakes her head.

'Look. You've been terribly sweet, and thanks, but perhaps I should go. You've got enough on your hands.'

That's true. But a part of me is glad she's here. I don't want to be here on my own with Martha. 'You don't have to. Go, I mean.' I cast an involuntary glance back down the hall to Martha's room.

'Is she totally snooker-loopy then?' Tara asks.

'What?'

Tara falters a little – my query came out unexpectedly sharp.

'Sorry. I just – Roo always said she was a bit odd.' As a distraction, she nods at the answering machine in the alcove. 'You've got messages,' she says.

She hovers by as I turn the volume down super-low and listen with my ear jammed at the speaker.

'Allie, it's Sue. If you get this before . . .' A hissed argument in the background, then she comes back, '. . . before four, give me a call. If not . . .'

More hissing, then Billy's voice breaks in, 'If not, ring Mrs T next door. She's got the kids. Same number as us. Just a seven, not an eight.' Then Sue comes in again, 'Seven four one two, he means. Seven four one two.' Then a long pause. '*Christ, where are you?*' This last bit is shouted.

'What's the matter?' Tara asks, bending down.

'What's the time?'

'About half three.'

I ring Sue's number – casting a wary glance down the corridor. What do they mean – *she's got the kids*? Mrs T always seemed to be a relatively innocuous old bird to me. Even if she didn't own a TV set. Have everyone's neighbours simultaneously gone barking mad? Is Mrs T holding my nephew and niece at knife-point?

'Allie?' Sue's voice is strangulated, heavy with mucus.

'What's up?'

'It's Dad. He's in a coma.'

The cab-driver is a sour, drizzly sort of Mancunian with a moustache made from three, or perhaps four ginger hairs. He has no reason to be sour, standing as he does to earn at least sixty quid for the journey from Manchester Piccadilly to Fazakerley Hospital. As soon as we're in, and the fare negotiated, he tunes his radio into *Heart of Lancashire Supergold 108.8* and leaves it there, loud. It's Country and Western Hour, but I'm well past protesting.

There's a yellow circle of plastic attached to the panel in front of us. I twist it at first, thinking it might be a volume control for the radio. Then I look more closely. *Cab-Fresh*, says a sticker on the circle, *supplied with compliments of Manchester City Council*. It has made my fingers smell like the bottom of the Irwell.

At least he doesn't want to speak. I am cold, wet, wrapped in a blanket of bleak thoughts, running over the events of the last hours: all trains to Liverpool cancelled; power lines down all across the country; trees strategically blocking every line and tunnel; me, swearing at the gentle clerk behind the glass; Tara, at my elbow, pulling me away; the policemen, called to calm me down. Then the cortège of five dark, empty trains through the wild, screaming night. Bedford in the rain. To Birmingham. In the rain. To Rugby. Where we – myself, Tara and four other, twitching passengers stood on a dark, power-cut platform for an hour and fifty minutes before the train to Manchester crept in. We had a cup of acrid coffee at Crewe and I laughed when they announced that the train would be held up for a short while. The trolley-lad, pouring my coffee, looked sympathetic. 'Worra night, eh?' he said. He didn't understand.

'What were you laughing at?' Tara asked, when the lad had moved on.

'Held up at Crewe. It's a sort of family joke. Was, I mean. My dad stood my mum up at the altar and that was his excuse – held up at Crewe.'

Tara smiles. 'Sounds like an interesting man.'

'I suppose so. Never really thought about it like that.' And I find myself wishing I had. Before it was too late.

Tara squeezes my arm. '*Unconscious*, they said. He's not dead.'

Sue was hysterical on the phone. Normally tougher than a Finnish fish-wife, she had to pass it on to Billy, who sounded little better himself. 'He's not regained consciousness,' he said, ponderously, as if reading the words off a card. 'They don't know if he'll come out.'

'Shit.' I said. Not a great speech, but a passionate one, nonetheless.

'Ye'd best come,' Billy said.

'Shit,' I said.

My father: struck on the head with a steel chair. Massive contusions, whatever they are. My father, examining GCSE German Conversation (Part II) in Walton prison, slipped up, fatally.

'He just asked this bloke where he was going for his summer holidays,' Billy said, slightly embarrassed. *Wohin fährst du auf Urlaub?* Not the sort of thing you ask, when the bloke in question is doing fifteen years.

We're on some orange-lit stretch of the motorway, cars creeping along like Chelsea Pensioners, swerving around the bomb-site of debris which litters every lane, flashing lights and ambulances every few feet of the hard shoulder, and weary-faced men in glowing jackets. Familiar signs to St Helens, Warrington and Skem look faintly frightening now in this apocalyptic setting.

'Pimbo,' says Tara, in a puzzled sort of voice, reading a passing sign. I look at her face, pale in the passing lights of the motorway. I said she didn't have to come, but she insisted. *May as well be in on your crisis darling. Better than sitting here with mine.* 'Wi-gan,' she says, reading another. 'Golly. Wigan. I never thought I'd go to Wigan.'

The girl on the radio announces that Bobby Blues Broke Her Heart in Boytown. The taxi driver spits *Bass-tid* at a passing lorry. My father is dying – perhaps already turning blue in some over-sized filing cabinet.

'You can cry if you want to,' Tara suggests. 'I shouldn't mind at all. In fact, I rather think you ought to.'

'I can't.'

I don't feel like crying. There's something like a British Airways Standard Issue ice-cube lodged tight in the place that tears start from. But I care. It surprises me how much.

'I'll make myself scarce when we get to the hospital,' Tara says. 'I shouldn't think your folks will want me around.'

'Don't know why they want me either.'

'That's just being silly.'

Which it is. But it's true. I was an unwelcome intrusion. Sensed it, from the moment I could sense things. Saw it confirmed that hot summer afternoon when I barged in on my father in the bathroom – I was only nine – and I saw the angry scar on his forearm. He'd pulled his shirt on, hurriedly, pushed past me out of the bathroom. Later, out in the garden, they all pretended I'd made up what he said to me. *Don't tell fibs*, they all said.

'What did he say?' asks Tara, listening to this in polite fascination, as if it was an anecdote at a cocktail party.

'He said: *Never trust an Estonian.*'

'An Estonian? Crikey. Then what?'

'Then nothing. He just ran out.'

'But why?'

I shrug, hopelessly. 'That's just what they're like. Weird.'

Tara clicks in exasperation. 'That's *ridiculous*. I'm sorry. I know I'm supposed to be being nice, but it is. You can't just shrug your shoulders and say they're all weird and write them off as if they don't matter. That's seriously awful.'

'Easy for you to say.'

'No it's not. Nothing's easy for me to say right now. I've just found out Mummy's been shagging Ben Fielding and my dad, my *poor*, stupid, fat old dad, isn't my dad at all. But that doesn't mean I'm just going to bury my head up my bum and pretend it's not happened.'

'So what *are* you going to do?'

'Oh f. off,' she exclaims, crossly. 'You know arsing well I don't know what I'm going to do. But as soon as I'm back down there I'm f. well going to get to the bottom of it and get some answers. I want to know what Mummy's feeling and I want to know what Daddy's feeling and I want to know what they're going to do about everything that I'm feeling!'

She stops herself, as the emotions within her gather a dangerous momentum, moves away from me, angry, and stares out of the window. My head is pounding now, just as it always does when the matter of my family comes under review. Just as it did the last time I spoke to Sue. *He's just special*, she'd tried to tell me. Because I'd sworn, and demanded to know why we couldn't have proper parents like everyone else. Parents without secret scars. *Just special*. Which was typical Sue: forgiving to the point of folly. During the James Bulger trial, she dubbed the suspects 'poor little bastard A' and 'poor little bastard B'.

'But *what* Estonian?' I'd demanded. 'Why an Estonian? What the fuck did he mean?'

'Oh I don't know,' she'd said, a touch irritably. 'Worrier.'

(That's Sue's pet name for me. Worrier, or sometimes Worry-bum.)

'Small wonder I worry. With a dad like ours.'

And, as always, she'd gone and leaped to his defence. 'Give him a chance, Al,' she'd said. 'He tries, you know. And you haven't always been brilliant to him, have you? Remember when he tried to pick you up from school?'

I got shirty then. That was so like Sue. Always pulling out grotty little stories from when I was about five to support her claim to know anything about what I'm like now. 'That was eighteen years ago, Sue,' I'd snapped.

'So you should've improved by now then, shouldn't you?'

She was referring to the one time my father tried to pick me up from school and I saw him waiting – pretending, in the midst of all the mums and the shift-working dads, to be reading his *Neue Zürcher Zeitung*. I sneaked out of the girls' gate and ran away, went for tea with Martin Cleary and his wild, Irish family and walked home alone at nine o'clock, straight into the middle of a nuclear meltdown.

'Well I still remember that speech day,' I'd countered. Our father made it a point of honour to use the oldest, most obscure terms for everything. Siam, *the* Iraq, the Home Service. And in the packed foyer of the Philharmonic Hall, he looked at the book they'd awarded me and said, sonorously, 'I expect you would have preferred a gramophone record.' They all heard. Everyone in my year, all their brothers and sisters and their normal, straight parents, the ones I wanted to belong to – watch films on their videos, go with them to Tenerife, eat McDonald's in the backs of their Volvos. Like Tara, sitting next to me, wiping her eyes again. Because I have upset her.

Suddenly, the taxi jerks to a halt. We've pulled off the motorway and we're in the outskirts of somewhere that could be Liverpool, could be anywhere. We're on the forecourt of a fiercely lit garage. The driver is filling up. ' 'S norron the meter,'

195

he says, defensively, leaning in through his open window. I shrug, watching the patterns of the raindrops on my window. Tara nudges me with a bony elbow.

'Sorry,' she says. 'Bet you wish I hadn't come now.'

'No I don't. I'm glad.' And I am. Because if she hadn't, it would have just been me and my worries. I doubt they'd have let me get as far as Crewe.

'Have they told your brother?'

I don't know what they've said to Gus. Or if he even knows a thing. It seems improbable that Sue could have left him out of the equation, knowing that secret connection they've always had.

What could family life have been like before I was born? What sufferings bonded the saintly Sue to the self-absorbed Gus? My own memories aren't of suffering, but just of a frugal existence, left to my own devices, provided my nose wasn't bleeding, my clothes were unmuddied and I asked no questions. It's as if my parents, strangers themselves in a foreign quarter, got their etiquette confused, mixed up parenting skills with ideas of hospitality. Because this is how it is up North. If you visit a Northern household, don't expect offers of a cup of tea and a cherry slice. You'll be invited in, certainly, but then made part of the surroundings, expected to sit down, shut the fuck up and quickly get as absorbed in whatever's on the telly as they are. My parents seemed to believe parenting was the same. They just showed you in and left you. '*Shush. I'm watching my programme.*' But this is how Northerners are with guests. Not their children. And my parents aren't even from the North. Mum is from Peterborough. My father is from. From . . .

I look at the meter. The fare, so far, is forty-three pounds. I have spent a hundred pounds already on this joyless night. Going to stand at the death-bed of a near-stranger.

'Gaah!' the driver exclaims, shaking himself, as he gets back in the cab. 'Never seen it bad as this before.'

196

'Aah,' says Tara – well practised at silencing talkative cabbies. But she's on foreign turf here and her noises, as I could have told her, only encourage him. He commences a lengthy, free-ranging soliloquy, touching on the storm, the climate, the recent follies of Man City FC, his knees and the need for less lorries, all the way to Fazakerley. I'm scarcely listening. It's just a dull hum at the edges of my awareness, one ear muffled in the fur of Tara's collar. Only one thing he says has any impact on me. As we all watch a large corrugated sheet of metal sail over a playing field as if it was a till receipt. 'All that bloody *energy*,' he says. 'Going all over the place. Wish we could get hold of it. All that energy. For free.'

He's right. That's what's wrong with the whole universe. All the energy's in the wrong places. Misplaced, it turns relatively clever men like Fielding into villains, whose only concern is the next swindled pound. It has twisted my father into some obscure, eccentric scholar who barely knows his sons' names, and sent Martha to the darkest corners of bedlam. And me – all that energy. So powerful it sparks and shudders in my knees and rumbles in my guts. And what do I do? I leg it. And when not legging it, I set it to writing giant head-essays on the stuff of late-night telly. Some of them are funny, some might even be right, but no one ever sees them. All that energy – and it doesn't *do* anything.

15

There's a chillingly industrial quality to Fazakerley Hospital, whose portals I haven't crossed since pitching headlong down Jill's stairs after a series of bucket-bongs on an empty stomach. (The sweet joys of youth.) At least the last time I was in here, there were some visible differences between doctors, nurses, porters and the patients. Now – we're finally here at one in the morning – there are only pyjama-clad ghouls, padding the corridors in sterile gym-shoes. Machinery, like a vigorous canker, has bubbled and boiled its way into every crevice of the place – even the people are bleeping. The wards, called units now, spring off a central glass-sided walkway. Scary signs, cactus-like, sit in clusters at either end. Names that make you feel ill just to see them. Nuclear Medicine. Oncology. Trauma.

My father, P.P. Strange, is in Trauma III. The numbers denote degrees of sterility and, by inverse relation, the likelihood of the patient ever getting out of there. There isn't a four.

Tara makes to leave me by the coffee machines but, witnessing my confusion, takes a deep breath and leads me off into the labyrinth of the hospital. She accosts a set of technicians by a lift door. 'Excuse me,' she demands, imperiously – a tone that doubtless sends Knightsbridge shop assistants scurrying for cover. 'We're looking for Trauma.'

One of the technicians chuckles. 'Plenty of that outside love,' he quips.

'Oh fuck off, you scruffy little man,' she says. 'This is an emergency.'

Sobered, the men direct us to the third floor. We start walking down a narrow corridor, through sets of plastic doors. In windows and the cracks of open doors I see ever more complex machinery, ever decreasing signs of life. The hurricane outside is silent, may as well not be happening. In here, there is only the struggle to draw another breath. This, I realise, is the sort of place they'll take Martha if they find out the thoughts she's having, where they'll smoke them out with high voltage, glue them to the rim of her skull with foreign liquids. Then, just as suddenly as the spectre of Martha appears, she steps to one side. I haven't got space in my head to think about her. She is filed in the wings. I have, without consent or conscious decision, become a librarian.

The doors ahead of us fly open and they hit me straight in the mouth. A gaggle of scientists are running full-pelt with a bed towards some darker place, like medical students on some charity dash. Except the bed contains no lagered-up first-year, instead a liver-green walnut of a person, croaking its last. We flatten ourselves against the walls, not to avoid the trolley, but what is on it. The ghastliest thing – worse than anything life can offer. The end. 'Soz!' shouts one of the technicians over a gowned shoulder, and then they are gone.

More carefully, we pass through the next set of doors and round a corner. A gaggle of grey, weary people are on chairs by a desk. They all look up. My mother shrieks and bolts for the door marked toilet.

'Allie lad, what happened?' Billy, stubbly and awkward in a diamond-patterned jumper and trackie bottoms, standing up, a hand outstretched as if I might fall. What does he mean – what happened? We all know what happened.

'Here.' Sue proffers a stiff, aged ball of tissue from the depths of her handbag. *Why are they all staring at me?*

A black woman, encased entirely in a suit of crackling white plastic, walks past with a clipboard. She leans across to Tara, nudging her with an elbow. 'Does he know his nose is bleeding?'

My mother refuses to come out of the toilet until I have cleaned up the blood. Tara helps me, in the Gents, with cold water and scratchy tissues and, when we come out, I am handed a gown and a hairnet to put on. This strikes me as a little unfair, as no one else has to wear them. 'You might infect someone,' says the nurse in the plastic jumpsuit.

Leaving Tara outside, we all go in together, me feeling a prat in my sterile robes. Billy keeps a gentle hand in the small of my back as if I might bolt for freedom. And believe me, when I see my father for the first time, I feel like it. They've shaved his head. If you ignore the clump of gauze and stitching covering the left side of his head, you might think this is some aged Nazi, captured at last in Paraguay. He is bare-chested – suckers sit like a second set of nipples and run to a monitor which, unlike the ones on TV, does not emit the steady blip-blip of submarine radar. It displays a squiggle of green light, roughly every second, which is our sole assurance that he lives. He looks tiny and vulnerable as I stand far above him in the bed. Reminds me of the only time I saw him drunk. The night the Berlin Wall came down. He made himself sick on Cointreau and passed out on the sofa.

Everyone else, by prior arrangement, seems to have taken up a distinct role at my father's deathbed. And there is none left for me. Sue is being hysterical, crying unashamedly. Billy is being grim, grey-faced, keeping a hand on Sue's shoulder so she doesn't fall to bits. And my mother has the trump card. Instead of being in sodden, quivering pieces, as I expected, she is composed, in a distant sort of way. She's stroking his hand, but her eyes are blank, uncomplaining, like those refugee faces we see on the TV. As if her life had not been composed of Tai Chi classes and the Number Nine into town, but only of grisly sights like this. The green crystal droplet at her throat, habitually rubbed and murmured over in times of domestic crisis, hangs ignored, powerless. The only event, so far, to have produced a visible reaction in her, has been my appearing with a nosebleed. After that a dry, mechanical, coffee-flavoured kiss on my cheek. And since then, she hasn't noticed me. No one has noticed me.

I steal out unobserved and, in the corridor, ignoring the signs, I take a cigarette from Tara and light it.

'You can't smoke in here,' she points out. 'I just got told off by that plastic woman.'

'I don't care. He's dying.' I look at her, for the first time my eyes growing watery. 'I don't think I really – you know – realised it. Until I saw all that stuff.'

'Why don't you go back in?'

I shake my head. I'm not needed in there. Any more than I was ever needed. The third child, a regrettable moment of passion that drove my mother crazy, then hung around for twenty-one years asking awkward questions.

Billy comes out, giving a huge yawn. I suddenly feel sorry for Billy. They don't need him here, either. He never fitted into this secret coven called Strange. At Christmases he always sat, dinner on his lap, trying to fix the lamps and radios and clocks that his other-worldly in-laws had buggered up, ignoring the weird conversation that crackled around him like a Chinese banger. And now here he is, two in the morning, stranded in Fazakerley – probably on earlies and knackered already, to the point of collapse.

' 'Lo,' he says, eyeing Tara. 'Are you his girlfriend?'

Tara adjusts an earring discreetly.

'She's a friend, Billy. I work with her.'

Billy nods. 'You just missed the bizzies.'

'The police? What did they want?'

'Told us the bloke's prob'ly gonna get life. On top of the rest.'

'The rest?'

'He was in seclusion – that's how come they never got to your dad. Not till he'd had a right kicking.'

'He was teaching people in seclusion?'

Billy nods. 'Yeh. Rapists an' that.'

'Is that what he was?'

Billy leans in, lowering his voice a notch. 'He was out of that lot that did that kid in the sand-dunes. The ringleader. Frigging huge bloke.'

My heart starts in terror. Static roars in my ears. 'Gibbo?'

Billy frowns. 'Oo?'

'Was he – were they from round here?'

'Didn't you read about it when they caught 'em? It was a 'ole big gang. Doing it all over the place.'

'But where were they *from*?'

Billy's face shrugs with the struggle to recall. 'What's that place that's like Aintree?'

'Haydock Park?'

Billy frowns. 'Naa. Sounds like it, I mean.' Billy has always had a degree of trouble coping with regions beyond the borders of Merseyside; it gave him great pleasure, I recall, to discover that there was also a Tuebrook in Libya.

'Braintree?' suggests Tara. Billy nods, excitedly.

'That's it. They were from Braintree.'

'That's in Essex,' pronounces Tara, knowledgeably.

Saliva finally floods back to my mouth. So I was wrong. The incident among the sand-dunes was nothing to do with Gibbo and his woollyback cronies. All that agonising. All that running away. To end up here.

'Ey luv – pull that chair over,' Billy calls to Tara. 'I think he's gonna faint.'

So who sent the brick?

Gentle hands ease me into the chair. 'I'm not fainting. I'm

fine,' I protest. 'I'm. I forgot to set the video. I've missed *Cell Block H.*'

'It's been quite a day,' Tara offers, apologetically. Billy nods.

'It's good you could get here, lad,' he says, tapping my knee to recover my dissipated attention. 'Yer mam appreciates it.'

'You reckon?'

Billy's bloodshot eyes look askance. ''Course. You're her son.'

'One of them.'

Billy lets out a puff of disgusted air. 'Oh aye. *Jeremy.*'

'Someone should tell him,' I say, feeling suddenly matured, responsible in the presence of death.

Billy laughs, joylessly. 'They did, la.'

'What do you mean?'

'We rang him up. At the workshop. In Kirby.'

'Corby.'

'Oh aye. Sue told him. She says, yer dad's in a coma. Gerr'ere quick.'

'And what did he say?'

'He said, "Oh that killer. Call us when they read the will." '

'Jesus.'

I am, I think, more disturbed by this than anything else I've seen or heard today. Maybe I don't love the man in that bed, but I don't hate him. And I am related in blood to someone else, who is unashamed to wish him dead. It unsettles me. It's fine to dislike the cool and the cruel – they are not just powerful, but everywhere, in every bar and bus. But to hate this quiet, strange old man, whom we barely know. That's madness. And it's in my blood.

Billy's nodding. It's clear he thinks the same. Perhaps now's the time. *Perhaps Billy knows.*

'Billy. Why does he always call him that? Do you know? Why does Gus always call him a killer?'

And Billy goes all quiet, studying, as if for the first time, the pattern on his jumper. A familiar sequence, repeated throughout my youth. I ask a question and suddenly designs on tablecloths, stains on the ceiling acquire a magnetic fascination for those around me. But even as he looks away, I can see that Billy is scared – peculiar, in a man built like a barrel of Higsons Bitter, but he is. He knows something. 'Look,' he starts. And then Sue comes screeching through the plastic doors, a giant warship of panic. Billy grabs on to her, as if her massive bulk might propel her past us and beyond. She is breathlessly repeating over and over again the same phrase. It sounds like Sidcup.

'Sue!' Billy snaps sharply. 'Breathe in.'

She stares, wild-eyed, her jowls shuddering, like a suffocating fish, but obeys him. Then she tries again.

'He's waking up!' she splutters.

When we run in there, my father's sitting bolt upright in bed, talking in a low voice to my mother. His eyes look haunted, and of course there's a clotted wound on the side of his head, but otherwise he could just be suffering a touch of the flu. It's only when we get close that I see he's talking utter gibberish.

'Dubček, you see. Hopeless idealist. Said to me once, "I will eradicate corruption." I said, "How can you? You're just one man." And he said, "But I have the soul of a poet." Soul of a poet.' Here my father spits, drily, on to the blanket spread across him. 'He was a lumberjack. Division knew what I meant. But those Curzon Street bastards wouldn't listen.'

My mother nods, solemnly. Then she looks up. 'Ooh,' she exclaims brightly, as if to a baby. 'Look who's here!'

My father's pale blue eyes narrow up as he looks at Sue, and then Billy. 'Who are these cunts?'

My mother looks flustered. She mouths something at Sue.

'It's me, Dad. Sue. And Billy. And look who else.'

Sue nudges me forward. My father squints to see me. Then he

falls back on his pillow, turning sheet-white with horror, his fingers twitching. 'Angus!' he croaks. 'Gussy.'

I look wildly from him to my mother, to Sue and then to Billy. They all look as worried as me, certainly, but there's something else there, too. A sheepishness, almost embarrassment, a definite reluctance to look me in the eye. 'Say something to him!' hisses my mother. 'His chakras are all over the place. He's very confused.' Not half, I think.

I clear my throat. 'It's not Gus,' I say, in a voice that sounds high and wobbly. 'It's me, Dad. Strange. I mean Alastair.'

My father is trembling, big bug-eyes fixed on me like I am some gory vision of the Death he has just evaded. 'I'm sorry, Angus. So *sorry*, boy. Lilly, where's the toolbox? I'm going to fix that drawer.' And he makes to get out of the bed.

Hands push him back there. I'm frozen in his glare. 'All that *blood*,' he says to me, puzzled. 'And you were so . . .' Suddenly he's a little boy, his face crumpled in tears, with horror at the precious thing he has just broken. '*So small.*' He covers his face with his hands.

'Right,' says Sue, yanking me by the elbow. 'I'm telling him.' My mother, who is wiping my father's clammy forehead, looks up, alarmed. But Sue, it seems, is not to be stopped. 'NOW, Mum,' she says.

In Sue's iron grip, I am propelled, between her and Billy into the corridor outside and back on to the orange plastic chair. 'Will you bloody stop pushing me about?' I whisper petulantly, wondering, as I say it, why all hospitals make us whisper.

'Sit,' she orders – all her bossy attitude recovered. 'Billy!' She snaps her fingers. 'Get him a cup of tea.' And Billy trots off, meekly – relieved, I think, not just to be going somewhere else, but to have a new, more familiar position in the hierarchy of mourners.

Tara gives an embarrassed cough. Sue notices her for the first time. 'Shall I—'

Sue gives a very definite nod, and Tara follows Billy off down the corridor.

Sue sits down next to me, taking up most of my chair as well as her own. A homely smell of mints and fabric conditioner wafts around.

'Why's he going on about Dubček?'

'He's very confused. He thinks he's still back in Prague.'

I am none the wiser.

'You can't not know now, it's just not fair,' she carries on, mysteriously, placing one hand on my knee.

'Eh?'

'We never wanted to tell you,' she says. 'But you can't not know now. It's all you've had, Al, half-truths, all the time. They aren't any use to anyone – you usually get the wrong half. And we're all, we're all very sorry about that.'

We're all very *sorry*. That's the thing about families. Unless you spend an entirely inappropriate amount of time thinking about them, you never see them as people with faults and strengths at all. You might rail at all their quirks, but in the end you know you may as well talk about the lewdness of an apricot. It's how they are. Crap. Weird. Or special – if you want to talk like Sue. The idea that they're capable of *sorry*, of regret, that knocks me as she says it. I'm not sure I believe it. But I let her carry on.

'You know,' she says, trying to find a place to start, 'you know our dad, right?'

'Not really.'

'*Stop* it. You know ... No. I'll have to go back to the beginning. You know he was in Eastern Europe and stuff after the war?'

And I give a nod. 'The wine business.'

'Yeah. Well no. All that wine thing ... that wasn't really what he did.'

Which figures. A man who can drink himself sick on Cointreau makes an unlikely wine-buyer. Now I think about it.

'He was working for the Government really, a lot of that time. On Special Duties – deep-cover, they called it. He was away.' She says 'away' with meaning. I'm clearly meant to understand.

'Away where?'

'All over. Very dangerous places.'

My mouth is getting sticky at this point. My eyes feel full of grit and I don't know where to look. Sue is looking straight at me, as if in an effort to make up for all the past shiftiness, but I don't want to look back. Even if I want answers. Instead, I settle on the blue-and-white sign on the wall in front. Trauma III. It seems oddly appropriate. Trauma times three. Martha. Then Tara. Now me.

'What was he doing in Eastern Europe then?' I ask, mechanically.

'All sorts. No. Always either import-exports, or an interpreter, or a buyer or an engineer or something. That wasn't really his job, you see.'

I almost laugh then. My father, an engineer. Who cannot even set the oven-timer without the aid of a small child. Of course he wasn't an engineer. Why would anyone have thought he was?

'He had papers that said he was. And he was a good actor. His job was . . . He used to find out if people had reasons to, wanted to defect. You know – go over to the other side.'

'I know what defecting means,' I say, automatically, like a nine-year-old. Which is, unavoidably, how I am in the presence of my family.

'Shut up. Then he'd sort of pass it on up to . . . to his people. The information.'

His people. I have heard him say this before. That one, odd time he came to see me at university. 'Got to go and see my people,' he'd said.

'Listen,' Sue says, a little crossly. 'Stop looking at that sign. You're not listening. It's important. Once he got friendly with this bloke, a top sort of . . . engineer, in this factory in Estonia. They made rockets. The man had a daughter and a son. Dad liked kids and he always used to go round there a lot and play with them.'

My father never played with me. If he stumbled across me looking inactive, he might teach me the names of a few trees and test my irregular verbs, but that was all. He wasn't the sort of a father who played with you.

'When they got more friendly, Dad realised this bloke was doing the same job as he was. For the other lot.'

'Spying you mean?'

Sue winces a little, as if I'd said something crude in a church.

'Dad's people wouldn't send anyone else in to help, so Dad had to. He had to sort it out himself.'

'What do you mean – sort it out?'

'They had this fight, but Dad won it. And then they got him out. If he hadn't done it, dozens of people would've got killed, Allie. In bad ways.'

Killer. Gus' curses. '*Up yours, Killer.*' Gus knew!

She lets out a long sigh and waits for me to say something. In the silence, my father yells something about Khrushchev. My mother shushes him. Then he shouts, three times, hoarse but still clearly, 'Angus!'

I look at Sue.

'Gus knows all this, doesn't he?'

She looks briefly helpless. 'It's not . . .' she says. Then frowns, rummages in her bag for mints.

'It's not finished. He's not talking about Gus. Well he is. But not THAT Gus.'

So I let her finish. She tells me some more, very strange things

208

about my father, and my mother. And Gus. And another member of our little family, whose existence has successfully been kept from me for twenty-one years. Billy and Tara never come back with the tea. I don't blame them.

And when Sue finishes telling me, we argue. Then she goes back into the room where my mother and my father are, telling me to come back in when I'm ready. But I don't – because I will never be ready. Instead, I run for half an hour around the corridors of Fazakerley Hospital until I find the exit. Another taxi takes me to Lime Street as the storm breathes its dying gusts across the flatlands of Merseyside.

Tara catches up with me as I'm sitting on the freezing station, waiting for the first train, the only person there, it seems, except for some muttering bag-lady, who studies every timetable as if she had the power to go anywhere she liked today. All around me are the clatterings and the sudden bangs of machinery, occasional shouts from people lifting heavy mail-bags in the chill air. And louder than them, louder than the departing storm, in my own head, are Sue's words, again and again – her final address, as we stood there in that empty hospital corridor, at the close of the bitterest of rows:

'Don't you get it? Do you really not get it? Don't you see – I'm not saying what they did was right or wrong. All that. The lying and the spying. But don't you see – sometimes, it's just a fine line. And you do what you have to do.'

I offer the approaching Tara a sheepish sort of smile, which she returns with a brief, peremptory wiggle of the corners of her mouth. She is torn between the need to be sympathetic and the fact that she is angry with me. And why wouldn't she be? I've just done what I always do. I legged it.

They're just opening the shutters to John Menzies. The girl in Casey Jones Fried Chicken is looking nervously my way, thinking I am some scarier version of the bag-lady. Who, it turns out, works in John Menzies.

'Come on,' Tara says, briskly. 'It's too cold.'

I frown at her. 'Come where?'

'Back to the hospital. I said I'd fetch you.'

'How did you know I'd be here?'

'Sue said you'd be here. Said it's what you always do. Run off.'

I give a moody shrug.

'What's that supposed to mean?'

'I'm not coming. I'm not going back there. I can't.'

'Why not?'

Numbly, I walk off to buy us coffees on auto-pilot. I catch myself wondering if my father was ever like this under pressure, out in *deep-cover* – body diarrhoeic, but mind numb, covered in scar-tissue where there should rightly be a swarm of raw feelings.

As Tara sips her coffee, I am reminded of our afternoon in the pub, still vivid, though a thousand years ago; the crushing sense of power she seemed to gain from knowing all the answers at last. *And now we know why* . . . she had pronounced, with sorry contempt for those who had, until that point, been her masters. That same knowledge has come to me in the last hour as well. But I feel more like Shoni, off *Jacaranda Cove*, the night she learned her brother was from Doncaster and her mother was really her dad. No wonder she had a miscarriage.

Suddenly, every mystery makes sense. The secret life, the dread of photographs, the scar. My mother, who never went, every summer, to visit an active volcano, but really to visit some field of milled granite and hewn marble. A tiny tombstone. Where my dead brother is, even now. *Angus.*

'Do you want one of those . . . croissant things?' I suggest, swivelling back to look at the Fried Chicken stand. I would offer her anything rather than sit here and review the events of the last hour: croissants, cigarettes, my fingers and toes . . .

Tara clicks her tongue in exasperation. 'I've got all the time in the world,' she points out. 'I'm not going anywhere.' She reminds me of my Latin teacher, demanding to know who'd stuck the Blu-Tac cock and balls on the statue of the founder. I'd kept quiet that time. Something tells me that's not an option here. 'Just tell me what you're so angry about.'

'I can cope with all the spy stuff. I really can. It's Sue and Gus and the other one. That's what hurts. That they wouldn't tell me. They *knew* him. Gus would have just been three. But they knew him. And they never told me.'

'Knew who?'

I sigh. It all seems too much, too vast to recount. But Sue managed it – even though it must have been worse than giving birth. So I start where she did. 'I had another brother. Called Angus. He was seven – and they were all living in Geneva. And he died.'

Sue and G-Jeremy adored him. Their seven-year-old brother who, in spite of his knock knees and his non-existent bum, had schooled his ever-twitching limbs into learning to row like a man and whittle sticks into intricate filigrees.

One day, in the summer of 1964, my parents' tenth wedding anniversary, my father took my mother out on Lac Leman. He'd bought her a locket – which he kept in his desk. But then, because he is my father, he lost the key and, to get the locket out, he had to jemmy the drawer open. My mother hated the idea of au pairs and nannies because in those days, before it all went crazy, she was a real hands-on sort of mother. But just for a day, she left the three kids with the au pair of the family next door. The girl had a bit of a thing for the man who mowed the lawns of the communal gardens, a wild gypsy type, who could do bird impressions and always worked with his shirt off. She was in the garden with Sue and G-Jeremy making light, fluttery conversation with the gypsy, so she didn't notice when the insatiably curious Angus slipped back into the house and went to my father's study. He wanted his rock collection. It was only a month old at the time and consisted of four lumps of quartz, stored in a shoebox to prevent G-Jeremy from putting them in his mouth.

Things were quiet for my father in those days – after they got him out of Estonia. His job consisted, largely, of monitoring radio broadcasts from a nondescript office on the Rue des Gavroches. But he still had to have his gun. For his own safety. And – so his people ironically put it – for the safety of his family as well. It was this gun, a revolver, that Angus took from the drawer of my father's desk. And everybody heard the bang, ran in and saw the mess.

The mess. It seemed a funny word for Sue to use, very house-wife-ish. The pink and purple porridge of a child's future spattered across the walls and the desk. My father's desk. With the one bust drawer.

I remember now going in to his little office to steal his Gitanes once – about thirteen or so. Him catching me, screaming, red-faced, terrifying, at the top of his voice, the only time ever, '*Get out! Get out! Get out!*'

Sue, implacable and forgiving, even at the age of four, mourned her brother for precisely eight weeks and then recovered. There was never any suggestion for her that my father was to blame. And to all intents and purposes, G-Jeremy also took the loss in his ever-increasing stride, appeared, in that way children have, to cope with tragedy in the same way they can cope with Father Christmas and dragons in the airing cupboard. Until, as he approached fourteen and a new brother emerged from his mother's belly, the memory of what befell the Strange family emerged from the lusty swamp of his teenage mind. And with his unique talent for mischief, Gus hit upon the cruellest means to show that he would never forgive them. *Said he wasn't Jeremy any more. Started writing Gus on his school bag and making all his mates call him Gus. So in the end, even his teachers and everyone except us called him Gus.*

Just as Sue told me that, back in the hospital, the top of my mother's worried little face had peeped out through the glass window in the door to my father's room, then ducked away again. Maybe because she was scared. Or perhaps just because she is five foot bugger all and couldn't reach. 'Don't GO!' Sue had shouted as I got up from my chair in the corridor and started to pull the gown off. 'Don't you see? It wasn't that they never wanted you. They *did*. But they'd lost two sons. Gus hated them and they were frightened, if you ever found out, they'd lose you too. So they were scared. Scared of getting too close.'

'Cock.' That was my response to that. So she lost her rag, said she was going to go back in, if all I could do was talk nasty like that.

I was wrong to run away again. But how could I have gone back in there and looked at them? Knowing they knew what I knew. What could I have said? *Don't worry, Dad. Don't worry, Mum. You raised me at arms' length, brought me up to believe I just wasn't particularly welcome. Now I'm to understand that you did all that, actually, because you loved me? Oh, and that all the subterfuge, in fact, was just because Dad happened to be an MI5 assassin who inadvertently murdered his own child? Fine. How's your fucking weather?*

Tara listens to this as it pours out of me like some grisly haemorrhage. When I've finished, she takes a cigarette from me, but does not light it, just rolls it back and forth between her finger and thumb. 'So that's why your mum's so . . .'

'No. That's not it.'

My mother coped with it, too – without recourse to Valium, or mysticism, or the bottle. She was – they all were, in their way – tougher than a squadron leader's scrotum. Which, I suppose, is how the families of spies turn out: able to keep a tragedy deep within their bowels like some stolen piece of microfilm. My mother coped with the loss of her first-born, her

214

husband's oppressive sense of guilt and his subsequent withdrawal from all but the most obscure forms of life. Even found the courage, eleven years later, to conceive another child. That was her mistake.

Thing is, Allie. When you were born, you were the dead spit of him. And when you got bigger, it didn't get any better. Right down to the nosebleeds. And that . . . that shuffling thing you do. That was when Gus started on them. And it sent Mum a bit . . . Well, you know. She got all sorts of ideas.

'That's why they all watch me like they do. Even Gus. I always thought there was just something weird about me. Like maybe I just did everything wrong or something. That's why – well – I always thought it was better to just sit still and watch the TV. Out of the way.'

Tara finally lights the cigarette. '*Poor* Strange,' she says. She makes as if to continue, but is interrupted by a vast, involuntary yawn. I catch the stale scent of her morning-breath on the motionless air. She glances at the station clock. 'They'll be getting worried.'

I shake my head. She sighs. 'I'm sorry,' I offer. 'You don't need all this. Not on top of . . . You know.'

She tosses the cigarette away, unfinished, and stares down at the marble floor, remembering her own peculiar disasters. 'I'd almost forgotten.'

'What are *you* going to do?'

She does another of her peculiar, multivalent snorts. 'Don't know. Tell them all to sod off. Then maybe . . . Well – I'll need a job. Or perhaps I'll finish my Ph.D.'

'Ph.D? How old are you?'

'I'm thirty,' she says, diffidently.

A single life can never contain enough surprises. At the outside, I'd have put Tara at twenty-two. I glance at her face, seeing it for the first time without make-up, in the unflattering

215

lights of the station hall, and suddenly it seems probable. Tara blinks, self-consciously. 'What?'

'Nothing. What was your . . .' I can't help but ask. 'What was your Ph.D about?'

'I had to stop when Dad went into partnership with Ben. Needed the money. Sorry. You asked what it was about. Knots.'

'Knots?'

'Have you heard of Coomaraswamy?' And in answer to my numbed head-shaking, she continues: 'He was this nineteenth-century Indian mathematician, the one who worked out that V was a node of Q. Totally blew those German boys out of the water. Except he was as wrong as they were.'

'He was?'

'Yes. That's what I was working on. If you plot the Gugger quadrants of V on a straight line, you see, then there aren't any nodes of Q at all. If V's related to anything, anything at all, then it's F. But *of course* Coomaraswamy wouldn't have included anything Gugger did, because they got in that fight over the chair at Heidelberg.'

'Of course.'

'Anyway,' she concludes sadly. 'I doubt I'll carry it on, not really. Haven't got any money.'

Finally, the silence of the hall is broken as the indicator board flickers like a thousand geisha-fans and the first train to London appears in red letters. Change at Crewe. Tara nudges me. 'You could probably do one on knots as well.'

'Eh?'

'*Knots Landing*. That's a soap opera, isn't it?' There's a lengthy pause. Tara nudges a lolly-stick with the tip of her shoe. 'It was meant to be a joke.'

'Oh. Sorry.'

'So what do we do, Strange?'

An invisible string pulls me to my feet and drags me, and my

216

mathematical friend, down towards the barriers. Perhaps this is what Sue meant when she said *you do what you have to do*. You just numbly grope around until some idea appears and you follow it. Not making your mind up, noting the pros and cons, just doing it. Finding where the energy of the storm is headed, and sailing along in front of it. Because the only other option is to be like wee, dead Angus – my brother, my doppelganger. With no mind left to make up.

By nine, I am back in the flat. I left Tara in the rush hour crowds at Victoria. She was grey, but full of grim determination to find her mother, as she squeezed my arm and told me to stay in touch. I said I would call her later, but Tara shook her head. 'Don't worry about me,' she said. 'Go and find Martha. She's the one who needs you.'

Feverish with lack of sleep – or lack of television, I am uncertain which is more damaging to the psyche – I creep down the hallway of the flat, holding my breath and my socks. The door to Martha's room is wide open, the light on. I look in. It no longer smells of bergamot in there, but of birdcage, and worse. There are feathers all over the carpet, drifting in the draught from the open window, mingling with roughly hewn handfuls of her auburn hair. The storm's over now, but there's still a cold breeze. The birdcage has a big hole in it. Deirdre has gone. Martha has been stuffing her clothes into one of Gus' kitbags.

On the kitchen table she's left a glass of murky water, into which she has spooned vast heaps of white sugar. Crystalline boulders of the stuff are all over the table cloth, all over her big black scribble-pad, which I don't dare look at. The little door to the balcony – really a fire-escape which doesn't go anywhere – is open. Knotted tight, several times around the bottom of the railings is a ring of familiar fabric – yellow and black, like a wasp. My school scarf.

No.

I bolt out on to the balcony and look down. The scarf is taut. It leads down to another cluster, where she has knotted it together with another striped scarf – green and magenta – her own school scarf, I guess. And further down, beyond that, almost where the window to the Sikh's bathroom sits, is the top of Martha's head, swinging eerily in the weak morning sun, the grey line of her scalp like a fishbone. She's hanging there.

Please no.

'Oh shit,' I say, quaveringly. 'Martha.' If only I'd been here for her – instead of upsetting people in Fazakerley – I could have stopped this.

A nasty cackle floats up from below and the scarves start to swing. *The body's moving.* Martha grunts and I know she isn't dead. And all my fear vanishes because I've heard her grunts, in some very different situations to this, and I just feel a rush of relief, which turns swiftly to anger. She kicks at the wall with her boots – my boots – and slowly, torturously, crab-walks her way up towards me, pulling with her hands on the scarf-rope which is knotted, not as I thought, in a noose around her neck, but into Gus' thick leather belt around her waist. She's wheezing with the exertion. I hold out my hand to her as she straightens up at the balcony and haul her over to safety. She's dirty, streaked with smudges of grey and gleaming with a brackish sweat that stains her light-blue vest at the front, a jagged V of damp marking out her cleavage. 'Wow,' she exclaims, breathlessly. 'That was fantastic!'

Her eyes are bright with a nervous, nasty elation. All at once I seem to pity, fear and hate her. 'What the fuck are you doing?' I demand, pushing her hard into the kitchen.

'Mountaineering,' she says, innocently. She looks at me quizzically, bites the top of her hand, naughty, guilty. 'Oop sorry – borrowed your boots.' And she flops down to the floor like a rag doll to take them off.

'Martha,' I say, very carefully, reminding myself that this is not Martha, not really. 'You're not well.'

'I know,' she says. 'I'm knackered.'

She's holding my boots out to me, and when I reach for them, she flings them over her head behind her. One bounces on to and off the balcony – we listen to it hit the trees below. 'Whee,' she says, quietly, flashing me a grin like those little cousins at wedding receptions, the ones who grow up with alarming haste to know you will not refuse them a sip of your drink. 'Got any cigarettes?' she asks, chirpily, as she fingers a remaining rat-tail of hair.

'What am I supposed to do without my boots?'

'Swim,' she offers. A mirthless laugh.

I ask her, still very calmly, what she thinks is going on. To which she answers that it is all the Christmases and all the birthdays. Temper reappears and I lose it then. I punch the wall – a very Hollywood sort of gesture. Except that my soft white hand cracks and crumples against the plaster and for some time, I'm doubled up with pain. It hurts enough, but does more good than you might expect because, as my hand throbs and I stand watching Martha watching me, impassively, all the nastiness in me fizzles away. I realise why I am so angry. Because we should never have to see people we love like this.

Calmer now, I sit down at the table. Martha does the same thing, almost as an impulse. Born I suppose, painfully, of the times we sat like that with our Whisky Queers, when everything was still good and funny. 'Talk to me,' I say, softly. She is humming, and breaks off.

'I want the world to explode so I never have to talk to you again,' she says, rubbing one index finger with the other, very carefully, like stropping a knife.

'Why?'

'Because you're ugly and you're slow and you're queer.'

'What does all that mean?'

'It means I'm selling the house and I'm going with your brother.'

And what can I say to this? Why did you fuck my brother? Gus who you don't know, Gus who knows nothing of you. Should I, like a mobster in a movie, push her up against the wall: *Jew fuck my brudda?* Even newly cut and sewn, like some bloodied cactus, was Gus better than me? Pointless. I may as well ask her why she is ill. Because she just is.

'You won't sell it in time,' I point out. She shrugs.

'Got enough anyway,' she replies, childishly.

'Martha,' I start again, slowly, gently, 'Do you remember that time we sat on your floor? When we had the Indian Potato Thing?'

A pause. 'A Team,' she finally observes.

'What?'

'You said I was like the A Team. And—' she laughs, almost fondly, 'I said you were full of shit.'

'That's right!' I exclaim, inappropriately happy, like some zealous Latin teacher whose pupil has finally mastered the ablative. My pulse quickens. 'Do you remember what you asked me? What I promised you?'

'You were funny,' she offers, by way of an answer. 'When you did that voice. Robert de Niro. Used to try and not laugh. So you'd keep on doing it.'

Her face softens and without any further preamble, she starts to cry. I lean forwards to mesh my fingers with hers, over the table. She does not pull away.

'You were just lying,' she sniffs. 'You're always lying.'

'When? When I promised you? I wasn't, I never lied to you.' She starts to grip my hand in mine. 'You have to believe me. I said I'd help you if it started again. And I will. I will, Martha.'

With patient devotion, she unknots the scarf from her waist and starts to wind it around her head, until she is all scarf.

'Will you?' says her fabric-muffled voice.

'Yes.'

'Say it. Say it properly.'

'I promise you. I'll help you.'

'Not like that. Like *him*. Make me laugh.'

Shutting my mind to the absurdity of the situation I say *I prammiss you. Marta. I'll help yuz*. Wondering, all the while, if psychiatrists have to do this sort of thing on a daily basis. It fails to make Martha laugh. After a moment, she says something indistinct.

'What?'

With her free hand, she drags a portion of the scarf away from her chin. Two heavy lips protrude from the cloth as she says the word 'Frightened.'

'You don't have to be,' I assure her. 'Just stay here.'

She does not answer me. I go out to the bathroom, taking a series of deep, long breaths, making sure I feel each one at its coming-in and going-out, determined not to let my feelings make me play it wrong. I know what I have to do.

Her words to me, as I leave the room, are inconsequential, indifferent: 'You know you've got tissue paper all up your nose, don't you?'

As indeed I do – from the nosebleed in Fazakerley. Just like the very first time we met: me on the doorstep, my stuff still in the bin-bag I'd carried down from Widnes, a forgotten, stiff horn of tissue paper in each nostril, to staunch the blood which came minutes after the elation of being offered my first job; she'd let me sit in the kitchen for an hour, flirting with her – so I imagined – before she even mentioned it.

Clear the shreds of rusted paper from around my nose. Splash cold water on my face, and spray deodorant under the armpits of my T-shirt. I go through the routine, step-by-step, like a chemistry experiment. *Work methodically, without undue haste*. I'm not going to cry. I'm going to brush my teeth. On the wall of the bathroom, I notice Rory has affixed something new:

a little wrought-iron clock in the shape of a mythic sun. Ten o'clock. I'm late for work. The idea almost makes me laugh. Because I really am going to go to work – to pick up my money and tell Noakes and Fielding, face-to-face, where they can stick their job. Then I'm going to take her away.

I have trouble finding clean socks amid the clutter of my room. It's more untidy than when I left it, definitely. She's been in here, rummaging through my things. The prehistoric fish is gone from off the mantelpiece. I call the office, quickly, to stall Noakes with some short lie – don't want him sacking me before I can quit – but he seems distracted, not really interested. Keeps breaking off to shout at someone in the office, perhaps Asuncion. 'I'm just waiting for the locksmith,' I tell him. 'Then I'll be in.'

'Fine,' Noakes says, vaguely. 'Don't open that! Put it down.'

'What?'

'Nothing. What were you saying?'

I start again. Noakes interrupts me. 'Hang on a tetch,' he says. He puts the phone down – I hear him shouting in the distance. I look down at my feet. Martha comes out of the kitchen and walks down the hall straight past me, the insect-whirring of a Walkman singing out from her ears. Doesn't even look my way. 'Martha,' I call out. 'I love you, you know.' Thinking, somehow, it might *do* something, stop her in her tracks and perhaps wake her out of her gruesome dream. But it comes out all whiny and wrong, not at all heroic – more like saying she still owes me a fiver. I love you.

'Come again?' says Noakes.

I watch, wordlessly, as Martha heads back along the hallway past me, and slams the door to her room shut. Quickly, and quietly, I dial another number.

'Are you the lad I talked to before?' asks Martha's dad, sharply. He's on some building site – the sounds of industry

223

hammer in the background as I try to tell him I'm taking his daughter with me to Ireland.

His response is tired, but businesslike. 'Has she been seeing rats?' he asks, sharply.

'Well, yes. She isn't well. She's very – very odd. But it's okay. I know what's going on. I'm going to look after her.'

'Listen, son,' he says, slowly and calmly, as if I am possibly as disturbed as his own daughter. 'You're not going to take her anywhere. You can't look after her. Lock her up somewhere and wait for me. I can't be away till tonight, but I'll be down. Do you understand?'

'I'm *not* locking her up. She's a person. Stay out of it. I know what you'll do if you come and get her. She's told me all about it.'

There's a long pause. 'She makes things up you know,' he says, with deliberate solemnity.

'What about giving her electric shocks? Did she make that up?'

Another expanse of silence. 'No she didn't. I'm a builder, son. Do you understand? I build houses.'

'What's that got to do with anything?'

'I thought it would help. I didn't know how to help her. Do you understand?' He seems to share his daughter's lack of faith in being properly understood. 'I did what I thought was right.'

'Yeah? Well that's what I'm doing.'

'You take her away, son,' he says, with gentle menace, 'and I'll have you. The law will have you. The courts will have you. Do you understand?'

Slamming the phone down, I go and check on Martha. She has climbed under the duvet.

'*I* fucking love you,' she says, bitterly, into the pillow, like a banished child. '*You* don't love me. *I* love you.'

'I do,' I say, ignoring the heavy kick her words aim at my heart. 'I want you to come with me.'

'Sod off. I want to go to Ireland.'

'We're *going* there. I just need to get my money first. Come on.' I shake one of her protruding legs and, in response, she shakes her head – the fringes of the scarf wiggle petulantly.

'I'm tired,' she says.

'So am I.'

'Get your money,' she says. 'Honey.'

I sigh. This is impossible. I think about dragging her from the bed. But she's a strong woman. Even if I got her out of bed, out of the flat, how could I keep a firm grip on her all the way to Pendennis and back again?

'Look—' I start a different tack. 'If I get the money – will you wait for me?'

'*Yes*,' she says, indignantly. 'Arsehole. Where else am I going to go?'

Thus reassured, I waggle her motionless foot by way of a farewell and close her door behind me.

'I'm not staying here!' she shouts, as I'm walking back down the hall. I hear a thud as she leaps up from the bed. I swivel round just in time to see her opening the bedroom door. Before I'm aware of it, I've slammed the door shut and am holding on to the handle with all my strength. She pulls, I pull. The door opens a wedge as she gains the advantage, then shuts as I pull back. I hear her grunting with the exertion. 'You bastard!' she shouts, as my hands begin to burn.

I hate myself for admitting it, but what her dad said was right. I could get back and find her dangling off the balcony again. I've got to keep her here, and safe. For her sake. Just until I can get the money.

'Just relax!' I suggest, uselessly, turning the little brass key in the lock and pocketing it. I wait for her to shout 'Bastard' again, for a battery of fists against the door, but she is silent, because someone else she loved has just locked her up.

225

Asuncion, I suspect, as I meet her on the office stairs, has some remarkably sophisticated surveillance equipment at her disposal. Since we first met, she has come to regard me as some sort of ally in the pursuit of woe, possibly because I'm the only person too polite to ignore her. She corners me now, her bucket and brush in her arms, to tell me there has been an explosion at a petrochemical plant in a remote region of Northern Portugal. 'Berry terrible. Many men burn,' she says, in the manner of someone contemplating hot bacon sandwiches, or a soft, warm bed.

I smile politely. I'm on automatic again – a ramrod of restraint passing right up my arse to the top of my head – stiff, frozen. *Go through with it.*

'Tooth?' Minty asks me, as I come in to the main office. She holds the phone against her neck. And then, in furtherance to my frown, she adds, 'Floyd Tooth. "A Firm Hand for Rosie"? He hasn't received his report.'

'It's pending,' I say. 'Charlie Watts has had a . . . family crisis.'

Minty looks vexed. 'Well how long? He's getting like, seriously stressed out.'

I pause. Nothing could seem less relevant, at that moment, than the matter of Mr Tooth's stress levels.

'I expect he's got a few ways of relieving himself. Just tell him to get on with it.'

I'm not sure this was such a good idea, coming in. It calls for pleasantry. Composure. Reserves of patience and tolerance – which I just don't have. I'm full of a crazy, twitching sort of power; the Voices, on Angel Dust.

I hadn't expected to see Fielding there at all, not now, but he's come and, instead of lounging at his desk, paring fingernails or doing crosswords, he's bent over a manuscript, glasses affixed to the very tip of his nose and a pair of flashy elasticated arm-bands around his Jermyn Street elbows. 'Picture of an editor what?' he says to me, with no trace of embarrassment, as I stalk in there, the words of my resignation oratory dividing and multiplying between my tongue and my teeth. Noakes, at the other end of the desk, gives a little harumph. 'Been rather lax lately,' Fielding carries on. 'Time to start running this like a proper business. That's what I say.'

I look over at Noakes, who is now nodding, approvingly. 'We wanted a word, Strange-oh,' he says. *Strange-oh?* 'I'm extremely pleased with your progress.'

'So am I,' Fielding chips in, eagerly. 'Fastest evaluator we've ever had.'

I blush, honourably, thinking of the Tragic Pile, all the manuscripts I couldn't bear to tackle, now secreted in various unvisited corners of the office. And wondering what sort of an honour it is, to have some pack of rats elect you King Rat. 'I'm—' I start to speak, but Noakes holds aloft a silencing hand.

'No no,' he says, in a grandfatherly tone. 'None of that Pommie modesty here.' He goes on to say that they are going to promote me, to reward my responsible attitude with yet more responsibility. And more money. My ground-breaking ideas for the cover of the haemorrhoids book have delighted the author and, in honour of that, I am henceforth to be known as Senior Production Manager.

One-eyed, crack-crazy scallies on the last bus have offered me fights which I have received with greater enthusiasm than this. 'You've got it all wrong,' I say, sternly.

'Hogan's ghost!' Noakes declares, mysteriously. 'Stop putting yourself down. You're a sight more sensible than most of the young galahs out there in the pubs. Sight more sensible than I was at your age, to be fair with you.'

I make a noise to suggest that this could never be possible. A deep, careless contempt for Noakes and Fielding is rising in my gullet like morning bile. It's the last ever day of school again. But this time, no handshakes and platitudes for Strange, A. This time, the truth will out.

Noakes shakes his head. 'I was bloody crackers when I was your age. Totally mad. I tell you, right. I went to university, okay? And I did GEOGRAPHY! Imagine that? Turned me mum's hair white.'

I fancy that Fielding just emitted a soft groan, but I can't be sure. I get no chance to reply, because Jo comes in.

'Mr Sammaddi's on the phone?'

Fielding and Noakes cast each other a nervous glance. Noakes puts a paternal hand on my shoulder, easing me out of the room. 'If you can just give us a moment, Strange-oh,' he says.

'I quit,' I say, loudly and clearly, a flush of anger forming on my cheeks.

Noakes looks at me quizzically. 'No need for that sort of language,' he says, mildly. 'You're management now. No cursing.' And before I know what's happened, the door closes in my face.

For want of anything better to do, and to provide some distraction from the series of low, conspiratorial murmurs coming from the inner office, I go and sit at my desk and flip skittishly through the folders. Willing time to move on so I can be away from here. My official task for today, had I chosen to fulfil it, would have been the third edit of a book entitled 'Drama Exercises For Youth Groups', featuring a host of situations which might, just might have been challenging to a few rather sheltered boys and girls back in the twenties.

The author is furious with us. '*When I saw the latest proofs of my book,*' she writes, '*I became depressed.*' She then furnishes us with a twenty-four-page list of precisely the things that have made her depressed.

Introduction, Page ii, line 43: 'The author is a devout Mormon', not 'Moron'.

   Pages 1, 2, 3, 4, etc. – end (see text): standardise leader dots. The International Federation of English-language Proof-readers recommends three dots as standard. Your editor has, throughout this book, used between two and eight. I can only assume that Pendennis Press is pursuing some kind of anti-IFEP agenda.

And, like her, I become depressed. I glance at the clock. 10.45. The door shows no sign of opening. Twitches and shudders in my shins counsel me to forget the speeches and the P45s. Remember Martha, back in her room. What if she panics? Tries to climb out of the window? Kicks the door down and runs to the Himalayas? I need to calm down. I mustn't blow it now. If I can just give it a few minutes more. How long can Mr Sammaddi possibly want to talk to them?

Thinking of the weeping Indian, something strikes me. That my leaving, however rudely I do it, will not hurt them. They will replace me, probably with a further Sloane, and merely carry on as before. That isn't enough. But there *is* a way. Something I can do. A way I could hurt them, on my behalf, on Tara's, and for all the broken, cheated souls out there on the Tragic Pile. Sowing the seeds as I do it for future and great calamity. It will only take a few minutes. Then I can go – not happy, certainly. But having *done* something.

So I swallow the rush of impulses boiling up inside me, trap my tongue shut painfully between my teeth and stare at the final proof of 'Drama Exercises' on my computer screen. 'Who's editing "Cherry Gizzard"?' I ask, quietly.

'No one?' says Jo. 'It was, like, supposed to be Tara?'

I lean over to Tara's desk and scan the mayhem. There, amid the back issues of *Company* and the sweet wrappers, sits Yelevadze's folder. I reach for it.

I'm just completing the revenge of Strange when the door to the office finally re-opens, and a fraught-looking Noakes comes out.

'Can we have a word?' he asks me.

'I wouldn't mind a word too,' I say, with what I hope is an element of threat. Time to go. I switch the machine off and stand, smoothing my trousers down in preparation for the conversation to come.

Noakes locks the door behind me. Fielding is pacing about with his jacket off. I look warily from one man to the other. Could they know what I was just doing?

'Strange-oh,' says Noakes, squeezing his testicles like the last of a tube of cheese spread. I guess he's given up on the earlobes. 'We've just had a call.'

'More of a rocket up the arse,' says Fielding.

Noakes shoots up a silencing hand. 'He's joking!'

I try a laugh. Meanwhile, the spirits of the Kalderash send hot chilli whispers up the marrow of my bones: *Punch them in their fat, greedy bellies! Tear the yellow folders of fraud from their moorings in the wall! Invite them to eat shit and die!*

'I don't care about your phone call,' I say, boldly. 'I quit. Give me my money.'

'Okay,' says Noakes, with mystifying simplicity.

'What?'

'I said okay. Go back to your choc-ices if that's what you want. But first, we need you to do a little job for us.'

'It's a *very* little sort of job,' says Fielding. 'Tiny, really.'

'He's right. It's a tiny job. Barely a job at all. More of a jaunt. A little outing, call it.'

'What?' I ask – I hope, a little stonily.

Noakes and Fielding look at one another, like two grubby boys lacking an excuse. Noakes reaches beneath his chair and hands me one of the grey, badgerskin briefcases. It's bulky and heavy, crackles as I squeeze it.

'This may sound a little erm . . . off, as it were, but we need you to take this to a hotel . . .'

'*An* hotel, dear boy,' interrupts Fielding, tapping a little dictionary on the table.

'Quite, quite. Take this to an hotel and er . . . give it to someone.'

'What's in it?' I ask.

'Papers,' says Fielding.

'Books,' says Noakes, at the same time. They glance at each other. I undo the buckles on the briefcase and look inside. It is cash. A great deal of dollars. I ask them, reasonably, what is going on.

Noakes does his best to explain that the Indian gentleman who visited the other day has just telephoned from his hotel. Subsequent to information received, from sources unknown, the Indian has, according to Noakes, discovered 'things'.

'What things?'

'Well. Things about the way we do things,' says Noakes.

'That the way we do things is perhaps a little radical,' adds Fielding, now unashamedly smoking a cigarette, 'in terms of the way other people might do things.'

'Exactly,' says Noakes. 'Well said, Benno. Pendennis Press is in the business of breaking boundaries and you can't break boundaries without erm . . . breaking other things.'

I put the briefcase on the table and stand up. 'You're being blackmailed because Mister Sammaddi has discovered some- how that Sarah Gaskell isn't dead. She doesn't and has never existed. He's discovered the whole thing is a fraud. And you're a pair of crooks.'

It is a fair and brave summary of events. I think I am expecting the two men to wither and die in front of me, shrivelled in the white-heat of truth, like those old cancerous noses you sometimes see on the Australian soaps.

They seem fairly affable about it all.

'That's about the face of it,' agrees Fielding.

'Yep,' says Noakes. 'Fair cop.' He pops the final segment of a Bounty Bar into his mouth.

'So why should I help you?' I ask.

'Because we'll give you money,' says Noakes. And he flashes me a number of fifties, tossing them on to the table. A thick wad. Enough to set me and Martha up for ever. I reach for them. Quick as a lizard, his thick hand pulls them back.

'I don't want that stuff,' I say, nobly. 'I just want my wages.'

'Tough titty,' observes Fielding. 'Make the drop. It'll only take you half an hour. And we'll pay you.'

'Or fuck off now,' adds Noakes, genially. 'And see what you get.'

19

The Midnight Lounge of the Masada Hotel, W12, has none of the atmosphere of midnight, but a fair spattering of Masada. Its carpets are blood-red, its walls the colour of curry. The bar, inexplicably, features as its crowning glory a series of agricultural implements, a collection in which scythes, prongs and blades are prominent. It is, in short, quite possible to imagine a massacre taking place here.

It took me an age to find the place. Noakes, pressing the heavy grey briefcase into my hand, told me it was on Bat Man Street, and appeared to be deadly serious. So, for half an hour, I trudged around the Goldhawk Road area, being skitted in cafés and kebab joints as I asked for directions. Finally a Ugandan taxi-driver, suspecting me to be some bewildered new arrival, and possibly remembering his own bewilderment, took me on a two-hundred-yard trip, left off the Askew Road, into Bateman Street. Some wag had removed the E from the roadsign.

At the reception desk, I was scowled at by one of those cheerless East End girls, with skin like a sore elbow. She instantly suspected me of trying to oppress her.

'I'm here to see Amjit Sammaddi,' I said.

'I'll page him,' she said, warily, reaching for the phone, but watching me all the time in case I made a sudden lunge for her breasts.

I waited. A clan of Glaswegians came up to the desk and conducted a lengthy debate concerning their mini-bar. She was delightful to them. When they finally left, happy in the knowledge that twelve chilled cans of Jaguar Lager would await their return, she wished them a pleasant day. I allowed myself a soft clearing of the throat. She glared at me as if the passage of phlegm had maybe carried some sinister innuendo behind it. 'You can always wait in the Midnight Lounge, sir,' she said. Pronouncing 'sir' as you might 'shagsack'.

In the bar, I put the briefcase between my feet and grip it with my ankles. I haul myself on to a torture device, the seat a leatherette olive skewered on a steel cocktail stick. With my every movement, it lets out squeaks and groans, like a series of sturdy farts. I order a whisky. No point buying a pint. I'll be in and out in minutes. Like Fielding said. A simple drop.

The barman resembles some kind of part-time executioner. A young man with just a faint fuzz of white blond hair – like the early Action Man – and a beetling forehead which reminds me of the Cape of Good Hope. He eyes me for a long while as I sip at my drink. I smile at him – which turns out to be a fairly bad move.

'Ey – man. Do you play any sports?' he demands, suddenly, in an impenetrable South African accent. *Ju pleni spawts*.

'Well,' I say. 'You know . . .'

He warms to this remark.

'The two sports I have mainly enjoyed since being here,' he recites carefully, as if from some autocue just beyond my head, 'are cricket, and water polo.' *Kruk uten war dap aylay.* It seems to be his chat-up line. Just what I need. Half an hour to rescue Martha and I end up being seduced by some Afrikaaner body-fascist.

'From South Africa?'

He spits on to the floor of his bar. 'Fuck no!' *Fac nay.* 'I'm from Zimbabwe.'

He introduces himself as Ray. His friends, he says, call him Cosmic, meaning, I suspect, that I can too. He is living in a house in Dollis Hill, he tells me, along with some forty-eight other Zimbabweans, South Africans, Kiwis and Australians. They each pay five pounds a week rent, he says. It seems damned steep to me.

'It's great in the house, man,' Cosmic Ray insists. 'We've got a whole fridge full of beer.' *Ole fruj.*

'Nice,' I say, casting a glance towards the door. Mr Sammaddi is nowhere to be seen.

Cosmic Ray leans in a little closer, more insistent. 'I don't mean just a couple of four packs,' he says, threateningly, as if I might, silently, be thinking him capable of such foppery.

'Perish the thought,' I say, easing away a little. He smiles.

'I mean full of beer.' He pauses, gazes lyrically into the distance. 'Man,' he sighs, 'I love being pissed. I just LOVE it!'

Rising from my stool, I say that they certainly go about their drinking in military fashion, the Zimbabwe boys. Cosmic Ray grabs me by the wrist then, painfully, professionally, like one with A levels in torture. 'Hey!' he says. 'Let me tell you about military drinking, man.' *Lemi telyu.*

He proceeds to tell me, tightening his grip on my wrist, that he had once been an army doctor out on the Angolan border. Work being long, and breaks being scarce, the established recreation was for a party of four or five doctors to attach themselves to glucose drips, and commence playing poker, accompanied by a crate of Angolan cane spirit. As one passed out, it was the duty of his neighbour to open up the glucose drip thus ensuring a speedy awakening, in time for yet more poker, and cane spirit.

Even I, no stranger to the dark side, think this a little bleak. 'Sounds jolly,' I say. He releases my wrist. I tell him I have to go.

'See you just now, man,' he says, companionably, crunching a piece of ice.

*

235

The receptionist has vanished. I hang about the lobby, staring at the cork tiles, listening to the xylophone music which seems to come cheesily from their pores. Is this all going to work? Suddenly I have a feeling I'm being watched – about to be arrested.

I ring the bell. No one comes. This is ridiculous. I glimpse a blur of blue and silver over by the door. Someone tall, in uniform. *The police!* But it isn't. It's a porter. I wipe my forehead with a corner of my shirt. I look all around the lobby. By the potted palms, the graceful black porter stands hands on hips like a ballet dancer, staring directly out of the glass doors. I go close to him and follow his gaze. On the forecourt, the poisonous receptionist is talking to some uniformed official with fluorescent stripes around his jacket. I pass out between the sliding doors, on to the forecourt.

'*Do it!*' At first, I think it's the whisky. I maybe misheard. But then it comes again. Right from the upper reaches of my bowel. Not *leg it*. Not *do one*. *Do it!* The little briefcase knocks shyly against my knees, seeming to urge them on.

The air outside, under the grandiose awning, is choked with exhaust fumes. Two men are loading a stretcher into the back of an ambulance whose engine keeps up a threatening hum. Its siren is off, but the light spins around still, casting shafts of blue on the eerie scene, every few seconds. I look at the stretcher, see only a pair of smart, unscuffed soles. The rest covered with the sort of gory, danger-red blanket favoured by emergency staff.

'I think the boy is dead,' says a small, satisfied voice at my elbow.

I look down. Asuncion is standing next to me, clad in a dark blue apron which carries the emblem of the Masada Hotel. Her doggy little eyes shine with wonder.

'Who is it?'

She shrugs, frowns a little. Why do such trivial details matter, she seems to say. All that matters, surely, is it's death. Death is here, among us, like a cousin. Glorious, victorious, all-levelling death. *Muerte*.

'What happened?' I suspect this might be a more fruitful line of enquiry. The briefcase grows heavier all the time in my hand. I shift it to my armpit, where the bony handle goads my flesh. Asuncion stares at me in sudden fascination.

'Jew working here too? *Te despedieron*?'

'Eh?'

'Jew got sack from Pendennis?'

'No. I'm just . . .'

'They *should* give jew sack. Jew no editor. Jew a *burro*. Always throwing away all the best books. Hiding under jour desk many beautiful stories. Sad stories, *poemas*. Berry bad. I take them home for reading.'

The stretcher is stowed and the men make to lock the doors. Asuncion nods delightedly at the ambulance.

'The *Indio*.'

'Mr Sammaddi? What happened to him?'

'I clean room. He no drink – berry clean boy. Today – two bottles whisky, brandy, don't know. *Muy triste* . . .'

'What?'

'Berry upset – after coming back from jew. So I am bringing him many folders from Mister Nowaak, for reading. To make him happy. *Muchas cartas* . . . many letters . . . *de Señora Gaskell*. But he is not becoming happy. Two bottles. *Muerte*.'

She turns to me – her black eyes aflame with some spooky charge. She pulls out her tongue and croaks, in perfect, awesome, haunting imitation of a death rattle. And I do it.

I am running faster than I knew I could run, down on to the Goldhawk Road, in giant strides which jar my knees with every landing, the briefcase, it seems, like an outboard motor, alternately pushing and pulling me as it swings in my arm. People around me scatter as I come haring out; outside a bookmaker's someone shouts as I knock them, but there is no time to say sorry. I leap out into the road, trying to save time, to be closer to the tube station and a moped flies at me like a violent wasp swerving with a squeal. I am safe. Martha will be safe. We will be safe together, I think, as, in a fanfare of horns, I am knocked to the ground and the air rushes out of me with a shout. The briefcase skitters across the harsh tarmac of the road, away from my grasp. Like Ireland, I think, curiously, as for no good reason at all, night falls.

I am watching the world in Mincer-Vision. Every image, every thought comes, not as a whole, but a series of wiry strands, that make no sense and hurt as they go on through. I catch on to things, but that's worse. They have barbs which snag like stitches.

A strange, almond-eyed creature with gentle hands brushes my forehead with something then retreats into the shadows. Some odd tribesman I tell myself – Komi, Mari, Karakalpak or plain old Kalmuck. Where the arses am I? In a yurt?

'You're okay,' whispers the voice of John Thomas Long-fellow Lamb. 'Go to sleep.'

I obey him, because he seems to have a definite authority. But all I can dream of is sudden, fierce pain in ribs and shoulders. Shouting voices. Hands lifting me into the sky. The back of a van that smells of old carpets. More pain.

I open my eyes, expecting light to assault them with scissors, but it doesn't. I am somewhere in the darkness. I feel light, weightless. There is choral singing. *I'm dead!*

'Do you want another pillow?' asks a softly passing cherub. It perches lightly, with a flutter of wings, on the end of my body. Fearfully, I crane my neck to gaze at it. 'You shouldn't really move about too much,' says Lamb, idly paring one tapered fingernail with another.

'Lamb?' I gape in astonishment. 'What's going on?'

'Well I ran you over,' says Lamb, simply.

'Why?'

239

He laughs gently.

'It wasn't *deliberate*, Strange. You just ran out in front of me. I don't know what was the matter with you. You didn't seem to notice me at all.'

With superhuman effort, I try to piece together the events that preceded this peculiar interlude in the Everafter. I remember being in a hotel. With money. Running away. Where?

Oh Christ! Martha!

I shoot bolt upright and a dense, dragging pain all over assures me that I am well and truly alive – covered in blankets on the sofa in Lamb's flat. I look around me in distraction. 'I had a—' And I am gripped with a paroxysm of coughing. Lamb pushes me gently back on to the pillows. 'Where is it?' I croak.

'I picked it up,' he says. 'It's in the kitchen. That *is* what you're worried about, isn't it? Your money?'

'It isn't mine.'

Lamb laughs. 'You don't say.'

'I mean – it is. I was stealing it. For Martha.'

The memory of Martha blips up like rotten gas from a muddy field. That's why I was running over the road, to unlock the door and take her away. I try to sit up again, but this time, waves of nausea crash down.

'Relax,' says Lamb, firmly. 'You're not going anywhere for a while.'

Hopelessly, I flop back and let the sickness pass.

'You're very lucky,' Lamb tells me. 'If I hadn't got you in the back of the van you'd probably be under arrest or something.'

A brief, vivid memory of old carpets and a dirty corrugated floor flicks across my mind. I *was* in a van.

'What van?'

'It's my new job,' Lamb explains, blandly. 'I deliver carpets.'

I don't know why I am surprised. What else could Lamb do? He failed most of his O levels, and all of his A levels, a slow boy with a scratchy pen, unable to finish a single sheet of paper in

240

an hour. And I know why. Not that Lamb seems to mind. He has the permanent detachment of a buddha, dazed even, smiling warmly with those red lips at the thin air, as if he's found his energy, pushed it in all the right directions, and now wants nothing at all.

At least, he doesn't want any of my stolen dollars. A crazy idea strikes me that if I pay him, he might let me out of here. Lamb doesn't seem surprised at the offer. His reaction suggests that he's always thought anything possible. 'Everything will work out,' he says. 'Really, Strange, I don't want your money. Just go to sleep.'

Suddenly, all this enforced Eastern tranquillity begins to irritate me. I *won't* sleep, I think, like some wilful child hearing the sounds of a grown-up barbecue in the garden. I've got to get back to Martha. Lamb doesn't understand. 'Get off my sodding feet, Lamb!' I shout, twisting and writhing under the blankets. 'I've got to get back to Fulham.'

'Your feet, Strange, wouldn't get you as far as the landing, whether I was sitting on them or not. So just be cool.'

Just my fucking luck. When I need to be in Fulham, I end up in Islington with some transvestite buddha sitting on my broken feet and ordering me to be cool. I sigh, crossly, then glance around the room.

'Where's Jill?' Jill, it strikes me, is my only hope now. Ten minutes of me being obnoxious on her sofa and she'll carry me to Fulham herself.

'Still at the drop-in centre. She'll be back soon.'

'Drop-in centre?'

'There's a lesbian drop-in centre place on Clerkenwell Green.' Lamb smiles at some distant memory. 'That's how I met her, actually. Used to run the coffee bar there.'

So very Jill. To make a play for the only man working in a lesbian drop-in centre. Novelty value.

'Are you still going to have babies?' I ask, cautiously, trying,

241

as I've heard hostages do, to distract my captor with chatter. *Look away, Lamb*, I think to myself, *just for a second, and I'll be out the shagging door.* 'You were going off to give sperm, weren't you?'

Lamb rocks with silent laughter for a moment. 'It was *mad*,' he confides, leaning across to me. 'They stick you in this cubicle. Not a room. I mean just a curtain around it. And you know they've all got blokes in them. You can *hear* them for Christ's sake!' He smooths out my blankets with nurse-like professionalism. 'Anyway, they give you this little pot. It's like an ink-pot. I mean. I said – how'm I going to get it in there? They said – oh, we'll get you some magazines. I said no, I mean . . . Well you know. It just sort of shoots out, doesn't it?'

Lamb seems surprised by this basic function. But then, I guess he spent his adolescence rather differently to me.

'In the end, I got Jill to come in and stand a few feet away to try and catch it. She was *livid*!'

I laugh, in spite of myself, in spite of the fierce pain it causes me, at the thought of Jill standing like some eager mid-leg fielder in a hall full of wanking men. To catch the seed of her lesbian lover in an ink-pot as it flew into space. If only I'd known that was going to happen when I went out with her.

Then, as the pain of the laughing ebbs away, there is silence. Lamb rises. 'We've had to sort of put things on a back burner for a bit,' he says. 'Till we can get some more money together.'

'I'm sorry. If I'd known—'

'No.' He raises a placatory hand. 'It wasn't your fault.' He turns and pads off into the kitchenette.

It's now or it's never. Lamb hums something to himself as the kettle begins to boil in the little kitchenette. I shrug the heavy blankets off and swing my legs round – a moment rewarded with pains which extend to the crown of my skull. On trembling wrists, I lever myself up and stand. To my surprise, both feet are in place. They feel slightly woolly, as if encased in several thermal socks. I take my first step, become jelly, and crash to the floor, rendering a bamboo coffee table into naught. 'You don't understand!' I shout urgently, as a stricken Lamb extricates me from the matchstick chaos and pulls me to my feet. 'I've locked her in her room! I've got to get her out before her dad comes!'

'What do you mean?' asks Lamb, patiently as, with perplexing strength, he resists the desperate blows which rain down on him and lifts me back on to the sofa. In jabbering bursts, I tell him about the call I made to Martha's dad.

'When did you call him?'

'This morning. Before I went to work. He said he couldn't get away until the evening. He'll take her back to that hopsital. I know he will.' Like someone in the grip of fever, I cling on to his wrists, urgently. 'You've got to drive me there. NOW.'

Lamb shakes his head, regretfully.

'Strange,' he says, patiently, 'that was *yesterday*. It's the next day. It's eleven o'clock in the morning. Look.' He extricates himself from my grip to go and draw the curtains back. Crisp autumn daylight floods in. And as it penetrates every corner of the room, so a terrible, sickly understanding descends on my head. I am filled with loss, which seeps out in throbs of pain. *She will be gone by now. Taken, helpless, to that place. And she'll never forgive me.*

'I promised her—' I start to say. My voice cracks. All that former strength, just gone – a thin sheet of ice. I bury my face in my hands. Suddenly, Lamb is at my side again, perched, weightless, on some minuscule ledge of the sofa. An arm across my shoulders – so light.

'When she's better, she'll realise. You were trying to keep your promise. But you couldn't. For the same reasons you made it.'

I like that – even caught up in the throes of self-pity, his words strike me as neat and admirable. Why couldn't *I* have

243

put it like that? I could never have kept that promise for the very same reasons I made it. Because I loved her.

'But what if she doesn't ever realise?'

'You just can't think like that. You have to do what you think is right. If she forgives you, then it's okay. If she doesn't, then, well, you did what you could.'

'What I had to.'

'If you like. Yeah.'

He slips away to the kitchen and returns, moments later, with a steaming mug. It's heavier than his slender wrists can bear – he trembles as he delivers it to me. The liquid is hot and brackish. I make a face as I sip it.

'Is this some hippy shit?'

Lamb makes a slightly impatient murmur.

'It's just tea. I put thingies in it. Co-Proxamol. Jill gets them for her—'

'I know. I remember,' I say, taking another draught. 'I used to nick them.'

'She said.'

A strong, but unalarming warmth floods over me, as I drink more of the loaded tea. Lurking fatigue, freed from its bonds, clambers on to my chest, and everything is odd again.

'Does she talk about me much?' I ask Lamb, suddenly, as I let my head fall into the welcoming embrace of the pillows.

'Not if she can help it, Strange,' says Lamb. I nod, peaceably, as if this is the most reassuring thing he could have said.

Everything's all alright. For ever and for ever and for ever, says a voice that's like Lamb's, but also like the voices in my bones. *Shut your eyes.*

But when I next open my eyes, seemingly just seconds later, everything is not alright. Not at all. And I have a strong, scary sense that it never will be. There's no sign of Lamb. I call out his name hoarsely. 'We're in the bath,' shouts Jill, slightly irritably, from behind a door I had always assumed to be a broom cupboard. 'What's the matter?'

I shake a vivid image of Jill and Lamb, plus soap suds, from my mind and stand, shakily, but without passing out. With a grunt for each footstep, I hop into the kitchen. It's one o'clock. Grabbing the grey briefcase from the tiny formica work-top, I unbuckle it and scatter a thick, random tribute of the dollars out across the kitchen. Then, shoving the remainder tightly under my arm, I hobble on feet of fire out of the flat.

Half of one trouser leg flaps in the breeze like a pendant as I limp towards the Angel. My shin, grazed to jam, is exposed to the chilly air. I am covered in dried blood and dirt. I don't know where I think I'm going. I don't care. I am trying to hold on to the last fragments of the codeinated dream I was having before I woke.

She was in it. Martha at the table. Laughing down the aisles of the Tesco, knocking against my shoulders, wrapped in my coat. Wrapped in me, in bed, her lips tucked as she slept, in the little hollow at the foot of my neck. Never again.

The journey back to Fulham is torturous and slow, matching my own movements. Someone under a train at Goodge Street. Signal failure at Westminster. Changing at Victoria, the whole station seems filled with the odour of frying bacon and there's a gaping chasm at the centre of my body which is far from spiritual. I'm starving hungry. I inch my way along on the District Line platform for a while, ignoring it. But every other commuter is, inexplicably, tucking into some overladen sandwich or pungent burger. I never knew that a major side-effect of having six tons of transit van up your arse would be a raging hunger.

The station tannoy announces severe delays on the District Line. Wearily, I inch my way back along the platform to the stairs in painful pursuit of a taxi. Mounting the steps, I glimpse a minor altercation taking place at the top. A willowy creature in black chiffon is standing at the centre of a knot of behatted inspectors, talking with some agitation. One of the men is making notes in a little notebook. 'I didn't *know*,' she is declaiming, as I draw near. 'You can't blame a girl for not knowing. You can smoke on the underground in Paris!'

'Vivien?'

The woman stops talking and looks at me in surprise.

'Good Lord,' she says, breaking into a girlish laugh. 'Whatever happened to you?'

I point to myself, by way of a cryptic answer, and shrug. 'What's going on?'

Vivien casts a hateful glance at the men around her. 'These *beastly* little Nazis are trying to prosecute me. Just for lighting a cigarette.'

'Are you going to pay or not?' asks one of the inspectors, irritably.

Vivien gives an exasperated sigh. 'How many times do I have to explain? I'm cash poor. Temporarily embarrassed. Otherwise I'd be in a taxi, wouldn't I?'

'Then you'll have to come with us, madam.'

Vivien gulps, and looks at me. *What the hell*, I think, grimly, fumbling with the briefcase. Who am I saving it for now?

After I've paid Vivien's fine and the men have dispersed in search of a bureau de change, she insists on taking my phone number. So she can 'thank me properly' she says, ominously. 'It's been a frightful morning,' she confides. 'Three hours up Bond Street and all I found was this.' From a glossy bag, she draws forth a tiny, diaphanous slip of material. 'It's for Tara,' she says. And in the face of my raised eyebrows, her own sparkling eyes cloud over.

'How is she?'

Vivien looks uncomfortable. '*Livid*. Positively purple with it. Says she's going off to India and no one can stop her. I'm just on my way to the hospital now. Try and make her see sense.'

'Hospital? What's happened?'

'Oh no no, Silly. There's nothing wrong with Tara. It's that ridiculous Raja she's always had a thing about. Did you meet him? He writes terrible poems.'

'Mr Sammaddi? I thought he was dead.'

'Mm? Good gracious me no.' She gives my arm a spidery brush which makes me wince in pain. 'Sorry. Just poisoned himself with cheap rum, the silly arse.'

'And Tara's with him?'

Vivien nods. 'Pelted off there the minute she heard. Says he's asked her to marry him. And she's accepted. Poor child says she's in love. As if she knew anything about love.'

'And you do?'

Vivien looks at me in much the way her daughter looked when she first learned about my love of TV. 'I *was* going to tell you I've always believed in the kindness of Strangers,' she says icily. 'But now I'm not so sure.'

And she turns from me theatrically, drifting, ghost-like through the barriers, her scent a slip-stream on the fried-food winds of the ticket hall. I watch her go for a moment, my fingers crossed. Not for Vivien. For Tara. She can go East if she wants. I hope she does, and, for what it's worth, revolutionises our understanding of knots while she's there. She helped me unpick a few.

At the entrance to our mansion-block, I pass a broad-shouldered man in his fifties, carrying a heavy box. I hold the door open for him. 'Cheers,' he says, smiling at me through his sweat. 'Could do without this.' Not a London voice – not designed for speaking to strangers. This is a Northerner. I watch him cross the road with the box – over to a high red van – his strong back sweating through the check shirt.

Martha's room is bare, the door crudely levered open, bed stripped, the walls dotted with tell-tale spots of Blue-Tac in place of the horses and the kids and Gus' map. A small pile of rubbish, screwed-up pieces of paper, cardboard packaging from hand lotions and spot creams and lip balms, sits in a corner beneath the window-sill. The carpet is still flecked with Deirdre's shit, her feathers, Martha's hair and, in the middle of the room, a little pyramid of talcum powder.

As I come out of Martha's room, I run smack into Rory, who is dressed in a tasselled night-robe, and attempting to move a large, ornately framed painting of some cubes into the kitchen. 'Alastair!' he exclaims, as if I've just emerged from a crack in the earth. 'How BRILLIANT!'

I push past him and limp out of the flat, down the stairs, light-headed now with the pain, my forehead filmed in clammy sweat. I pass the man again – Martha's father, it must be. He's wiping the bald spot on his head with a handkerchief.

'Only one more trip!' he says, pleasantly, as I hobble out, over the road, to the van parked next to the post-box.

Martha is sitting in the front passenger seat, still wrapped in my overcoat and leaning her head against the glass, creating a little patch of steam around her. Her eyes are open. She isn't smiling. She looks at me, but still seems to end her gaze in the thin air just before me. I tap on the window. Her eyes roll. I try feverishly to open the door – it's locked. So is the other side. I pass round to the front of the van and bang on the bonnet with both hands. 'Martha! It's me!'

Slowly, she turns her head and sees me. Deliberately, as if all the air around her is glue, she lets her tongue poke out of her lips for a second, focusing cross-eyed on the tip of her nose, strains with the effort of holding it out, holds it there until it wobbles and then lets it slip back. The tiniest grin scissors faint fjords at the sides of her nose. Then she turns her head on to the cold glass of the window and won't look again.

'Martha! Wake up!' I shout, hammering again on the van.

'She'll be very sleepy now,' says a deep voice next to me. I swivel round in alarm and stare into a pair of mauve-tinted Lennon glasses in a white-bearded face. I take the figure in – a stocky, middle-aged man in a Grateful Dead T-shirt; he looks like someone who took the bad acid at Woodstock and never quite came back.

'Who the hell are you?'

His smiling face screws up in sudden distraction as his tongue seeks out some trace of flavour in a recess of his mouth. He sucks, gently. 'Cardamom,' he pronounces, beaming beatifically at me. 'One of nature's finest little pods, wouldn't you say?' And when I say nothing, only stare, he grasps my good hand in a greasy paw and pumps it vigorously. 'Rourke. Doctor,' he continues. 'Who are you?'

I pull my hand away from him roughly. 'Given her a shot of something have you?'

Dr Rourke gives his mighty nest of silver hair a sad shake. 'I don't give anybody shots of anything, son,' he says, patiently. 'That's not the way I do things.'

'So why's she like that?' I say, pointing accusingly at the moribund bundle that is Martha.

'Because we've been up all night with the child. Getting her ready. She didn't want to come.'

'Funny that,' I observe, nastily. 'I'd have thought she could hardly wait to get those electrodes on her head again.'

'That won't be happening ever again,' says Martha's dad, coming over to us with a final boxload of bric-à-brac. 'She's going to Dr Rourke's.'

'I've got a special centre,' the doctor explains. 'Up in Scarborough. No drugs. No shocks. Just sea air and herbs.'

'Herbs?'

'Herbs and vegetables. Turnips, cauliflowers – that sort of thing. It works.'

Martha's dad nods. I can only give a sceptical snort.

'If you don't believe me, come out and see her in a few weeks,' suggests the psychedelic doctor, twisting a little yin-yang round his neck.

Martha's dad nods again as he starts to pull on his coat – a heavy, waxed jacket – and fumbles for his keys.

'I wouldn't be saying it if I hadn't seen it myself,' he says. 'Do you understand me? I just build houses. But it works.' He looks at me eagerly, willing me, it seems, to approve. But when he receives only a chilly silence, he relents, with a final shrug. 'Anyhow. We've left you the address.'

'I've a feeling she'll be wanting to see you,' adds the doctor, with a slightly inappropriate son-of-a-sea-dog sort of wink. 'The tincture of turnip has some funny side-effects.'

'Soon have you there, girl,' I hear Martha's dad say, as he climbs into the driver's seat.

'But—' I observe, feebly.

Dr Rourke gives my sore arm a companionable squeeze as he

heads round to the passenger door. 'I've a wee book coming out. Just been accepted. Give it a read. Then you'll understand.'

Martha's dad starts up the engine and the truck swings out into the road. I move to avoid it. Briefly, he pauses to wind the window down. 'You tried your best, lad,' he says. 'And I don't blame you for it. Do you understand me? You're a good man.'

After the truck has fed its way into the roaring traffic joining the Great West Road, I turn, slowly, and head back into the flat. Sucked, inexplicably, to the things which make me saddest, I go and look in at Martha's room again. Too many cheesy episodes of *Hotel* lead me to fancy she might have left something for me in there. A note or token. Even a sock would do. But it's just a room. Soon to be someone else's London cupboard. Stuffed, in between the bed and the wall, is a bright orange box, the cheery, trippy colour of some healing product. *Modecate* is the word on the box. Somewhere, at the top of a building, someone has sat down and thought of that name and been paid for it. A brilliant act of commercial fusion: *medicate, moderate, modify.* Three grim sentiments in the one handy pack.

Dragging the thing out, I read some of the blurb on the side of the packet. *Modecate*, it announces, proudly, *is the original British lithium.* Which almost makes me laugh. As if anyone taking it cares whether it's home-grown or imported from Lithuania. *Some people notice that Modecate makes them feel detached or less sensitive to moods. This is not necessarily to be seen as a side-effect.* No wonder she wouldn't take it. Preferred to ride the tiger of her own emotions rather than walk round with a head full of porridge – whatever the cost. I screw up the gaudy packet and throw it out of the window, wondering if the tincture of turnips could possibly do her any more good.

My mouth feels sticky and dry. I go into the kitchen for some water. Rory's fussing over his painting – kneeling on top of the fridge trying to fix it in place on the wall. 'What do you think?'

he asks, intensely. 'Don't you think it's quite exciting here?' And then when I don't answer, just keep on pouring glass after glass of warmish water down my throat, splashing down my shirt, Rory clambers down from the fridge, lugging the painting over to the other side of the kitchen. He holds it up against the wall by the windows. 'Or perhaps people will enjoy it more here? Where the light strikes it.'

I say, half-drowned, that I don't really know much about art. Rory frowns. Starts to hammer a nail into the wall.

'Your boss has been ringing for you,' he says, turning round to look at me. 'All morning.'

Dazed and numb, I go and stand by the phone, and am halfway through dialling the number when I glance down at the dirty grey briefcase I dumped on the floor when I first came in. And realise that ringing work would not be a good idea at all.

Rory sails past, this time clutching a fragile-looking wire sculpture. It looks like a pair of twisted kidneys on a stalk. He seems to think it would be nice in his bedroom. I can't imagine sleeping with it anywhere near me.

'I've met Gus,' he breathes. 'What a fascinating guy. A real character.'

I think, for a moment, I maybe misheard, but when I open the door to my room, Gus is there, stuffing his worldly goods into his rucksacks. No wily Northern 'Naa then kid' greets me this time. Just a humid silence. He ignores me until it becomes impossible and then stretches up to his full mighty dimensions to face me. He stands oddly, his sequoia-size legs a little too far apart – no doubt still pained by the surgical assault on his Gus-hood – but above all else, he looks frightening. A vengeful thing from the myths, a brother who straddles the earth.

'Spoiled that one for us alright, didn't you? Cheers.'

Oh brother.

His face, which I've always freely admitted as handsome, is twisted-up and ugly. He looks away, and starts folding up the big map of Nepal, which is on the floor all crumpled, two of its corners torn away. I bend down to help him. He snatches the map away. 'Just fuck off, kid, will yer? Before I really hit you.'

'No,' I say. 'I won't.'

And Gus doesn't try to hit me. He looks a little surprised.

'She wasn't well, Gus,' I say. I watch him screwing up his face, in patent disbelief, making ready to pour a dose of contempt upon that statement, thinking – how can this tiny creature, my tiny, little brother, be right about anything? Know anything I don't know? But before he can speak, I've started.

'It would have gone wrong. I know you thought she was cool. So did I. She just wanted to die. That would have been good – stuck up some mountain with a girl who wants to die. You'd have had no time for it, Gus. You know it.'

He turns back. Away from me. His voice, I've noticed, goes very high when he's angry.

'I get one crack at something good, man, and you spoil it. You're jealous, so you have to ruin everything, don't you?'

This, from Gus, the Great Hob-Nailed Bespoiler. My answer wells up and I spit it out, fiercely. 'Sorry Gus. When you first said it, I couldn't quite see how putting you up, and feeding you, and letting you leave all your stuff here while you screw my girlfriend . . . MY girlfriend . . . and then drag her off to Nepal right in front of me could be called ruining it for you. But, now you mention it, 'course, I *have* ruined it for you, haven't I? Just want to fucking tell me how?'

Gus listens scornfully to all this, and then he bends down to my height. Hisses the words in my face like some pissed-off dragon.

'You ruined it when you were born, you little shitter! Ma going mental like that, everyone fussing about her, and you. Everything was alright till *you* came along.'

'I didn't have much choice,' I say, with a shrug. Gus shivers, and looks away.

'You're too weird,' he says.

'Look at me Gus.'

'No.'

'Why can't you stand me? It's because I'm like *him*, isn't it? Because I look like Angus.'

Momentarily, he's knocked asunder. Flinches, as I say it, as if struck by a warm gust of fish-paste sandwich or garlic-breath. He sits down on the bed, the kitbag between his knees, fiddling meaninglessly with the straps. Even under his tan, he looks pale. Shocked.

He continues to stare at the floor. The words tumble out of him quietly, in monotone, as he twists the scarab ring on his finger like a rosary. '*I* wanted to be him. Why did it have to be you? You was just a fat blob in front of the telly. *I* should have been him. Not you.' He shakes himself, as if to dislodge the unsettling rhythms taking over his brain. He takes a deep breath. 'They've told you, haven't they?'

'Sue did.'

'I always tried to keep a lid on it, like,' he says, quietly, looking up.

Not especially hard, it strikes me. Referring to our father as 'killer' for the best part of two decades seems like a fairly half-hearted way of keeping a secret. Then again, that's just Gus. I sit down next to him. He tries very hard not to edge away.

'Thanks,' I say, more gently, 'for trying. I've tried not telling people things too, you know. Never works.'

Gus turns to me, finally, carefully, as if daring to out-stare the midday sun. 'I punched him,' he says, regretfully.

'I know. I remember. In our driveway. Right in the gob.'

Gus frowns.

'Not *that cunt*. Martha's dad. When he tried to take her off. I gorrim on the arm.'

Martha's dad, I think, seemed remarkably cheerful for someone who'd just been attacked by Gus.

'What did he do?'

Gus shakes his head, bewildered. 'He just said "Don't be daft, son". And he pushed her in the truck.'

I sigh, perplexed by the impossibilities of the situation. Have Good Men, truly Good Men, such as Jesus, or Harrison Ford, ever faced these problems? How did Christ feel when he cured a cripple, and then the cripple walked home and kicked the crap out of his wife? How do you become, and stay, a Good Man? How do you keep a hold of that energy for good-doing when the only things you know for certain are that 'good' is a very tricky word to define, and whatever good you do will probably be bad as well?

You just do what you have to do. And you can only trust people will understand why you do it.

'Was you at the hospital?' Gus asks.

I nod. 'He's not dead, by the way.'

Gus sniffs. 'Oh,' he says, blandly. 'Pity.' He pulls a length of chequered cloth back out of the kitbag. 'Want this?'

I look at it distractedly. 'What is it?'

''S a *kaffiyeh*. Like that geezer wears. Ararat. Or wharrever. Seen loads of students wearing them.'

'I'm not a student.'

'Naa. Suppose you're not.' And he rolls the thing up again. Looks up at me. 'You don't. You don't like me much, do you, kid?'

'You're wrong, Gus. You really are. I just don't understand you. You frighten me.'

He squints. '*I* frighten *you*?' he says, slightly aggrieved, as if he had the monopoly on being unsettled by one's brother.

'I just don't get why you still hate them so much. It's not their fault I look like him. Any more than it's their fault he's dead. Why haven't you worked it all out? It's not ... it's not like being a kid. Being old. There's no one to make decisions for you. You can't just hide away. You have to do it for yourself.

255

And sometimes you're wrong. But you still have to try. Like in Papua New Guinea.'

Gus stares at me as if I've just announced my intention to stand for Parliament.

'Papua New Guinea? What the fuck do *you* know about Papua New Guinea?'

'People *try* there. People try to be Good Men. I saw a film about it. Even poor people in the hills. Like this bloke I saw. Onka. They just try.'

'Lemme tell you about Papua New fucking Guinea kid. It's a shithole. 'Specially up there in the hills. They've got this thing going. Called a *Moka*.'

I lean forward excitedly straining, like a kid who knows the right answer.

'I know! I know all about them. We did it. At college.'

'Oh yeah? So what is it then?'

'Well.' I deflate a little. 'I was never really sure.'

'I'll tell you, kiddah. A *moka*'s like this big feast. And one village invites the village down the river, or up the hill or whatever. And they give them shit. Valuable shit – pigs, blankets, medicine, guns. Just give it. Free.'

'Well what's so shit about that?'

' 'Cos it's just to make them jealous. Just so next time round, the neighbours have to give them back twice as much – jeeps, helicopters, dynamite. Or it's war. That's what it's about. They're all tossers up there.'

He says this with such bitterness that I guess Gus might have had to learn the obligations of the *moka* in some rather brutal manner himself. I wish he'd never told me what the *moka* was. Onka, the beacon of my inspiration, has fallen in my esteem to a status no higher than some loan shark.

Still, I know what I know. And if Gus met with trouble in Papua New Guinea, it only really goes to prove my point. 'It's still *true*, Gus. Wherever you are. It's tough. But you have to

256

try. And you can't blame people all your life when they make mistakes. That's what it's all about.'

'Bull,' he observes, predictably. 'An' anyway. Why are *you* on their side all of a sudden? D'you not remember finishing college and they'd fuckin moved? That's not normal, mate. That's *fucked*.'

But of course I know why they moved now. Sue told me at the hospital. When I asked her about the brick through the kitchen window. *That was just the start of it, Allie. Someone started giving them funny phone calls – all through that summer. Sending nasty letters. Things he was going to do to them. Dad went down to Whitehall and saw his old people. They said they didn't think it was a real security risk. Probably just a local nutter. They told him just to move again.* So they did. And the calls and the letters stopped. And the bricks. It was Gus' fault. That mischief call to the *Clarion*. Its contents printed in the next edition – with my father's name beneath them. They moved, not to escape us, but what Gus did, and I failed to stop.

''Eck.'

This is all Gus can say, after I've explained. Then he goes silent for a long while, full, I think, of a dimly formed regret. He takes a series of deep, difficult breaths, as if crushed by the weight of his thoughts. At the end of each gulp of air, his mouth fills up with possible words and then he blows them, defeatedly, out of his nose. I understand, I sympathise – it's hard. He tries again. 'Anyhow,' he says, at last. '*Jeremy* sounds like a fuckin' dork. Ye can't hardly blame us for that.'

I offer, because there seems to be not much else to say, to help him finish his packing. He shakes his head. No rush, he says, no point. 'Trip'll have to be cancelled now,' he says, glumly.

'Why?'

'Norrenuff on it,' he says. 'If there's less than five, it can't go.

257

And she were five,' he adds, jerking his head towards the outside, meaning Martha, now somewhere on her way to the M1.

'Bit tight on the others,' I say.

'S'pose,' says Gus, as if this has never really troubled him before. He stares distractedly at the grey briefcase in my hand. 'What you doing with that?'

And soon after this, he's packing again. We both are.

I send him off to wait for me in the pub. Willingly, he takes half of my stuff along with his own belongings, swings it effortlessly on to his already-laden shoulders and stalks off. A mighty, walking Christmas tree.

Only one thing remains. A call. Special Duties.

I ring Fazakerley Hospital to speak to my parents. He's not in Trauma III any more, a nurse tells me. They've moved him on to Graeme Souness Ward. She puts me through and, while the phone rings and rings, I rehearse what I'm going to say if they'll let me speak to him, or her. That there's no need for remorse, not now, not ever. Let's not deliver lofty speeches about the fools we have been. We might be them again.

'You went off without a coat,' says my mother, accusingly, as a nurse hands her the phone.

'I'm okay,' I assure her. 'I'm sorry I ran off.'

There's a long pause, as if my mother is consulting a set of notes. As perhaps she is. She's had twenty-one years to prepare them. 'Well we knew you would, really. That's why we didn't want to tell you. You do understand – don't you? You're not angry?'

'No, Mum. I'm not. Not any more.'

'Good. We were so . . . Are you *smoking*?'

'I know, I know,' I say, wearily. 'I'll go blind in my third eye.'

'I wasn't going to say that,' she interjects, a little haughtily. 'It's a waste of money. That's all . . .'

She breaks off as a rumbling begins in the background. I hear her rest the phone on something and, behind that, a series of whispers. This conversation hasn't turned out remotely like I thought it would. From my mother's alarmingly practical frame of mind to her frank answers, nothing is as it was.

The phone rattles. 'Your father,' says my mother, solemnly, as if she appreciates the near-sacred novelty of the event, 'would like a word.'

'Ah yes,' my father notes vaguely, as if I am perhaps an ex-student accosting him in Dale Street when he has the wrong glasses. 'I'm *so* glad you rang. We've been ah wanting to get hold of you.'

'I know. I'm sorry. It's been hard.'

'I ah look . . .'

'It's okay, Dad,' I say, warmly. Because it really, really is.

'Good,' he says. 'Very good. I'm so glad. Listen.'

Dad: all ears.

'Lilly . . . your mother tells me you're working for some sort of ah publisher.'

I take a deep breath. Then I let it out again. There just seems no point explaining.

'Yes,' I say.

'Good,' my father says. 'Thing is, you see, the reason I wanted to talk to you – been doing a lot of thinking, lying here. And I've decided I'm going to write this ah book. Sort of informal, tongue-in-cheek history thing. "A Jovial History of the Liverpool Polytechnic". I wondered if you might consider it?'

Christ on ice.

'I'm going away,' I say. 'On business. We'll talk about it when I get back.' I must, I think, be growing up. Because only two-thirds of this is a lie.

On my way downstairs, the mad Sikh is standing in his doorway, squinting at me through red, telly-strained eyes. 'Hey,' he says, gruffly.

259

'Look, mate. It's no use starting on me. I don't even live here any more. Talk to Rory. Tell the Residents' Committee.'

But the Sikh's shaking his head. He peers at me sideways. 'Are you Str*aaa*nge?'

And I put my bags down.

'In a manner of speaking. Yes. Why?'

'Have you got a minute? I'd like a word.'

Baglung, Nepal

November 1996

Dear Martha,

You might wonder why I'm writing to you from a place called Baglung. So do I. Frequently. I can only say that I *was* going to send you a postcard from Buttwal, but no one had any stamps. I hope this reaches Scarborough intact. Give my regards to Dr Rourke – tell him I'll bring the herbs he wanted when I come and stay.

We're stranded here living on lentils while the company tries to find another driver to finish the trip. Nobody's seen or heard anything of Gus for weeks now. He met up with a certain Nola, a lady driver for one of the Aussie firms out here who had boots almost as big as he does. He left me a very rambling note, the main import of which was that Nola and he had found something very special in each other and were going off to enjoy it on some Thai beach. I would quote you some of it, only the note was seized by a more litigious member of our party and it now rests with the British Consul in Kathmandhu.

I'm having an ace time of it myself. There's a cobbler here who believes that, on his last visit, Gus cured his niece's club foot. Possibly he did, though I hardly wish to consider the method. Consequently, they have a little shrine dedicated to Gus with a very blurred photo of him at its centre. As a blood relation to the seven-foot shaman, I have a certain elevated status in the town myself. I've been accorded a rank which is somewhere between a cousin and a senior official and my main struggle at the moment involves avoiding bowls of rice and dhal, rather than procuring them. My fellow-travellers, meanwhile, who had not budgeted for this detour, are increasingly grateful for the wodge of Pendennis-dollars at the bottom of my backpack. I don't care. Pretty soon, I won't need them any more. Tara's husband has offered to fly us all out.

Good that you're reading again. You might like to take a look at the enclosed: 'Drama Exercises For Youth Groups', which marks the concluding stages of my revenge upon the Pendennis Press. In particular, page 117, where we suddenly leap from the dilemma *An older boy at a disco tries to encourage you to drink some cider* to a lengthy passage from that modern erotic classic 'Her Cherry Gizzard'. I think the author will sue. My dad says there was a piece on 'Roger Cook' the other night.

What next? When I was about nine, I once ate a whole Arctic Roll all to myself and kept my mother up all night being sick. And as she mopped up the fifth or the sixth deposit of polar puke, she said, 'Pray God you never get a taste for whisky, Alastair Strange, because you've got a greedy spirit in you.' And I'm beginning to realise she was right. Not about the whisky (she also used to warn Gus that smoking would stunt his growth, so let's not give her too much credit). But I *am* greedy, now. I spent a whole big chunk of my life missing my vardo and now I'm truly in the driving seat, and I know where it's all going, I'm never getting off.

Just before I left Fulham, that weird bloke – do you remember the mad Sikh from downstairs? – stopped me in the hall. It turns out, we had the founder of *TV Forum* living downstairs from us all the time. And he spent all his time at the window, not because he was crazy, or wanted to have us evicted from the building, but because (did I ever tell you? It all seems so long ago) I wrote a letter to

TV Forum just after I moved in and he noticed the address and was trying to work out if I was the bloke who wrote it. It seems he liked my letter so much, he wants to give me a job. His editor's gone off to write for *Chechen Heights* on Channel Four and he wants a new one: the only criteria being an autistic knowledge of twilight telly and a sound understanding of commas. I'm fixed up to start when I'm back in London.

So yes, I'm greedy. And so should you be. Do you understand me? Never give up, Martha. Do what you have to do, always, because this is all we've got. And never wish for the scaffolding, or the sky, to fall on your head again.

More anon.

Love,

Strange

A SELECTED LIST OF CONTEMPORARY FICTION
AVAILABLE IN VINTAGE

☐ THE MERCY BOYS	John Burnside	£6.99
☐ DISGRACE	J M Coetzee	£6.99
☐ BY THE SHORE	Galaxy Craze	£6.99
☐ CHARLOTTE GRAY	Sebastian Faulks	£6.99
☐ MEMOIRS OF A GEISHA	Arthur Golden	£6.99
☐ HERE ON EARTH	Alice Hoffman	£6.99
☐ THE MAGUS	John Fowles	£7.99
☐ AMSTERDAM	Ian McEwan	£6.99
☐ ENDURING LOVE	Ian McEwan	£6.99
☐ BELOVED	Toni Morrison	£6.99
☐ PARADISE	Toni Morrison	£6.99
☐ AMERICAN PASTORAL	Philip Roth	£6.99
☐ THE WAY I FOUND HER	Rose Tremain	£6.99
☐ A PATCHWORK PLANET	Anne Tyler	£6.99

- All Vintage books are available through mail order or from your local bookshop.

- Please send cheque/eurocheque/postal order (sterling only), Access, Visa, or Mastercard:

☐☐☐☐☐☐☐☐☐☐☐☐☐☐☐☐

Expiry Date:_____Signature:_____

Please allow 75 pence per book for post and packing U.K.
Overseas customers please allow £1.00 per copy for post and packing.

ALL ORDERS TO:

Vintage Books, Books by Post, TBS Limited, The Book Service,
Colchester Road, Frating Green, Colchester, Essex CO7 7DW

NAME:_____

ADDRESS:_____

_____

_____

_____

Please allow 28 days for delivery. Please tick box if you do not ☐
wish to receive any additional information

Prices and availability subject to change without notice.